FLAT WHITE

FLAT WHITE

Sandra Balzo

**SEVERN
HOUSE**

First world edition published in Great Britain and the USA in 2021
by Severn House, an imprint of Canongate Books Ltd,
14 High Street, Edinburgh EH1 1TE.

Trade paperback edition first published in Great Britain and the USA in 2022
by Severn House, an imprint of Canongate Books Ltd.

severnhouse.com

British Library Cataloguing-in-Publication Data
A CIP catalogue record for this title is available from the British Library.

ISBN-13: 978-0-7278-9057-3 (cased)
ISBN-13: 978-1-78029-766-8 (trade paper)
ISBN-13: 978-1-4483-0504-9 (e-book)

All Severn House titles are printed on acid-free paper.

Typeset by Palimpsest Book Production Ltd.,
Falkirk, Stirlingshire, Scotland.
Printed and bound in Great Britain by
TJ Books Limited, Padstow, Cornwall.

ONE

'Let me flatten her now. Please?'

My business partner Sarah Kingston was watching Christy Wrigley shimmy under the condiment cart at our Brookhills, Wisconsin coffeehouse.

'Absolutely not,' I said, as Christy's top half disappeared, leaving cable-knit knees visible. 'We need her.'

I could have appealed to Sarah's common decency. You know, 'It's not nice to squish people' – yada, yada, yada. But there were some days when Sarah was all about Sarah.

'I'll just kick out one of the casters,' she pleaded. 'It won't hurt her. Much.'

This was one of those days.

'Our neighbor very kindly volunteered to fill in at Uncommon Grounds while Amy is in Europe,' I reminded her. 'Can you show a little more gratitude?' And a lot less bloodlust.

'Fill in as a barista, but have you seen the woman make a drink?'

'Christy is a piano teacher,' I reminded Sarah. 'If you want her to make an espresso drink, you'll need to show her how to use the espresso machine. It's called training. Which is what I thought you were doing with her this morning.'

'I assumed she knew what she was doing when she started to dismantle the machine. So sue me.'

'If only I could,' I muttered, 'but I'd be suing myself.'

'Wah, wah, wah. It's not like you were here to put the thing back together. I did that.' She pulled a black rubber gasket from her apron pocket and looked at it absent-mindedly. 'Mostly.'

The missing gasket probably explained the rivulet of water trailing from the tip of the steam wand down our service counter.

'The espresso machine was filthy.' A yellow rubber-gloved palm appeared from under the cart. 'Brush.'

I leaned down to pluck a scrub brush from the pile of cleaning implements on the floor and slap it into the extended hand like I was a surgical nurse. Though if Christy were a surgeon, she'd never make it out of the scrub room.

'I don't know why you're encouraging her,' said the same woman who allowed our neighbor to dismantle our $25,000 espresso machine three hours earlier.

'She's just cleaning the cart's wheels.' I shrugged. 'What can she hurt?'

The brush shot back out and hit the front door, making the sleigh bells on the back of it jangle against the plate glass window.

'Hurt besides me, you mean?' Sarah asked, neatly sidestepping the ricocheting brush.

'If I had wanted to hit you, I would have hit you,' Christy's disembodied voice flatly stated.

'See?' Sarah asked. 'The woman is clearly unhinged and now, to make matters worse, she's marrying my jailbird step-cousin, who is as crazy as she is,' Sarah continued. 'They'll have litters of little lunatics.'

Oy vey, Sarah was on a roll. Though I did applaud the alliteration.

'You do know that I can hear you,' came the voice from down under. 'Ronny and I will not be procreating together.'

'Oh,' seemed my safest response at this point.

Sarah, of course, couldn't leave this potential scab unpicked. 'What turns you off most, Christy? Ronny's murderous past or the fact you'd actually have to have sex to procreate?'

'I'll have you know I have no problem with sex,' Christy said. 'In fact, I can be quite racy.'

I tried not to imagine the pale redhead in her yellow rubber gloves and little else.

'The fact is,' she continued, 'Ronny and I aren't seeing each other anymore.'

'Seeing each other' had been restricted to four hours per month anyway. Christy had only become interested in Ronny Eisvogel after he had been arrested and subsequently sentenced to state prison. My theory was that the little germaphobe needed to be needed and Ronny was safe, if only for the next twenty to life. If Christy ever had to live with the man and wash his socks, it would be all over.

Still, I felt badly for her. 'I'm sorry, Christy.'

'I'm not.' Her gloved palm flashed back out again. 'Toothbrush.'

If Christy didn't want to talk about something, she simply . . . didn't.

Sarah glanced at me, then asked, 'Ronny dumped you?'

'Toothbrush.'

I grinned at Sarah and then went to scan the other assorted items Christy had gathered from our utility room before she slid under the condiment cart. Sponge, pile of rags, bent table knife, used bar of soap, rusted razor blade. 'I don't see a toothbrush.'

'Impossible.'

I picked through the rags. Nothing. 'Are you sure you saw a toothbrush amongst this stuff when you brought it out?'

'No. But I assumed you both kept one here.'

'To brush my teeth,' Sarah said. 'Why in the hell would I give you my toothbrush to clean the condiment cart's wheels with?'

'You have a toothbrush here?' I asked her.

'Of course not. It was a rhetorical question.'

I sighed. 'No toothbrush, Christy.'

'My purse.'

Of course, she'd keep one in her purse. She probably had two toothbrushes, in fact. One for cleaning teeth and the other for the odd job. 'Where's your purse?'

'Under my coat on the rack by the door.'

I went to the coat-rack, removing first a stocking cap and then a plaid wool scarf from the hook before getting to the bulky full-length wool coat. 'My God, this is heavy,' I said, hefting it.

'It's January in Wisconsin and there's two feet of snow on the ground.'

Which was why Christy had also worn rubber hip-waders this morning. I had made her leave the tall boots outside on the porch, the pair of them forming a yellow lean-to next to the door.

'You live directly across the street,' Sarah pointed out. 'That's what? A twenty-five-foot journey door to door?'

'Sooo?' Christy's voice had gone up an octave. 'What if I got hit by a car as I crossed?'

'You honestly care whether your corpse is nice and toasty or not while it's waiting for the meat wagon to arrive?' Sarah asked.

'You can't be sure that I would die instantly,' Christy rebutted. 'I might linger.'

'You should be so—'

'Will you two stop?' I draped the heavy coat over the nearest chair and slipped an enormous robin's egg blue tote off the hook. Everything about Christy was oversized, except the woman herself.

Undoing the bag's drawstring, I peered inside. A mobile phone was peeking out of a pocket, but the contents below were a jumble. I could make out the handle of a pair of scissors, a can of something – likely spray disinfectant, knowing Christy – a single torn yellow rubber glove, an unlabeled bottle of brown liquid and, yes, a toothbrush.

I went to retrieve it and pulled my hand back quickly. 'Ouch!'

'What?' Sarah asked. 'Something in that rat's nest bite you?'

'No, something stabbed me.' I grasped the toothbrush by the brush end this time and held it up. 'Christy, why do you have a shiv in your purse?'

Sarah took it and ran her finger over the end that had been filed to a point.

Christy stuck her head out from under the cart to see. 'Oh, that was for Ronny. Give it here.'

'You planned on smuggling a weapon into the prison?' I asked. 'Have you lost your mind?'

Now *that* was a rhetorical question.

'Oh, I wasn't going to actually give it to him,' she said, still holding out her hand. 'It was just a craft project. You know, something to show him I cared.'

'Until you didn't,' Sarah said, slapping the weaponized toothbrush into Christy's hand a little harder than necessary.

'Exactly right.' Christy took the brush and slid back under. 'Dammit.'

'What?'

'This is the soft-bristled brush. I need the other one.'

I was not about to stick my hand back in that bag. Next, I'd likely come up with a file just waiting to be baked into a cake. 'Come out and get it.'

'Oh, for God's sake.' The hand shot back out. 'Give me my purse.'

I held up the bag and squinted at it and the space between cart and floor, trying to gauge the space. 'I don't think it will fit under there. I guess I could dump it out and—'

'Just give it to me!'

'With pleasure.' Sarah pulled the bag from my grasp and dropped it unceremoniously on the outstretched hand. Clunk.

'Ouch.' Christy scrabbled for the drawstring and used it to reel the bag in. Or at least she tried to reel it in. 'Damn. It's stuck.'

'No shit, Sherlock,' Sarah said. 'If you want your toothbrush, crawl out from under your rock and find it yourself.'

'Honestly!' The legs bent at the knee as she scrambled for purchase and the little redhead slid out, one hand still holding the drawstring.

Pushing herself up to sit cross-legged on the tile floor, back against the condiment cart, Christy opened the bag and started to remove items one by one and set them on the floor next to her. The disinfectant, the scissors, a sponge, a wrapper from—

'You carry your own disposable . . .' Sarah picked up the wrapper and read, '"Prophylactic toilet seat cover"?'

'Of course,' Christy said. 'I certainly hope you don't sit on public toilet seats unprotected.'

'Of course not. I hover.'

'Oh.' Christy's lips had twisted in distaste. 'You're one of those.'

'I'm one of whats?' Sarah asked.

'Toilet hoverers.' Christy's phone vibrated in the depths of the bag, but she ignored it. 'I'm just saying that people like you who—'

I held up my hands. 'Could we please focus? The first afternoon train from downtown Milwaukee will be here in a little over an hour, and not only is the espresso machine leaking, but our cleaning supplies and half the contents of Christy's bag are all over the—' I interrupted myself. 'Do you need to get that, Christy?'

Her phone had stopped ringing and then started up again, either with another call or the original caller trying again.

'Excuse me?' She acted like she hadn't noticed.

'Your phone.' I nudged Christy's bag with my toe and the mobile in question slipped out. 'Oh, I'm sorry,' I said, leaning down to pick it up. 'I—'

'Give me that!' Christy jumped up.

But Sarah was quicker. She had the phone in her hand before Christy could make a grab for it. 'Something you don't want us to see?'

'No, I—'

But my partner was dancing away with the cell phone. So far, Sarah had been hazing Christy for fun, but now my partner seemed intent on turning up the heat. 'Whoever do you think is calling? Must be an emergency if they are so persistent that—'

'Give me my phone.' Christy seemed to be trying to hide her irritation, but her foot was tapping, her arms crossed. 'Please.'

'Barry Margraves,' Sarah read and then held the phone out for me to see. The photo of a good-looking man beamed back at us. 'Now who could that be?'

'None of your business.' Christy reached out and snatched the phone away, holding Barry Margraves to her bosom. 'That's who he is.'

'He's none of my business?' Sarah was grinning, like a gleeful lion circling the wounded wildebeest. 'You dumped my poor incarcerated cousin for this guy and it's none of my business?'

But then Christy wasn't all that wounded. 'I did not dump Ronny for Barry. In fact, I went on the dating site because I had already ended things with Ronny, and I was lonely. Rebecca suggested it.'

'Rebecca Penn?' I asked, a little surprised.

'Yes, of course,' Christy said. 'You know she's moved back, right? She's living above the studio.'

Rebecca Penn and Michael Inkel had owned Penn and Ink, a graphic arts studio and marketing company two doors down from Christy. Michael handled the writing and marketing side, while Rebecca had been the artist. When the two called off their engagement, Rebecca had moved to New York. Michael, on the other hand, had returned to Brookhills after a short trip back to his native Toronto to lick his emotional wounds. 'No, I didn't know. When was this?'

'Like a month ago,' Sarah said. 'You should try to keep up.'

The Penn and Ink building was a converted one-and-a-half-story bungalow with a small apartment above the retail studio space on the ground floor. The studio had been rented out since Penn and Ink had closed, its retail tenants seeming to change every few months. I tried to keep up, as Sarah said, but it was hard. 'That Rowena, the one with the stationery store, she moved out?'

'Rochelle,' Christy corrected. 'And it was a fabric store. She's been gone for six months.'

You see why I don't bother. 'Rebecca and Michael aren't back together again, are they?'

'On and off, still,' Christy said. 'I told Rebecca that she'd be far better off making a clean break with him, like I did with Ronny.'

But then Christy was not going to run into Ronny on the street. Or in the building.

As I recalled, Rebecca and Michael had purchased the bungalow together, and I thought Michael still kept a workspace at the back of the studio. And now, according to Christy, Rebecca was living on the floor above.

'Damn shame Penn and Ink busted up,' Sarah said, pulling a chair out from a table and flipping it around so she could sit facing us over the chair back.

'Damn shame for the people or for the business?' I asked.

Sarah rolled her eyes. 'Like I care about their personal lives. But Michael was a damn good writer and Rebecca a passable designer. Did I ever tell you they did our ads and website?'

I assumed she meant for Kingston Realty, which Sarah had recently shelved after unsuccessfully trying to split her time

between it and Uncommon Grounds. And by 'shelved', I mean
sold the agency for a good sum.

'. . . says Michael is driving ride-share to supplement his
freelance writing,' Christy was saying with a pout. 'Serves
him right for trying to make Rebecca into something she
wasn't.'

'A nice person?' I guessed.

'That's a little uncharitable of you, Maggy.' Christy had
leaned down to retrieve items from the floor to return to her
purse and now swiveled her head toward me. 'Just because
Rebecca accused Sheriff Pavlik of having an affair with her
sister.'

'It was an honest mistake on Rebecca's part,' Sarah
said. 'She knew JoLynne had been having a fling with somebody. She was just wrong about who that person was.'

The 'who' being Michael, not Pavlik. But Rebecca had
forgiven him. And then, not. 'I'm just surprised she'd move
back after all the drama. And that I haven't seen her here at
the shop.'

'Rebecca's sister died in a giant coffee cup on our porch,'
Sarah reminded me.

Drama, like I said. But Rebecca did not strike me as a very
sentimental person. Especially if she were looking for a good
cup of joe.

'Now that I'm working here, I'm sure she'll come by regularly,' Christy assured us, straightening. 'We're like this.' She
crossed two of her rubber-gloved fingers.

That surprised me, too, considering how different the women
were, but not as much as the 'now that I'm working here' part
of Christy's statement.

Surprised Sarah, too, apparently. 'You know you're just
filling in while Amy is gone, right?'

Christy looked hurt. 'Well, yes. But who knows what could
happen down the road?'

Hell freezing over came to mind. 'Anyway,' I said, changing
the subject, 'you met this new guy online?'

'Yes.' Christy's feelings already hurt, she jutted out her chin
defiantly. 'You have a problem with that?'

'Not at all.' I had been lucky enough to find love without

an app, but not everybody can count on their potential soulmate suspecting them of murder.

The redhead squinted suspiciously at Sarah. 'How about you?'

'Me? How else can you meet people these days? In fact, I applaud you for getting out there again, especially at the expense of my cousin.'

Christy and I exchanged looks, not sure what to say to that.

'Thank you,' Christy settled on.

'Tell us about this guy,' I said, then hesitated as she glanced down at the phone in her hand. 'Or do you need to call him back first?'

Christy was reading a text message. 'He's about to board a plane, so he says he'll call me when he lands.'

'Then he's free to travel.' The words were out of my mouth before I could stop them.

'You just assume Barry is in jail, too?' She had this way of extending her neck when she was irritated, like a cartoon chicken.

'It did cross my mind,' I admitted.

'You can't blame Maggy,' Sarah said to her. 'You have a type.'

'Had.' Christy was stuffing the last of the junk back into her purse. 'I'll have you know I specifically steered clear of dating sites for inmates.'

'There are dating apps for inmates?' Swipe left for homicide, right for minor crimes.

'Maybe not apps so much,' Christy said. 'Prisoners wouldn't necessarily have cell phones, of course.'

Of course.

'There are websites though.' Christy's face had reddened. 'Not that I'd know anything about them. I'm done with prisoners.'

'You sure?' Sarah asked. 'There are advantages. You always know where they are, for one.'

Christy nodded in agreement. 'That's true. But fidelity isn't everything.'

Sheesh. I cleared my throat. 'But tell us about Barry. Is he from around here?'

'No, Denver.'

I guessed a long-distance relationship was a step up from a life-sentence one.

'He's moving to Brookhills,' Christy assured me. 'Or at least to the greater Milwaukee area.'

Brookhills was a far west suburb of the City of Milwaukee, which was situated on Lake Michigan about 100 miles north of Chicago. 'That will be nice for you.'

But apparently, I hadn't been quick or enthusiastic enough in my reaction for Christy's liking. 'What?' she demanded with a sniff. 'You think this is just another arm's length relationship?'

Well, yes.

'Well, it's not,' she said like she had read my thoughts. 'Barry *is* moving here. Why else search southeastern Wisconsin for matches in the first place?'

It made sense. If you were relocating, it would be nice to know somebody in town before you got there, even if it was virtually.

Sarah was wagging her head at me. 'I don't know why you're being so negative, Maggy.'

That made us even. I didn't know why Sarah was being so positive. Positivity and supportiveness were not her thing.

'I've just never had any experience with dating apps,' I said, rubbing the small of my back. Long days standing on hard tile floors were taking a toll. 'Why? Have you?'

'Maybe.' Was that a touch of crimson on the tip of Sarah's nose?

Christy had noticed it. 'You have! Tell us.'

I wanted to hear, too. Sarah had pulled a gun on the last guy she had dated, but that was a few years back. And she had saved my life in the process, so I couldn't be judgmental.

Now my friend held up her hands, uncomfortable but maybe a little pleased, too, that we were interested. 'I just put up my profile to get the kids off my back. I have to admit, though, that it's kind of fun.'

Sarah had adopted Sam and Courtney Harper after their mother Patricia – one of our original threesome who started

Uncommon Grounds – was killed. In fact, it was Patricia's death that had brought Sarah and me together in the first place.

The third of our trio, Caron Egan, had stepped away after one year in the coffee business – albeit a year filled with three or four murders, a couple of betrayals and one coffeehouse destroyed by a freak May snowstorm.

Wuss. But then she and her lawyer husband Bernie had just purchased Brookhills' historic Hotel Morrison to renovate it, so perhaps she was a glutton who decided she missed the punishment of the hospitality industry.

Meanwhile, Caron's defection left only me to resurrect the coffeehouse until Sarah raised the possibility of a partnership and offered the historic train depot at Brookhills Junction as our site. The rest is recent history.

'Why Courtney and Sam's sudden interest in your dating?' I asked Sarah now. 'Are you getting on their nerves?'

'More Courtney's,' Sarah said, crossing the store to straighten the espresso cups and latte mugs on our retail sale shelves. 'Sam just blocks my messages when I get annoying.'

Sam was away at his first year in college, but Courtney was still in high school. Having to hit the ground running with two teenagers when Patricia died four years ago had not been easy for Sarah and she'd done a damned good job from what I had seen.

Still, I empathized with Courtney. Being Sarah's sole focus could be exhausting, as I'd found out since she sold Kingston Realty. Every day, it seemed, my partner came in with a new idea for growing Uncommon Grounds and I had been relegated to stick-in-the-mud status in her mind, because I hadn't jumped on each and every one of them.

Even Amy was getting worn out. Or maybe she was just tired of being stuck in the middle of the push and pull between Sarah and me. Her vacation had come at an opportune time for Amy to get a respite from us. And, for whatever reason, Sarah's stream of schemes had slowed to a trickle since Amy had been gone.

Or maybe she had been focusing all her energy on the dating site.

'By the way,' Sarah said, turning with one of our colonial

blue teapots in her hand. 'I was thinking we should expand our line of teas. Maybe host a high tea once a week or something to promote them.'

'Not a bad idea,' I said, automatically. 'But back to your dating profile. Are you getting likes or swipes or whatever they are?'

'Of course I am,' Sarah said, setting the teapot back on the shelf. 'I have a kick-ass profile and—'

An unseen hand pulled open the door and a cold blast of January air whooshed through, threatening the stack of napkins on the condiment cart. I made a grab for them and missed.

'What the hell is that?' Sarah snapped. The door had gotten away from whoever it was, slamming open against the outside of the building.

'A customer,' I said as I chased down the last of the napkins. 'You don't recognize one because the shop has been empty all day. Be nice.'

'Come on in and get out of the cold,' I said, raising my voice so I could be heard over the gust.

'I'm so sorry,' a petite woman in a puffer jacket said, managing to pull the door closed behind her. 'The wind just took it out of my hands.'

'There's an Alberta Clipper moving through,' I said with a smile. 'We're supposed to get snow overnight.'

Again. But, as I said, it was January. And this was Wisconsin.

'An Alberta Clipper?'

Tourist. 'Yes, it's a fast-moving low-pressure system from Canada. We get them a lot here. Like nor'easters out east.'

'Oh, yes,' the woman said, slipping off her gloves. 'Of course.'

'But hopefully with less snow.' Having recovered from the shock of seeing a customer between commuter trains, Sarah had manned the service window. 'What can I get you?

'Oh, um . . .' The woman was looking around, seeming surprised to find herself in a coffeehouse. 'Yes, yes. I should have something.'

'A latte, maybe? Or a cappuccino? Flat white?' I suggested.

'Please.' She was still glancing around at our empty tables, taking in me, then Christy on the other side of the condiment cart and then Sarah behind the counter.

'Which?'

'Sorry.' The woman pushed her hood off dark hair, revealing bangs. 'You must think me a flake – no lame snow joke intended. I'll have a latte.'

'I'm Maggy Thorsen,' I said, as Sarah got the drink started. I was warming to the woman, since I do love me a pun. Lame or otherwise. 'Is this your first time in Uncommon Grounds?'

'Yes, yes, it is. I've never been . . . I mean, I'm new to the area. I'm looking for a piano teacher and stopped across the street. The sign tacked to the door said she was here? A Christy Wrigley?'

'That's me.' Christy, who did not like to shake hands au naturel, realized she still had on her gloves and circumvented the cart to stick one out.

'You?' The woman looked hesitant.

Christy cleared her throat. 'Yes.'

'Oh, well, yes. I'm pleased to meet you.' The woman gingerly shook the rubber-gloved hand.

'Christy is helping us out while our barista is on vacation.' I was trying to make our neighborhood clean-freak/piano teacher seem normal.

'She was about to scrub our condiment cart's wheels with a shiv,' Sarah explained helpfully. 'Skim, whole or two percent?'

'What?' The woman could not seem to take her eyes off Christy as she stripped her rubber gloves off.

'Milk,' Sarah explained. 'Or we have soy, almond or oatmeal. Which are also milks. Kind of.'

'Skim, please. That's a beautiful bracelet.' This last was directed to Christy.

'Oh, this?' Christy held up a skinny wrist.

'This' was a diamond tennis bracelet.

'Shit.' Sarah had stopped midway to frothing to look. 'My cousin didn't give you that. Unless it's fake.'

'Or stolen,' I suggested.

Christy was frowning. 'Don't be silly. It's Tiffany's.'

'A gift from Barry?' I guessed.

Christy's head ducked and she just smiled.

'Geez.' Sarah placed the pitcher under the wand and turned up the steam. 'Maybe I'd better take this online dating stuff more seriously.'

Our customer was standing uncomfortably, seeming to have stumbled into an episode of *The Bachelor*, minus the bachelor.

'Don't mind us,' I said over the noise of Sarah's frothing. 'Christy has a new beau. Can I get you something besides the latte?'

'The sticky buns are wonderful.' Christy was gesturing toward the pastry case a la Vanna White, probably to show off the bracelet.

'Yes, they are.' And sold out. I moved to peer into the pastry case and offer an alternative. 'But even better for a cold day, we have some nice crusty rolls to go with a bowl of chili or—'

A frigid wind cut through the shop, and I whirled round to see the door slam shut. The woman – our only customer of the afternoon – was gone.

TWO

'You chased the woman out, annoyed her with your chattering,' I said crossly, sitting down at a table with the unclaimed – and unpaid for – latte. 'The two of you.'

'No such thing,' Sarah said. 'She obviously didn't want coffee in the first place. She came here looking for Christy and felt obliged to order once I'd greeted her with my signature smile.' She bared her teeth in what was more snarl than grin.

'So she took the opportunity to bail out when I turned my back? Maybe.'

She'd probably been plotting her escape ever since she had shaken Christy's rubber-gloved hand. Nobody needs piano lessons that badly.

'I don't teach piano with my gloves on,' Christy said, as if I'd said it out loud. Then she added in a mumble, 'Usually.'

I didn't want to know. But we had twenty minutes to kill before the first afternoon commuter train returned from Milwaukee, hopefully filled with customers. 'You've honestly taught piano in those gloves?'

'Of course not,' she said indignantly, folding her arms against her chest. 'I have a pair of white cotton ones I can use for playing, if need be. 'You have to be able to feel the keys, after all.'

Silly me.

Best to wade back to the shore of sanity. 'So, Christy – Barry. Was he your first? Online date, I mean.'

'It probably depends on what you mean by date,' Christy said, taking the seat across from me. 'I've communicated with a few other guys through the site, but Barry was the first one I felt comfortable giving my phone number to. He said it was the same for him.'

'And you have arranged to meet?'

'As I told you, Maggy, Barry doesn't live here,' Christy said primly. 'How could we meet?'

Get on an airplane perhaps? The guy was sitting on one – probably in first class – as we spoke, after all. 'I thought since he'd given you the bracelet and all, that—'

Her lips were pursed. 'We talk on the phone every day.'

'That's it?' Sarah leaned back against the counter. 'Talk?'

'A telephone call can be very intimate,' Christy said. 'In fact—'

I held up a hand to stop her before I heard something I couldn't unhear. Or unsee, every time I closed my eyes. 'I think we can stipulate that point, right, Sarah?'

'Phone sex? God, yes.' Sarah seemed to be trying to figure out where she was going wrong Internet dating-wise. 'I haven't gotten up the nerve to talk on the phone, much less meet one of these guys in person. I could text, I think, or s—'

'We're not having phone sex,' Christy said. 'Or sexting, before you ask.'

'Hmm.' Sarah was still thinking. 'Are you withholding sext? Maybe that's why he sent you that bracelet. Why buy the cow diamonds when you can get the milk at current data rates?'

'We have *talked* – sometimes for hours – nearly every day for more than three months.' Christy said, exasperated. 'That's a kind of intimacy *some* people can't understand.'

Some people came over to examine the bracelet. 'Can't argue with the results,' Sarah admitted.

Christy pushed up her sleeve and, resting her elbow on the table, flexed her wrist so Sarah could get a better look. The bracelet slid down the skinny forearm to be stopped only by her elbow on the table.

'Should you have it sized?' I asked, as she slipped the bracelet back up to her wrist. 'You could lose it.'

'What?' Sarah asked, 'and remove a diamond or four?'

'I wouldn't want to change a thing,' Christy said. 'Besides, I have big hands, luckily, so it's unlikely to fall off.'

She waggled the fingers of her right hand and I felt myself involuntarily pull back. Christy did have unusually large hands for such a small woman. With the gloves and all, I guess I had never really noticed. Now I was hard put to see anything but.

Must be good for playing the piano though.

'. . . barely stand the excitement when he said he had a surprise for me for our three-month anniversary,' Christy was saying. 'It arrived just last week because it was caught up in customs. Barry had to pay extra tax or something to get it released.'

'Customs?' I asked. 'Where did he buy it?'

'Paris. That was on his last trip.' She did a little wiggle in her chair. '*Champs-Elysées*.' She pronounced it 'champs-elsies'.

'Very nice,' Sarah said, stepping back. 'Looks real.'

'Of course, it's real,' Christy said, indignantly.

'Hey,' Sarah said, holding up a hand. 'Just looking out for you.'

'That's very kind of you,' Christy said, rotating the bracelet so it shimmered in the overhead compact fluorescents. 'Especially given that you're jealous, *and* I dumped your cousin for Barry.'

'I'm not jealous, I'm just trying to up my online dating game,' Sarah protested. 'As for dumping Ronny, no big deal. He did try to kill Maggy, after all.'

'While wearing an Elvis costume.' Ronny, not me.

'Very true.' Christy suddenly looked earnest. 'But I don't want you two to worry about me. I was not born yesterday. I've researched Barry. Even Google-Earthed his house in Denver.'

'I'd expect nothing less,' Sarah said. 'How else can you know a guy is legit?'

'Right?' Christy's head was bobbing up and down. 'And it's wonderful. *So* much easier than sitting outside his house in your car for days on end. That can land you a restraining order.'

Something about the way she said it made me think she'd had experience. 'What was it like?'

They both looked at me, identically cocked heads.

'The house in Denver?' I elucidated.

'Oooh, it's just beautiful,' Christy said. 'Lots of land, in-ground swimming pool, Mercedes in the driveway.'

'The Mercedes may have been visiting,' I pointed out. 'The Google shot of the house where Ted and I lived still shows my mini-van in the driveway and it's going on four years now since our divorce.'

'I know. But I was able to find it more than once,' she said a little smugly.

'Well then, Mercedes Man can afford the bracelet,' Sarah said.

'And whatever he's sending for month *four*' – Christy's voice had gone up half an octave in excitement, but she lowered it now – 'I think it might be a diamond.'

'Just one?' Sarah asked. 'Have you noticed how many you have around your wrist?'

'But this is a special one.' Christy was glowing. 'It—'

The double blast of a whistle interrupted her as the sounds of a train pulling in reverberated through the shop. The building where Uncommon Grounds was housed was a historic train depot and our service windows were the original ticket counters. The three clocks above the counters were labeled 'Seattle', 'Brookhills' and 'New York City' for the Pacific, Central and Eastern time zones the original trains had traveled through. Nowadays, the commuter line just bounced back and forth between the western suburbs and downtown Milwaukee, where it connected to the airport spur.

'Five-fifteen train,' I said, getting to my feet.

But Sarah was more interested in Christy's prospects – love and financial – than the customers about to descend on us. 'You were saying, Christy? The diamond?'

'Oh, never mind,' Christy said, waving her off. 'I'm not supposed to talk about it. Besides, I don't want to jinx it.'

'But—'

Enough. 'Showtime, ladies,' I called as the platform door opened.

It was just touching seven on the Brookhills clock as Sarah and I finished closing the shop. We had sent Christy home, telling her it was because she was opening with me the next morning. In truth, if we handed the woman a vacuum cleaner, she would not put it down until midnight.

I didn't have that problem. 'Good enough,' I said, hanging up the vacuum hose in the storeroom. A coffee bean fell out of one end.

I kicked the bean into the corner.

Sarah was sitting in the adjacent office, balancing the day's books. 'Damn.'

'Off again?'

'Twenty-two cents.'

'Here.' I gave her a quarter. 'Balanced.'

'We have twenty-two cents too much, not too little.'

I took back my quarter and pulled two dimes and two pennies from the stack of coins. 'Problem solved.'

'You're pretty casual about our receipts, all of a sudden,' she said, leaning back in the desk chair so hard it squealed.

'Twenty-two cents one way or the other won't get me a diamond tennis bracelet,' I said, settling into the chair next to the desk.

'Tennis bracelets always have diamonds,' Sarah said. 'You're being redundant.'

'And why is that?' I asked. 'Who wears diamonds to play tennis? Except for engagement rings, of course.'

'Chris Evert,' Sarah said. 'The story is that the clasp of her diamond bracelet broke during a match at the US Open and she stopped to find it. From then on, people called them tennis bracelets.'

'That's pretty impressive for one broken clasp.' As was the breadth of Sarah's tennis knowledge since, so far as I knew, she had played for all of four months. As for her jewelry knowledge, I had never seen her wear any.

'Guess so.' Sarah was still messing with the numbers. 'I've always wondered if they'd have stopped play if it had happened at Wimbledon. They take their tennis pretty seriously at the All England Club. Have to wear white, you know. But then look at the fifth set tiebreak – you have to admit the Brits were groundbreaking with that.'

'They were,' I said, not having the faintest idea what she was talking about.

Sarah put down her pen. 'Sometimes don't you wonder if this is all worth it?'

'Owning a coffee shop?' I asked, surprised. It was a little early in our partnership for her to burn out.

'I mean working hard. Christy goes to an online dating site for the first time and meets a rich guy.'

'Who gives her a tennis bracelet.'

I must have said it a little wistfully because Sarah glanced at me. 'You don't like diamonds.'

'That's just what I told Pavlik so he wouldn't feel like he had to buy me an engagement ring.'

Jake Pavlik was Brookhills' sheriff and my man. I loved him enough to share my house, my bed and my sheepdog, Frank. We even had a chihuahua together, which was kind of an accident.

Now I leaned forward. 'Christy is such an enigma to me. She has no visible means of support other than teaching piano.'

'That's not true, Maggy. She did have that promising stint at the crematorium.'

'But that's what I mean. She's just the oddest little person, but she just keeps on keeping on.' I sat back in my chair. 'She has a good heart though. I'm glad she's found somebody.'

'Who isn't in jail.'

'Exactly. Though they haven't actually met.'

'That worries you?'

'Of course. Maybe on the phone she comes across as . . .'

'Normal?'

'Yes.' I sighed and stood up. 'Tomorrow I'm sure I'll hear about Barry Margraves ad nauseum.'

'Sure you don't want to change shifts with me?'

I hesitated. 'You would do that?'

'Nope.' She shrugged. 'Just messing with you. See you Wednesday.'

THREE

B y the time the door was unlocked and the 'closed' sign flipped to 'open' the next morning, I had been treated to an array of Barry emails, Barry texts and Barry photos. Happily, the man wasn't into weenie-pics or, if he was, Christy wasn't sharing.

Still, when Sarah snagged Christy's phone and outed her relationship with Barry, she had opened the floodgates, leaving me and our baker Tien Romano to be overtaken by the buoyant detritus of Christy's love life.

'She's certainly head over heels, isn't she?' Tien said, as she exchanged her chef's coat for a winter one.

Tien and her father Luc had run An's Market a few doors down from our original Uncommon Grounds location. Luc was largely retired, but Tien had turned her talents to baking and catering. Our new shop had a full commercial kitchen that Tien used for her business in exchange for providing us with our exclusive signature sticky buns and other treats she baked up for us.

Most of Tien's baking and prep was done overnight or in the wee hours, but the companionable hour of overlap as Tien wrapped up her workday and we started ours was usually spent catching up with each other's lives. Sometimes Tien even hung on a bit and helped with the morning rush.

Today, though, our baker could not seem to get out fast enough.

'Oh, Maggy, Tien.' Christy burst into the office, mobile in hand. 'Barry is on speaker. He wants to say hi.'

She thrust the phone at me. I had to admit the guy appeared nice enough from Christy's description. And, from his pictures, cute even. Maybe thirty-five, with sandy-colored hair and just enough stubble to give his round face character.

Didn't mean I wanted to talk to him.

'Umm, hi, Barry,' I said into the phone, waving to Tien that she had *better* not leave me. 'It's good to meet you telephonically.'

A chuckle. 'Hopefully it'll be more than telephonic soon,' a pleasant baritone voice said. 'I'm in the UK at the moment, but I told Christy as soon as I wrap up this project—'

'Pronounced prō-ject.' Christy was literally dancing a happy dance next to the file cabinet. 'Because Barry spends so much time abroad. He even says kilometers instead of miles sometimes.'

A little pretentious, but whatever.

'—to visit,' the man was wrapping up.

'That's wonderful,' I said, waving Christy down. 'I know Christy will be thrilled. Let me give the phone back to her.'

But Christy was gesturing for me to pass the cell on to Tien, who was holding up her hands and shaking her head no.

'Barry asked for you,' I told Christy as Tien threw me a grateful look.

Our fill-in barista took the mobile. 'I took care of that transfer yesterday just like you asked,' she said into it, switching off the speaker.

I exchanged looks with Tien. Mine felt concerned, hers just seemed curious.

Christy was listening. Then: 'Really? No, I will not open it until you're here and we can do it together. I promise.' A giggle. 'I'll just keep it safe until then. In my lingerie drawer.'

Ugh. Happily, we were not subjected to more of the one-sided intimate conversation as the little lovebird had disappeared around the corner.

'Sweet,' Tien said.

'I guess.' I was frowning. 'Did I hear right? Christy said she'd transferred something?'

'Took care of a transfer, I think, were her words.' Tien picked up snow boots. 'Maybe I'll leave these here. I don't know why I brought them – it was just flurrying.'

'She wouldn't be stupid enough to send this Barry money, would she? She hardly knows him. He could be a con artist.'

Tien stopped. 'Didn't he sound on the level? And thank you, by the way, for not putting me on the line with him.'

Now I wished I had, if for no other reason than to get Tien's opinion of the man. 'He sounded normal. Nice, even. But that's kind of the definition of a gigolo, isn't it?'

Tien snorted. 'Gigolo? You've been watching old movies again.'

Sunset Boulevard last night, but that wasn't the point. 'I just don't want Christy taken advantage of. She hardly knows the man.'

'*We* hardly know the man,' Tien said, setting the boots back down again. 'Because she didn't tell us about him. She probably was afraid we'd be judgy.'

Not a word. But a valid point.

'Besides,' Tien continued, 'Christy teaches piano for a living and picks up the occasional odd job. She's hardly a mark.'

'We don't know what she put in her profile,' I argued. 'For all we know, she told him she's a concert pianist.'

'Which doesn't pay zillions either,' Tien said. 'And don't you have it the wrong way around? He's the one who sent her a diamond bracelet.'

'Probably cubic zirconium.' I was grouchy, and I wasn't going to let it go. 'The man sends her a hundred-dollar bracelet and she reciprocates by wiring him her life's savings.'

Tien eyed me. 'Binge-watching old *Datelines*?'

'Am not,' I said a little indignantly. I had plenty of true crime in my life already, thank you very much.

'Anyway, if you're worried about Christy, ask her.' Tien went to the door with the sign 'To All Trains' over it and shoved it open. 'Oh, my God. What happened? There's a foot of snow on the platform.'

What happened was winter. I went to help her push the door open against the drifted snow, but she pulled back, shutting the door again.

'I hate snow.' Tien shook flakes out of her dark hair and pulled a cap from her coat pocket. 'I mean like pathologically.'

Most people would laugh and say then she was living in the wrong place, but Tien and I had braved the same freak May snowstorm together. Not only had we been stranded without heat and electricity in a strip mall, but the storm had ultimately destroyed both the market named for Tien's mother and the original Uncommon Grounds.

So I got it. 'I feel you. Now put on your boots.'

'Yes, ma'am.' She retrieved them and sat on a bench in the boarding corridor to pull them on. 'I must have missed the forecast. How much snow are we supposed to get?'

'Ten to twelve inches,' Christy said, passing through the corridor. 'I just heard they're canceling a lot of flights.'

'Ugh. Hope I make it home.' Standing, Tien donned her cap and then added mittens before she shoved the door open again and stepped out. 'You two ladies stay warm . . . Hey, Caron.'

I caught the door and stuck my head out to see my former partner, Caron Egan, passing Tien as she waded down the drifted steps from the platform toward the parking lot.

'What are you doing out in the snow, missy?' I asked, bracing myself and the door against the wind.

Caron stomped the snow from her boots before stepping in. 'Just finishing the night shift at the hotel, if you can believe it.'

'Sounds worse than getting up to open a coffeehouse.'

'It is.' She pulled out a tissue and blew her pert nose. 'But nobody has died yet.'

'Always a bonus.' I pulled the door tightly closed behind her. 'Don't tell me you're on foot?'

Hotel Morrison was just five or six blocks east of us, but the Egan house was probably twice that due south. Not a bad walk, in good weather, but . . .

'Only on foot this far,' she said. 'Bernie left the car in your lot to take the train to the airport yesterday. I'll drive home and then come back to pick him up when he gets in tonight.'

'If he gets in. Christy just said they're canceling flights.'

'Damn.' Caron swiped the stocking cap off her head, sending a spray of snowflakes onto the floor. 'Oops, sorry.'

My former partner was familiar with my need for orderliness. She had once accused me of trying to assign seats in the coffeehouse.

I waved her off. 'Not to worry. I've survived a year and counting of Sarah.'

'Don't tell me she's wearing down your OCD-ness.' Caron ducked into the utility closet for a tattered towel.

I took it from her to drop on the floor, pushing the thing with my foot to mop up the melting snow. 'Let's just say I've had to choose my battles.'

'I didn't know that was an option,' Caron said with a smile. 'When you're done cleaning up after me, can I get a latte?'

'Sure. For here or to go?' I tossed the towel back in the closet and beckoned for her to follow me through the door marked 'Employees Only' which led to our office, storeroom, kitchen and the serving area behind the counters. 'If you stay, Christy can tell you all about her new love.'

'Christy?' Caron asked, following me to the order window and craning her neck to see the front of house.

'Uh-huh. Filling in for Amy.'

'Oh.' Caron was an 'if you can't say anything nice, don't say anything at all' kind of person. Sarah was her bi-polar opposite.

Which was sometimes refreshing and most times not.

'We're getting a lot of cleaning done,' I told my former partner.

'Gotcha,' she said.

'She's in the storeroom, I think,' I told Caron, picking up the frothing pitcher. 'You can speak freely.'

'I'd rather not,' Caron said.

Stick in the mud. I opened the fridge and pulled out the skim milk.

'Two percent,' she told me. 'Frothed to just one-hundred-and-forty-five degrees Fahrenheit, please?'

I suppressed a sigh and switched out the milks. Pouring the two percent into the stainless-steel pitcher, I put it under the steam wand to start the frothing before I went to dispense espresso from the grinder into the long-handled portafilter.

'Decaf.'

Right. I took the lid off the can of decaf French roast I had ground earlier and spooned it into the portafilter before tamping and twisting it onto the espresso machine.

Hearing no objections, I pushed the button to brew a double shot and selected a clear glass latte mug.

'To go, please.'

I stood back. 'Want to make it yourself?'

'Sure,' she said, moving forward to commandeer the frothing pitcher and check the thermometer. 'You overheated the milk.'

'It's a cold day,' I said, sullenly. 'It'll cool down.'

She glanced over at me with a grin, as she dumped out the milk and started over. 'I've gotten picky since we bought the hotel.'

'Not true,' I said, folding my arms. 'You've always been a pain in the butt.'

'Maybe,' she said, raising and lowering the pitcher under the frothing wand to get just the right consistency of froth. 'How's business been? You're a little more off the beaten track here than we were at the strip mall.'

'It's true there's not as much walk-in traffic,' I said, uncrossing my arms. 'But the commuters are dependable. Not that you'd know that from this morning. The first train was practically empty.'

'The snow's coming off the lake, which means it's worse downtown.'

Downtown Milwaukee was situated on the shores of Lake Michigan. Brookhills was fifteen miles inland, so less subject to lake-effect snow. This storm, though, was following a trough from Canada – the so-called Alberta Clipper – so eventually nobody would be spared. 'Bet people will work from home rather than go in.'

'If they can. Which neither you nor I is lucky enough to be able to.'

'You could have stayed retired,' I told her.

'I know.' She took a paper cup and poured the espresso in, before topping it with steamed milk and then a cap of froth. 'I was bored.'

'So Bernie bought you a hotel.'

'*We* bought a hotel,' Caron corrected me, putting a lid on both the conversation and her drink.

I held up my hands. 'I know. Just messing with you.'

'And I know that.' She gave me a peck on the cheek. 'Miss you.'

'Miss you, too. See you later when you pick up Bernie.'

'If his flight doesn't get canceled. And the train is running tonight.' She pulled on her stocking cap then picked up the cup. 'Want me to pay for this?'

'Nope. That was our agreement. You get coffee for life.'

'But you probably thought that wouldn't be long,' Caron said, going to the door. 'People were dropping like flies all around you.'

'Still are,' I said, pushing the door open for her. 'You're just not here to see them.'

'Still miss you anyway.' A smile and she was trudging down the steps to the parking lot.

'Ooh!' Christy's voice came from the back as I was closing the door. 'Was that Caron? I wanted to show her Barry's picture. I caught her on the sidewalk the other day and was tempted to, but I didn't have my phone with me.'

'She said to say she was sorry she couldn't stay,' I fibbed, retrieving the same towel from the closet to mop up the snow that had blown in when I'd held the door open. 'She just finished a night shift at the hotel.'

'I think it's so exciting, owning a hotel like that,' she said. 'Every day is new people, new adventures.'

New problems.

'Speaking of people, or lack thereof,' I said, leaning over to pick up the towel. 'We're probably in for a slow morning, given the snow. If you want to lea—'

'I could do some more cleaning,' Christy interrupted brightly. 'It always cheers me up.'

'Why would you need cheering up?' I tossed the towel into a pile in the office that I planned to take home to wash. 'You just got off the phone with Barry.'

'I'm sad because I'm no longer on the phone with Barry,' she said, opening the utility closet to pull out a bucket. 'Parting is such sweet sorrow, you know.'

It was. Pavlik had been in New York last week, but it did not make me want to clean. It made me want to sit on the sofa and binge movie classics, accompanied by red wine, spray cheese and Ritz Crackers. Sweet.

But that was just me. 'Listen, I have to ask. When you were on the phone with Barry, you told him you made a transfer of some kind. I know it's none of my business, but—'

'But you want to know if I'm giving him money. Wiring it out of my account to his. Exactly how stupid do you think I am?'

Sarah would have had fun with the 'exactly' part, but I answered honestly. 'You are not stupid, not at all. But maybe . . . naïve?'

'Well, I'm not,' she said, folding her arms over her scrawny chest. 'Not naïve and not giving him money.'

She could shame me for asking, but I was not about to give up without a direct answer to my question. 'So the transfer?'

'Barry's money, Barry's account, if it's any of your business,' she sniffed. 'Which it's not.'

'He gave you his account information?' I asked, curiosity piqued even more.

'The man travels. All around the world,' Christy said, waving her hand in a circle over her head. 'You know how hard it is to manage your finances across different time zones?'

'He's never heard of Internet banking?'

'Shows what you know, Maggy. Trades have to be done when the market is open.' She jutted out her jaw. 'Nine to four eastern time.'

Not having money to invest in anything beyond my house and dog food, I didn't know if that was true, but I was still worried. 'Promise me you're not giving him access to your money.'

'Of course I'm not. But I am honored he trusts me with his.'

And I was astonished. Though I had to admit I had never known Christy to be anything but straight-up honest despite how odd she could be.

So I dropped the subject against my better judgment. 'I don't suppose shoveling cheers you up?'

'Shoveling? Like outside?'

I hesitated, not knowing what she would find inside to shovel. 'Yes.'

'I suppose so,' she said, going to the front window. 'I have my boots and all.'

In order to cross the road, as we knew. 'It's just the front sidewalk and steps up to the porch and the front door.'

'But what about the parking lot? And the train platform? Do we have to clear that, too?'

'The county is responsible for shoveling the train platform and plowing the parking lot, though I don't know where they'll go with the snow.'

The snow cleared from the parking lot and street so far this winter was piled against a light pole between the front of our building and the train tracks. If it got much higher, they'd have to bring in a front-loader to shovel it into trucks and dispose of it. Somewhere.

'They used to dump it in Lake Michigan, I think.' Christy was reading my thoughts again. 'During bad snow years, I mean. But the salt and sand they use on the roads in the winter plus all the other pollutants from cars and trucks is bad for the lake.'

Which was, after all, where Milwaukee got its drinking water.

Christy was peering out at the heavily falling snow. 'The steps are already drifted shut. And . . . oh, no. There goes my driveway.'

I joined her at the window to catch a garbage truck with a giant plow blade attached to its bumper blast past, sending plumes of snow up toward Christy's studio on the opposite side of the street.

'Ugh,' I said as the roar of the snowplow receded into the distance. 'I hate digging out the end of the driveway after the plows come through. If you want to go do it now, before it freezes—'

But Christy was craning her neck. 'Bury?'

'Bury what?' I asked, trying to see past her. 'Your car? Are you parked on the street? You should move it if you are. There's a snow emergency, so they'll tow anything—'

'No, no.' She was rolling up on and off of her tiptoes, like a toddler trying to see. 'I could have sworn I just saw Barry getting out of a black SUV.'

Oh, that kind of Barry. 'But he just called from . . . where exactly was he?'

'Heathrow. That's the airport in London.' She turned, her face alight. 'But what if he just said that? What if Barry was already in the States getting ready to surprise me.'

The States. Our little girl had grown so continental. 'He called what? An hour ago? And in the middle of a blizzard with the airlines canceling flights. He'd have to—'

'Mitchell International is still open for now,' Christy said, not ready to give up her dream of a surprise visit from her long-distance lover-to-be. Maybe. 'He could have flown in last night even.'

She cocked her head, her chin lifted. 'That's when flights from Europe arrive, you know. Afternoon or evening. Because of the time difference.'

The 'International' in Mitchell International pertained to flights from Canada, Mexico and the Caribbean, as far as I knew. 'There are no direct flights from Europe to Milwaukee.'

'Not to Milwaukee, of course. But to Chicago O'Hare. So, it makes even more sense that Barry flew into O'Hare yesterday and then either flew or drove up here this morning. He could even have taken a ride-share.'

From Chicago – that would cost a fortune. But who was I to dash her dreams? 'Do you really think it was him? Would you recognize him?'

'Of course.' She turned to me with her chin inching even higher. 'You saw the photos and all—'

The sound of footsteps pounding up the stairs interrupted her and, as Christy turned breathlessly toward the door, it swung open sending the sleigh bells crashing.

'Can I get a quick coffee? Whatever you got.'

Harold Byerly, one of our regular trash collectors, was standing on the rug, snow and slush clinging to his boots.

'You're melting,' Christy snapped, disappointment on her face.

'Oh, sorry,' Harold said, lifting one and then the other of the boots, like he hadn't noticed he had them on.

'Not a problem. Stay there and we'll bring it to you.' I leaned over the counter to reach a newly brewed pot to fill a to-go cup. 'Plow duty today?'

'Yup, drew the short straw,' he said, nodding gratefully. 'What do I owe you?'

'Coffee's on the house,' I said, handing it to him. 'Just try not to block our parking lot entrance.'

'Or my driveway,' Christy added.

'Deal,' he said, now rocking back and forth on his boots. 'Umm, could I use your restroom? I had—'

'Of course,' I said, waving him on before we had more than just snow on the floor.

Without another word, he shuffle-ran/sprinted around the corner with the coffee. Happily, the restrooms were just down the hall across from the train platform door.

'He could at least have wiped his feet,' Christy said, still pouting. 'And he took his coffee in there. Eeeew.'

'I'm sorry Harold wasn't Barry,' I said, retrieving my towel from the dirty pile and using it to wipe up the snow and slush trail. 'But he is a customer.'

'A non-paying one.' Christy, sounding remarkably like Sarah, had returned to the window and now did a double take. 'See? There!'

'There where?' Even without Harold's plow adding to the white-out by throwing up the already fallen snow, it was nearly impossible to see.

'Across the street,' she said, pointing. 'I think, yes, he's coming this way.'

A man emerged from the storm.

'Barry, Barry!' Christy was waving her arms in front of the window, trying to get the man's attention.

'And you're sure it's him?' I was squinting, trying to see between gusts of wind that were taking the snow nearly horizontal.

'Of course I am,' she said, now balling her fist to pound the base of it against the window. 'Who else would it be?'

Some random customer who is going to think you're nuts, was my thought. It honestly seemed more likely than having the man we'd just spoken to in London appear on the doorstep.

'Stop,' I ordered as she raised her hand to hammer the glass again. 'You're going to break the window and he can't hear you above the storm anyway.'

'You're right,' she said, dropping her fist and craning her neck to see. 'I think he's coming this way.'

How she knew that, I had no idea. I could see nothing and

nobody out there. 'He has your address, right? Won't he go up to your house?'

'I suppose. Though I did tell him I was working just before I put you on the phone.'

'Did you tell him where?' I asked. 'Or explain that the coffeehouse was across the street?'

'Of course.' Comprehension flooded her face. 'That's why Barry called this morning. To find out where I was.'

'And here you are.' I don't think I said it facetiously.

'That's right,' she said. 'I should go to him.'

'Yes, you should.' Whoever he was.

She stopped with her hand on the doorknob. 'But look at me. I can't meet the love of my life for the first time dressed like this.'

Christy was wearing a navy Uncommon Grounds apron over a cappuccino-colored Uncommon Grounds T-shirt which she had unwisely paired with black dress pants. The look, such as it was, worked best with jeans.

Not that I had ever seen Christy Wrigley in jeans.

'You said yourself that he knows you're working,' I pointed out. 'And, besides, you look fine.'

'You think?'

'As long as you didn't send him a picture of Sophia Loren or somebody and tell him it was you.'

'Sophia?' Christy asked, untying her apron and tossing it toward me. 'Is that Ralph's daughter?'

Not knowing the apron was coming, I missed it and had to bend to retrieve it from the floor. By the time I had straightened up, I'd worked out that Christy was talking about the designer. 'No. Ralph Lauren's daughter isn't named Sophia.'

'But same last name, right?'

'Wrong.' But I didn't bother to literally spell it out, instead leaving it at, 'Sophia Loren is a long-time actress. Incredibly famous, very beautiful.'

'And I look like her?'

Sure, let's go with that.

But Christy already had moved on. 'He must have gone up to the house because he's coming back down the driveway.' Christy was nervously running a hand through her red hair.

When the hand balled in a fist again, dangerously close to my plate-glass window, I shoved the door open with a jangle. 'Catch him now then.'

But the little redhead stepped back – distancing herself not only from the cold and snow blowing in, but the man standing across the street in it. 'I'll ruin the surprise.'

'Not as much as if he doesn't find you,' I pointed out, letting the wind slam the door shut. 'He'll leave.'

Christy considered that for a moment before stepping up to the door and shoving it open again. 'Barry!'

The man, who had hesitated on the sidewalk across the way to pull out his phone, now turned, slipping his phone back in his coat pocket. 'Yes?' he called.

'It's me!' Christy stepped out onto the porch now, arms crossed against her chest in the cold. I followed.

Barry held a hand to his ear, bracing himself against the wind as he crossed the street to us. 'Pardon?'

'It's me, Christy,' she tried again.

'Christy Wrigley?' It seemed clear that whatever Barry had expected, she was not it.

And she wasn't even wearing the creepy yellow rubber gloves.

Still, I felt horrible for her. 'I'm Maggy,' I said, trying for polite in the face of the man's rudeness. 'Why don't you come in for a coffee? You must be freezing.'

'Yes. Please.' Christy was advancing down the steps. The snow was falling in giant flakes now.

'No way.' His voice was half an octave higher than I had heard it earlier and he was backing away even as Christy advanced. 'I didn't expect this.' He waved his hand at Christy in her UG T-shirt, pants and sneakers. 'Whatever this is.'

Ass. 'That's just plain rude,' I said, coming to stand shoulder-to-shoulder with Christy, a united front on the bottom step of our porch. 'I suggest you leave before I call the police.'

Or freeze to death.

'Maggy, no.' Christy was sniffling next to me.

'You're going to call the police?' He stumbled backwards

down off the curb as he dug into his pocket and came up with the phone. 'Let me do the honors.'

A gust of wind blew, carrying his words horizontally away from us along with the snow. We were in a near whiteout now.

'Trust me,' I said to Christy as the cacophony of howling wind blended with that of snow removal equipment. 'You don't want this man in your life.'

'Shh,' Christy said, though there was no way Barry could hear me as the din grew. Nor could we hear what he was saying into the phone as he was eerily illuminated.

'Barry, come!' I ordered, like the man was my sheepdog. 'Come here now!'

I should have known that Barry would do exactly what Frank usually did. Ignore me. Even if Frank were equipped with opposable thumbs, though, I like to think he wouldn't throw me the finger.

Which was exactly what Barry was doing as the snowplow mowed him down.

FOUR

'Flat.' Sarah's phone-slash-camera was focused on the light pole where the plowed snow of this winter had been piled. It was here that the snowplow had come to rest. Sarah had already snapped photos of where Barry Margraves had been struck by the plow blade and then run over by the tires of the truck itself. 'White.'

We were standing on the porch of Uncommon Grounds, both of us in parkas and knitted hats. The snow was still coming down in great handfuls piling up on the bright blue tarp that covered Barry's body.

'That's kind of tasteless, don't you think?' I said, looking sideways at her.

'What?' She put the phone away. 'Taking pictures?'

That, too. 'Flat white. As in the man was run over. And snowed upon.'

The ambulance crew lifted the tarp-covered body onto a gurney, snow falling off in clumps as they half-wheeled, half-lifted the cart into the ambulance. The vehicle's destination would be the morgue, not the hospital.

'Flat white. As in I'm freezing my ass off and want one.' She pulled open the door. 'I can have a latte if you think that's in better taste.'

I glanced back at where the body had lain, outline already being blurred by the snow, and followed her in. 'Have what you want. Just don't say "flat white" in front of her.'

I chin-gestured toward the table where Rebecca Penn sat with Christy, the latter's red head next to the former's dark one. I'd had to physically restrain Christy from going to what was left of Barry's side. I left her sitting on the top step of the porch and made my way to his body on the street while dialing 911.

The man had been hit and run over from left to right as we had watched. I'd leaned down to check for a pulse, though the astonished, vacant eyes already told me there would be none.

Standing up from Barry's body, I'd surveyed the empty street. No looky-loos or helpful neighbors emerging from the surrounding buildings. The storm meant everybody was inside and probably unaware of anything but the passing of the snowplow. The eerie blanket-like quiet of the storm was broken only by Christy's sobbing and the rhythmic engine noise of the still-running truck sitting plow-end into the snow pile.

I had started toward the truck to check on the driver when the first Brookhills County squad car pulled up and Deputy Kelly Anthony emerged. I'd told Kelly that Christy's friend had been hit by the plow and she, in turn, pointed out that I was not wearing a coat and would freeze to death if I didn't go in. Getting Christy to her feet, I'd taken her inside Uncommon Grounds, wrapped her coat around the shivering shoulders and let her cry.

I'm not much good with emotion-fraught situations, so when Christy had quieted a bit, I asked if there was somebody I could call to be with her. She'd sobbed something that sounded like 'Ruh . . . ruh . . .' and that was good enough for me to go looking for Rebecca Penn's number on her phone.

I had found it and dialed Rebecca for her and Sarah for me. Not that Sarah was so much a comfort as a familiar thorn in my side. Being right across the street, Rebecca had been there straight away, not even bothering with gloves or a hat. Sarah had filled her gas tank and picked up her dry cleaning on the way.

Now back inside with Sarah, I slipped off my boots, hung up my jacket and padded sock-footed over to Christy and Rebecca at the table.

'. . . and I just don't understand,' Christy was saying. 'Am I so ugly that he . . . he—'

'Stepped in front of a snowplow?' Sarah was shrugging out of her coat even as she disappeared around the corner to the service area. She popped out behind the ordering window, peeling the cap off her head. 'Nah.'

Rebecca bristled, which saved me the energy of doing it myself. 'That's a horrible thing to say, Sarah.' She awkwardly rubbed Christy's shoulder. 'Of course he didn't, hon. Don't you listen to her.'

Awkward or not, Christy seemed reassured. Or at least diverted. She lifted her tear-stained face. 'It's not that I think he stepped in front of the truck on purpose. Suicide by snow-plow would be too odd, don't you think? And unnecessary. It's not like we were married or anything.'

Even then, divorce seemed the better alternative. 'Absolutely,' was all I could think to say.

'But he certainly didn't want to come into the coffee-house,' Christy continued. 'In fact, he seemed focused on leaving.'

'Escaping, from the sounds of it,' was Sarah's contribution.

'I'm sure that's not true.' Now Rebecca was patting Christy's head like she was an Irish setter. This *I* could have done. 'Maybe he forgot something in the car and went back to retrieve it. Right, Sarah?' she asked pointedly.

'Righto.' Sarah was pouring milk into a stainless-steel pitcher and did not look up.

'He was dropped off by a ride-share, I think,' Christy said, chewing on her lip.

'So he forgot something and was trying to catch the driver before he left,' Rebecca said, nodding at me to hop up on the bandwagon Sarah had already joined.

'A gift for you, maybe?' I offered feebly.

Sarah twisted a portafilter on the espresso machine and pushed the button to pull a shot before commencing frothing. She said nothing.

But Christy had brightened a bit at the thought of a prezzy. 'You think?'

'Of course,' Rebecca said, throwing me a grateful smile. 'Didn't you say he was bringing you something for your four-month anniversary?'

'Sending it, he said.' Christy seemed to be buying into the scenario we were weaving. 'But maybe that was all part of the surprise. He said it would probably arrive today or tomorrow, but I shouldn't open it until he was able to be here to see me do it.'

Rebecca flung out a hand, sending the coffee mug next to

her sliding. She steadied it. 'That must be it! And then he shows up with it in person.'

'I think it's a diamond,' Christy confided breathlessly. 'For an engagement ring that we'll pick out together . . .'

She let the rest of the sentence go, the reality that there would be no 'together' seeming to slap her in the face.

'He must have loved you very much,' Rebecca continued gamely. 'I bet he was just setting up another surprise, leaving like that. Right, Maggy?'

Having witnessed the leave-taking myself, I was pretty sure Sarah was right and Barry was fleeing the scene when the plow hit him.

Before I could say 'righto' like Sarah had, the door opened. Deputy Kelly Anthony was stomping the snow off her boots on the porch.

'Should I take my boots off?' the deputy asked, stepping in and seeing my sock feet.

'Only if you want—' I started.

'Cold feet.' Sarah finished. 'The tile floor is freezing and Maggy's the only one anal enough to keep slippers here.' Sarah disappeared behind the counter and reappeared with my slippers, setting them on the counter itself.

'Don't put those there,' I protested. 'It's unsanitary.' As I went to take the slippers, my right foot landed in a cold puddle, likely left by Sarah's defrosting boots as she had made her way into the serving area. Without stomping.

Anthony grinned. 'You sure you don't want me to take them off? I don't mind.'

'So you, too, can have cold, wet feet?' I put my hand on the counter for balance to slip my wet, socked foot into dry slipper. I considered stripping off the sock first, but it did not seem a good look in the dining room. Especially after I had criticized Sarah for being less than sanitary.

'Wah, wah, wah.' Sarah came around the corner and snagged the drink she had just made – presumably a flat white – from the service window where she'd left it for retrieval. 'Anybody want one?'

'What is it?' Rebecca asked, cocking her head.

'Small latte,' I said before Sarah could answer. Putting the one slippered foot down, I stepped sideways with the other foot, landing on a small pile of melting snow cut with sand and salt from the street. 'Damn it.'

'We should wipe that slush up,' Christy said absently from the table. It was a measure of her grief and confusion that she already wasn't on it.

Anthony did a double-wipe of her shoes on the rug and came over to me as I slipped on my other slipper. 'I'm trying to get the picture,' she said, keeping her voice down. 'You told me out there that the deceased is a friend of Ms Wrigley?'

'Virtually,' Sarah said, joining us.

'Virtually?'

'They met online, Sarah means,' I explained. 'A dating site.'

'Dating?' She seemed surprised.

'I know,' I said. 'But I guess it's the way to meet people these days.'

'"These days" being the last two decades,' Sarah said mildly. Or mildly for her.

'No, I was just surprised,' the deputy said. 'Wasn't she—'

'Dating my cousin, the killer?' Sarah asked. 'Yes. Christy and Ronny started up in your county jail and continued to state prison. But apparently it's over. Though who knows given . . .' She chin-gestured toward the street, still teeming with emergency vehicles.

'Anyway,' I said, taking in Anthony's puzzled expression, 'Christy met Barry Margraves online, but this was the first time they'd met in person.'

'Which is why he had stopped here in the first place,' Anthony said, seeming to recover. She flipped a page of her notebook. 'Quite a shock.'

'Especially for him,' Sarah said under her breath.

'For the deceased,' the deputy said.

Sarah shrugged. 'From what I hear, he got a gander at Christy and stepped in front of the truck.'

Anthony cocked her head. 'You're saying Mr Margraves killed himself with the snowplow?'

'No, no,' I said, holding up my hands. 'Sarah is being . . . Sarah. I saw the accident and that's just what it was. An accident. Margraves stepped back off the curb onto the street in front of the plow.'

Christy's head had swiveled our way and now she left Rebecca to join us.

'I'm Christy Wrigley,' she said, holding out her hand to the deputy.

'I'm very sorry for your loss, Ms Wrigley,' Anthony said, shaking Christy's hand.

'Thank you. We were to be married.'

Anthony glanced at me. I shrugged.

Christy caught it. 'Barry was bringing me a diamond. You said it yourself, Maggy.'

I grimaced. This is what I got for following Rebecca's lead and trying to be nice. 'I didn't actually. You said he was sending you a gift and that you thought it was a diamond. I merely didn't . . . disagree.'

'See?' Christy asked, sticking her head out like a chicken.

'Yes,' Anthony said, her face saying just the opposite. 'This diamond, did you say he had it on his person or was sending it?'

'We don't know,' I said, before Christy could further confuse things. 'Barry told Christy he was sending her a gift, which she presumed was a diamond. When he surprised her by showing up here in person, she thought—'

'That he might have it with him,' Anthony said, nodding. 'There's no sign of it.'

'Do you need me to identify Barry's body, deputy?' Christy asked, her hand playing at her neck like she was wearing a string of pearls. 'It would be terribly difficult, but—'

Rebecca had jumped up and was now at her elbow. 'You don't want to do that, Christy. Think about it: is that how you want to remember Barry?'

'No.' A wistful smile had come to Christy's face. 'I want to see him forever as he is in his profile picture, I think. Smiling up at the camera with French bulldog Buster. But if the authorities need a formal identification, it's my duty.'

Kelly Anthony cleared her throat.' No need for that, Ms Wrigley—'

'Christy.'

'Thank you, Christy. For now, the deceased . . . Mr Margraves did have picture ID on him.'

'His passport, I'm sure.' Christy's head was bobbing up and down. 'He was just in Europe.'

'We didn't find a passport, but he did have a Colorado driver's license. Is he—'

'Going to get a Wisconsin one?' Christy anticipated, seeming to want to prove – at least to herself – that she knew the man. 'I'm sure he planned to. It is state law, isn't it? Once you move here permanently?'

'Within sixty days of relocating,' Anthony told her. 'So where was Mr Margraves staying for now? With you?'

Christy colored up at that. 'No, I . . . well, not yet. He would not just show up at my place of work with his suitcase. I mean, he was a gentleman.'

'Of course,' Anthony said. 'A hotel then? Or a vacation rental.'

'I don't know,' Christy had to admit. 'He had stopped by to surprise me, as Maggy said.'

'Maybe the driver who dropped him off could help,' I said quickly.

'Another driver dropped Mr Margraves off?' Again, Anthony seemed puzzled.

'Ride-share, I think,' Christy said, head bobbing up and down. 'Barry prefers them to cabs. Not that money is a consideration. Barry gave me this.' She held out her diamond bracelet but kept on talking. 'It was the conversation he enjoyed, he said. People from all walks of life. He loves . . . loved meeting people.' Abruptly, she broke into tears.

Rebecca put an arm around her and led her away toward the restroom.

Kelly Anthony turned to us. 'How long has Barry Margraves worked in Brookhills?'

I cocked my head. 'I didn't realize he already had a job here, but I guess that explains why he's moving from Denver in the first place.'

'He didn't have a commercial license on his person, though,' Anthony said, taking out the Colorado license and laying it on her notebook. 'He should have.'

'A commercial license for what?' Sarah asked.

Instead of answering the question, Anthony asked another. It was a deflection tactic of Pavlik's, too. I assume they teach it in Sheriff 101. 'Just how well does Ms Wrigley know Mr Margraves?'

'I guess they talked a lot on the phone,' I told her. 'I think it was a real relationship, at least for her.'

'And maybe for him, until he got a load of the craziness that is Christy,' Sarah said.

'Be nice,' I said. 'She wasn't wearing her gloves.'

'Gloves or no, still crazy,' Sarah said and turned to the deputy. 'Why do you ask how well she knew him? Is the guy a crook or something?'

'Not that I can tell.' Anthony punched up something on her phone. 'Nice house in Denver, dog named Buster and' – she looked up from her phone – 'wife named Helena.'

'Wife?' Sarah repeated loudly.

'Shh.' I took a step back to check around the corner. Rebecca and Christy were standing in the corridor outside the restroom. The redhead's back was toward me, but Rebecca glanced up.

I lowered my voice and said to Anthony, 'You're telling us that Barry Margraves is married? I mean, like, happily married?'

'As opposed to happily cheating married?' Sarah clarified.

'They married fifteen years ago,' Anthony said. 'As for the rest, he apparently was happy enough to have booked a trip for two to London next week,' Anthony said. 'We found the ticket receipt in his coat pocket.'

Sarah shrugged. 'So? How do you know it wasn't for him and Christy?'

Good point, I thought. 'Their four-month anniversary was coming up and, remember, Christy was expecting a proposal. Maybe she's right and the trip was to celebrate, or he was going to whisk her away to get married.'

'Have to get divorced first,' Sarah pointed out. 'I think this engagement was in Christy's fertile imagination.'

'If so, the idea was planted there by Margraves,' I said. 'As for the trip, he apparently traveled to Europe extensively.'

'Expensive for a man in his line of work,' Kelly said, checking her notes.

The deputy apparently knew more about Barry Margraves than we did. I hadn't bothered to ask Christy what her new beau did for a living. 'My point is, if a man goes on a business trip, how's his wife to know if he's brought along a bimbo?'

'Bimbo?' Kelly Anthony repeated. 'I thought Ms Wrigley was your friend.'

'Sorry. Just an automatic reaction on my part,' I said, shamefaced.

'Maggy's ex-husband Ted used to take his bimbo on business trips,' Sarah explained.

'Got you,' the deputy said with the wisp of a grin. 'Anyway, the ticket was in the names of Helena and Barry Margraves.'

Hmm. 'We don't have to tell Christy right now, do we?' I asked, wanting to make up for calling her a bimbo.

'I would like to know if *she* knew,' Anthony said.

'That Barry Margraves was married?' I asked. 'I doubt it. In fact, I'd stake my life on it.'

'Let's not go overboard, Maggy,' Sarah said. 'Christy was dating a convicted murderer before this. A married man is peanuts by comparison.'

'Whose side are you on?' I demanded.

'The truth,' Sarah said, making me want to gag a little. 'The guy was too good to be true. Christy should have known it.'

'Maybe.'

'I still don't understand,' Anthony said, tapping her pen on her pad. 'We know Margraves was here long enough to be working for Brookhills County. How is it that he and Christy Wrigley just met today?'

'About time,' Rebecca's voice said huffily from the corridor.

'They've corresponded for three months, nearly four,' I said. 'But you say he worked for Brookhills?'

'Sorry, sorry,' a man's voice was saying. 'You might want to wait a beat before going in there.'

'Maggy?' Christy, this time.

'Can we keep a lid on this, please?' I asked Anthony again

before I stuck my head around the corner. A man was coming out of the bathroom, checking his fly. 'Harold?'

'Sorry,' the portly driver said with a sheepish grin as he snagged his parka from a hook. 'Spicy pad thai last night. I should know better.'

I glanced out to where the garbage truck/snowplow sat with its nose deep in the mound of snow. 'You can't have been in the bathroom the whole time.'

'Yeah, really sorry to hog it.' He nodded toward Christy, whose hand was on the knob. 'I kind of fell asleep. Or my butt did.'

'Wait,' Kelly Anthony said, picking up on my confusion. 'Who is this?'

'Harold Byerly. He drives the snowplow.' I waved toward the window.

The deputy was staring at Harold Byerly, but his gaze had followed mine. 'Whose truck is that?'

'It's not yours?' Anthony asked, her face gone white.

'Hell, no.' He went to the front door and threw it open to stick his head out. 'I left mine up . . . Well, will you look at that?' He pulled back in. 'It's gone.'

FIVE

'OMG. OMG. O.M . . . G.'

'Is it just me,' said Sarah, watching Harold Byerly, head in hands at a table by the window, 'or is there something disturbing about a sixty-something man whose pants are riding dangerously low using texting acronyms like some twelve-year-old girl?'

'You mean the man who just found out his unattended snowplow ran somebody over while he was purging himself of Thai food in our bathroom?' I asked, coming back to the counter. 'I'd say give him a break.'

Sarah had given me two steaming mugs of coffee which I had placed in front of both Harold and Deputy Kelly Anthony, who was sitting across from him at the table. Neither of them touched it.

Anthony had her notebook laid out on the table. 'What time did you park your truck?'

'Maybe close to eight?' He glanced over at me for confirmation.

I nodded. 'Thereabouts.'

'But it was nearly nine when you came out just now.'

'I told you, spicy pad thai. I love it, but . . . well, it doesn't love me.'

Sarah snorted and he glanced around. 'I wouldn't have ordered it if I knew it was going to snow this morning.'

And therefore, he'd be driving the plow, presumably.

'It was in the forecast,' Sarah pointed out, elbows propped on the service counter. 'Besides, if you weren't plowing, you'd be picking up garbage.'

'True, but that's not as stressful. Stress and pad thai' – he wound his index and middle finger around each other and shook his head – 'not a good combination, take it from me.'

I would do that, because I sure as hell was not going to ask any more questions about it.

'Why is that?'

I knocked one elbow out from under Sarah. 'Stop. If you want to do research, clean the bathroom.'

'I was thinking maybe Christy should do that.' She straightened up and glanced over her shoulder. 'Therapy.'

Rebecca had taken Christy into our office.

'I'll let you suggest that,' I said. 'On the other hand, don't.' Because she would and then tell Christy it was my idea.

'. . . sure you took it out of gear and set the brake?' Anthony was asking.

Harold Byerly bristled. 'Of course, I did. I told you that.'

'You'll forgive my question,' Anthony said, dryly. 'You left an unattended snowplow running for nearly an hour while you took a dump.'

'I like this woman,' Sarah whispered.

'I didn't leave it running,' Byerly hesitated. 'Or maybe I did. I remember thinking I'd only be a minute so maybe I didn't want the cab to get cold.'

Another snort from Sarah.

'Hey,' Byerly said, twisting in his chair. 'You try to start one of these trucks on a cold morning.'

'The commercial license,' I said to Sarah in an undertone.

'What?' she asked loudly.

I kept my voice low. 'Kelly said that Barry Margraves had a job here and should have had a commercial license. She was talking about a commercial driver's license, which would be needed to drive the snowplow for Brookhills County.'

'They thought Margraves stopped by to see Christy and had been run over by his own plow,' Sarah said, catching my drift.

'I guess so.' I rubbed my forehead. 'Though he wasn't dressed much like a truck driver. I think his coat was cashmere.'

'Bloody, smooshed and snow-covered cashmere now,' Sarah pointed out. 'They can be excused.'

'True.' Until autopsy, when all is usually revealed.

Rebecca came around the corner. 'Which coat is Christy's? I'm going to take her home.' She glanced at the deputy. 'Assuming that's OK?'

'It's fine.'

I pointed Rebecca to the hook with Christy's heavy wool coat. I had hung her bag back over it. 'There with the bag. She'll want that, too.'

'Thanks.' She turned toward them.

'Rebecca, one thing,' I said, stopping her.

'Yes?' We had never really been friends, and now her eyes regarded me suspiciously.

'It's just that I know you helped Christy with the online dating and all. You've gotten close.'

'Are you going to tell her about Margraves?' Sarah asked me.

'I was going to, but I don't know if I should,' I said, glancing toward the deputy's back.

'Tell me what about Margraves?' Rebecca asked.

'I don't know if I should say,' I said. 'The deputy may want to do it.'

'Deputy may want to do what?' Kelly Anthony had been speaking in low tones to Harold and now swiveled her head toward us.

I went over. 'Tell Christy about Barry being married,' I whispered.

'She's not a suspect,' Anthony said in a normal voice. 'If there's a crime here, it's vehicular homicide.'

Harold Byerly groaned. 'Oh, no. I . . .'

Anthony held up her hand to him before turning to me. 'If you want to break the bad news to your friend, have at it.'

'I was thinking we should tell Rebecca and she could help us decide when to tell Christy.' Or, even better, do it herself.

'Tell me what?' Rebecca asked testily. She had good hearing, but not much patience, and we were trying what little supply she had left at this point.

'That Barry-boy was married,' Sarah said. 'Happy?'

Rebecca closed her eyes. 'Damn.'

'Yeah,' I said. 'So what do you think? Do we tell her? And if so, when?'

Rebecca rubbed her face, thinking it over as she went to retrieve the coat and bag. When she came back, she was shaking her head. 'I don't want to tell her tonight.'

Christy popped her head out. 'Can we go?'

'Of course,' Rebecca said, giving her the coat. She held the bag as Christy pulled on the coat and then handed it to her.

'Is there anything else I can do for you?' Christy said, approaching the deputy. 'For Barry?'

Deputy Anthony stood. 'Not at the moment. But we'll be in touch.'

'Thank you.' Christy touched Byerly on the shoulder. 'I know it was an accident.'

'It was,' he said, tears coming to his eyes. 'I don't know how it happened.'

'I forgive you for killing the love of my life,' Christy said, making the sign of the cross before she curtsied. 'Go in peace.'

'Well, that was . . . nice of her,' Anthony said, as the door closed behind the two women.

I watched as they picked their way across the snow-covered road to Christy's studio, avoiding the still taped-off area where Barry Margraves had lain.

'She's had a shock.' Kelly Anthony had appeared at my shoulder as Byerly excused himself to go to the bathroom. Again. 'She won't be operating on all cylinders for a while.'

'It's up to debate whether Christy even has all cylinders,' Sarah said.

'Be nice,' I said automatically, as Christy stopped to pull a manila envelope from the mailbox before pausing at the door and looking down at her feet and then back across the road at us. 'She's just realized she forgot her boots.'

'Her shoes are already wet,' Anthony said, as a verbal push-pull ensued across the street, with Christy apparently wanting to come back for the boots and Rebecca arguing against it. 'Crossing back will only make it worse.'

'Which is exactly what Rebecca is probably telling her,' I said. 'But Christy is a creature of habit. I think it's what keeps her functioning.'

'We all need some semblance of routine in our lives, I guess,' Anthony said with a shrug.

'Maybe you should take Christy her boots,' I suggested to Sarah.

Sarah had been about to sit down. 'You're kidding, right?'

Yes, but only myself. 'Never mind.'

Seat taken, Sarah said, 'Best she and Rebecca have some alone time anyway. She can tell Christy about Margraves being married.'

'It didn't sound like she was in any hurry to do that,' I said.

'I hope she doesn't wait too long,' Sarah said, leaning back in the chair. 'Meeting the wife at the funeral could be awkward.'

An exceptionally good point. 'Has she been notified?' I asked Anthony. 'Barry Margraves' wife, Helena, I mean.'

'Margraves had a cell number for her on his phone, but it went directly to voicemail. I asked that she call us back.'

'Good thinking,' Sarah said. '"Your husband has been killed by a snowplow while visiting his mistress" isn't a message to leave on voicemail.'

'Christy wasn't his mistress,' I said. 'She had no idea he was a cheating bastard.'

'What are you saying?' Deputy Anthony asked, head cocked to look at me. 'That Margraves got what he deserved?'

I could feel my eyes go wide. 'No, of course not. I only meant—'

She waved me off with a grin. 'Just messing with you. I know how much you get off on this murder stuff.'

When I am not a suspect, thank you very much.

Deputy Anthony picked up her notebook as we heard the toilet flush. 'Happily, this is probably an accident or, at worst, negligent homicide.'

'Not so happily for Margraves,' I muttered to myself, as the door closed behind her and Harold Byerly a few minutes later. 'Or Harold, for that matter.'

'Is Harold in big trouble?' I asked. 'I mean, criminal kind of trouble?'

Pavlik and I were sitting on our living room sofa waiting for Thai takeout to be delivered. Maybe my ordering Thai food for dinner was as insensitive as Sarah hankering for a flat white as Barry Margraves' body was being scraped off the snowy ground. But pad thai had just sounded good. Minus the extended bathroom time, I hoped.

'Still to be determined,' Pavlik said. 'We do know a

twenty-ton truck apparently sat idling unattended for nearly twenty minutes before rolling down the street to kill a man.'

The twenty minutes was admittedly a puzzler. 'Was the truck in gear?'

'It was in neutral when the deputies found it.'

'Are garbage trucks manual transmission?'

'The county has both. This one was manual, from what Anthony said.'

'Was the parking brake set?' I asked, tucking one foot under me and turning to face him more directly.

'Apparently not.'

I cocked my head. 'Are you saying that because it rolled or is there a way of actually telling that mechanically?'

'You mean when we take the truck into the shop for processing?'

'Do you do that?' I asked. 'I mean, I know you do. But in a case like this?'

'There's always the possibility of mechanical failure, which will enter into the finding of fault.'

'So say if the brake was pulled, but the truck still rolled. That would be a mechanical failure.'

'Yes. The plow stopped in the pile of snow cleared from the depot parking lot. There's no indication the parking brake was on and failed, but we'll check, of course.'

'Why would Harold park the truck and not put the brake on?'

'He was in a hurry to get to your bathroom?' Pavlik checked his watch. 'When is the food being delivered?'

'Should be here soon,' I said, getting up to glance out the window. No action yet. I turned. 'If Harold did leave the truck without pulling the handbrake, he would be negligent.'

Pavlik patted the sofa next to him. 'I'm sure we'll hear when the delivery comes.'

I sat back down next to him. 'And?'

'And, yes, Byerly would be negligent. But it also begs the question I referred to earlier.'

'Why did it sit there idling before it rolled down the street?' I rubbed my chin. 'Maybe the heat of the truck melted the snow around it, freeing it to roll?'

Pavlik dipped his head. 'Good theory. I would think that's possible, but the crime scene investigators will tell us more. It's just a shame that a lot of the physical evidence has been lost.'

'Because of the snow.' I was trying to think back to what I had seen of the truck's path before impact with Barry. It had been moving at a good clip, or so it seemed in that freeze-framed moment.

I had just assumed the truck had a driver. Who wouldn't? It was obscured by snow and my attention was on Margraves as he stepped back into the street. 'Kelly and the first responders found a man dead on the street and an empty truck crashed nearby. Didn't they wonder where the driver was?'

'Of course. That's why they assumed the driver had gotten out of his truck for some reason and been run over by his own plow.'

'I told Kelly Christy's friend had been hit by the plow but didn't realize she thought he was the driver.'

'Believe me,' he said, perturbed, 'I'm not happy about Anthony's assumption. It wasted precious time and allowed the scene to be compromised.'

'You know what they say,' I said, shifting so I could snuggle my back against him. 'When you assume, you make an ass of—'

'Please don't.'

Fine. I wouldn't. I did smile just a little.

'But you're right,' Pavlik said. 'And that assumption stalled and confused everything until you produced Harold Byerly.'

Aw shucks. 'I didn't so much produce him as he emerged. Took us all by surprise, but Kelly more than the rest of us, given she thought he was dead.'

'And what did you assume?' Pavlik wrapped an arm around me. 'That Byerly had finished in the bathroom and gone back out?'

'Yes, though in hindsight he'd have had to use the side door onto the train platform and then gone down the stairs from there. Christy and I were standing by the front door or on the front porch the entire time, so we would have seen him go out the front.'

'The platform door is right across from the restroom,' Pavlik pointed out. 'So, it would have made sense for him to go out that way.'

Our sheepdog Frank wandered in, sniffing the air.

'I guess. When Margraves was hit, I figured it was Harold or even another snowplow completely. Either way, I didn't expect him to still be in our bathroom.'

Finding no aromas wafting here in the living room, Frank padded back out, likely to report to Mocha that dinner was not yet served.

'Harold left the truck in front of Clare's shop.' Clare's Antiques and Floral Shop was on the other end of our block, across the street from the former Penn and Ink.

Pavlik hesitated. 'Do you know that or are you fishing?'

I squeezed one eye closed and squinted at him. 'Does it matter?'

'Not really.' He snugged me closer to him. 'I usually get more information than I give in one of these consultations regardless.'

I pulled away. 'I beg to differ.'

'Which is exactly why we keep doing this,' he said, pulling me back. 'We both delude ourselves into believing we've won.'

Well, yes. But I win more. I leaned back into him. 'Anyway, Harold parked the truck in front of Clare's because the space in front of our shop isn't big enough for a truck.' There was a driveway leading to the parking lot on one side of our building and the train tracks on the other. 'Then he hot-footed it to Uncommon Grounds to occupy our bathroom.'

'We'll have to take the word of you and his irritable bowel. By the time Deputy Anthony realized Margraves wasn't the driver—'

'The blowing and drifting had made a mess of any foot-prints,' I guessed. Sarah and I had cleared our sidewalk three times before we had finally called it a day and closed.

'It was a full thirty minutes after the accident that Byerly re-emerged, as you say, and told Anthony where he had parked the truck and when.'

The dogs came trotting back in the room and I disengaged

myself from Pavlik's arm around my waist and stood up. 'An accident, like you say.'

The doorbell rang. The four canine ears and two canine noses were seldom wrong. I didn't know why I had bothered to look out the window earlier.

'Thanks,' I said, taking one big bag and one small from the driver. They had my charge card on file.

'Beef with basil, I hope?' Pavlik said, taking a bag from me.

I closed the door against the cold and led the way back to the couch and glass-topped coffee table, where I had already stacked plates and silverware. Plus poured a nice dry Riesling in two glasses. 'Beef with basil, pad thai with shrimp and chicken satay. A veritable Thai smorgasbord.' I was opening boxes as I spoke.

A string of drool landed on my bare foot.

Mocha. Frank's drool was usually absorbed by his beard, at least until it reached saturation point and rapelled onto the coffee table.

'You'll get yours after we have ours,' I assured her.

She gave me the chihuahua stare and sat down on Frank's foot. He pulled it out from under and harrumphed down next to her.

'Anyway,' I said, sticking serving spoons in the beef and pad thai. 'You were saying?'

'What?' Pavlik scored a satay skewer.

I slid the little plastic cup of peanut sauce closer to him for enticement. 'You were saying that it was an accident and Harold won't be charged.'

He took the sauce. 'Just because you voice something doesn't make it true, you know. Harold Byerly was careless to leave the plow unlocked and running, at the very least.'

'This is Brookhills, though. And it is winter. People start their cars and leave them running to warm up all the time.' Not one to let myself starve, even in the pursuit of justice, I dished pad thai onto my plate and added a bit of beef with basil.

'They shouldn't do that either.' Pavlik dunked. 'But at least most are smart enough to leave the car in their own driveway, not on a public street.'

I stopped, fork in the air with a rice noodle hanging off it. 'Do we know that he left the engine running? Harold wasn't sure when Deputy Anthony asked.'

'Odd thing not to be sure of.' Pavlik took another skewer and used his fork to push the meat off.

'You think he's lying?'

Pavlik shrugged. 'I think that Byerly knows that admitting he left his truck unlocked with the engine running will get him into trouble. With Brookhills County Services, if not with us.'

'You're both Brookhills County.'

'Yes, but one of us can fire him, the other can revoke his license and put him in jail.'

I put my fork down and picked up my wine glass. 'Tell me about commercial driving licenses. Kelly mentioned them in connection with Margraves when she thought he was the driver.'

'A CDL is required to operate a vehicle over twenty-six thousand pounds.' Pavlik had moved onto the beef with basil.

'But . . .' Out of the corner of my eye, I saw a string of drool coming off Frank's beard. Catching it with a napkin, I tidied his beard and set the napkin gingerly aside on the coffee table, oozy side up. 'Of course, Barry Margraves wasn't the driver at all so it's no surprise he didn't have your CDL. Is the license he had on him enough for identification? Kelly didn't ask Christy to ID him, even though she volunteered.'

'I bet she did,' Pavlik said. 'For as meek as Christy might appear, she has a backbone of steel. She was quite the champion for Ronny Eisvogel when he was in county jail before his trial and sentencing.'

To state prison. 'I found a shiv in her purse yesterday.'

This made Pavlik put down his fork. 'You're kidding.'

'Made from a toothbrush,' I told him. 'She used it to clean the wheels of our condiment cart.'

'Christy got it from Ronny?' Pavlik was appalled.

'No, she made it herself. She said she wanted to show him she cared.'

'Prisoners make shivs out of what they can get their hands on *in* prison. Visitors don't try to smuggle them in.'

'I see what you're saying.' I put down my glass as I considered what to add to my plate. 'Better to smuggle in a real weapon like a gun or knife.'

'Or not,' Pavlik said dryly.

Spoilsport. 'Anyway,' I said with a grin, 'we were talking about the identification of Margraves' body. Is the Colorado license he had on him sufficient?'

'Mrs Margraves will confirm the identification when she gets here,' Pavlik said. 'Can you pass the pad thai?'

I complied, pausing to add a hefty spoonful on my plate en route. 'You got hold of her? Kelly said she had to leave a voicemail message.'

'Yes, Mrs Margraves called Anthony back,' Pavlik said, cherry-picking shrimp from the pad thai. 'Tough one. The poor woman didn't even know her husband was here in Brookhills.'

'Where did she think he was?'

'He told her he was going to San Diego to meet about a property for some tech company.'

'Is that what he does?' I'd realized earlier that Christy hadn't told me what the man did for a living, which was kind of amazing. I did, however, know his dog's name. 'Technology of some sort?'

Pavlik shook his head. 'Property investment and management. Anthony asked the same question and his wife laughed. Said he was about as non-techy as they come.'

Techy enough to find his way onto a dating app, though he probably hadn't wanted his wife to know that. 'Did Kelly tell her why her husband was here?' I asked. 'About Christy, I mean?'

'No,' Pavlik said, moving on to the beef. 'It's not our place.'

'To tell her the truth?'

'Not our place,' Pavlik said again. 'Unless the fact is integral to the investigation and she needs to know.'

'But won't she ask why he lied?'

'That's not for us to answer. For all we know, Margraves may have had a business reason for being here. Or not. But that is up to Mrs Margraves to look into. If she wants to.'

I supposed it made sense. It was bad enough to get a call that your husband is dead. But to compound the pain by hearing from a stranger that he was cheating? Ugh. And the fact was, Margraves had not actually cheated – at least physically – yet. With Christy.

'Barry Margraves apparently travels – or traveled – a lot. Maybe his wife is used to him popping into different cities at a moment's notice and won't question it.'

'Maybe. Or if she suspects, she may not want it confirmed. It'll change nothing at this point. Her husband is dead.'

'Once you know, you can't unknow.' Even if your first instinct is to protect yourself by pretending it didn't happen. Or would not happen again.

Neither was an option in my case, since Ted broke the news to an unsuspecting me and went off and married his hygienist in less than six months. Ted is a dentist, by the way, not some patient who fell in love in the dental chair. That would be creepy.

'Damn, just hit a pepper!'

'I ordered hot,' I told him.

'Good,' said the masochist, taking a sip of his Riesling. 'Anyway, before you ask: Helena Margraves is flying in late tomorrow afternoon. But I'd appreciate it if you wouldn't share that information.'

'With Christy, you mean? Never.'

'Or with Sarah. Who might just tell Christy for kicks.'

'I don't think Sarah's quite that cruel.' But I was not willing to bet my relationship with Pavlik on it. 'Neither will hear it from me.'

I picked up my fork and stabbed a piece of beef. 'It's terrifying to me that a quick decision any of us might make – like Harold leaving the truck for what he thought was going to be a minute – can affect so many lives: Harold, Barry Margraves, Helena Margraves, Christy. All broken.'

'And it can't be undone.'

'Hopefully, something is wrong with the truck.' Always better to blame a thing than a person.

'Like I said, it'll be checked over.' Pavlik took my plate. 'Are you finished? I'll give the dogs some.'

'Not the pad thai,' I warned. 'It's too hot.'

Frank looked disappointed. I picked up the container of

beef. 'Both beef and basil, on the other hand, are fine for dogs. Just don't give them the green onion garnish.'

'Gotcha,' Pavlik said, leading the three of us to the kitchen.

'I keep hoping it wasn't Harold's fault,' I said, watching the sheriff at the counter, divvying up the beef leftovers into two bowls – one papa bear-sized, the other baby bear.

'We'll see,' he said without turning. Or commitment.

'He found the space to safely park the truck in front of Clare's, so even if he left the engine running . . .'

Pavlik set down the two dishes and turned to me as the two dogs tore into the beef and the basil. No onions. 'Is that the end of your sentence?'

'Yes, but not of my thought.'

Pavlik returned to the living room to retrieve the wine glasses and handed one to me. 'Elucidate, please. Before it's time to go to bed.'

I took a sip. 'So here's what I'm thinking. Clare's is half a block away on our side of the street, but it was only when Barry was backing away from us toward the street that I registered the sound of the truck engine.'

'And tried to warn him by yelling "come".'

Both dogs left their bowls and came to sit obediently on the floor in front of him.

'They never do that for me,' I said. 'And don't say it's because you're alpha.'

'I would never say that,' Pavlik said with a grin. 'Having already made that mistake.'

Though the fact was that Pavlik was alpha, dammit, at least as far as Mocha was concerned. Frank still humored me occasionally.

'Anyway,' I said, picking up the empty bowls. 'My point is that Christy and I were out on the porch talking to Margraves, and I don't remember hearing an engine idling or any engine noise at all.'

'Until it was too late.'

There was that.

SIX

'Sorry,' my partner said the next morning. 'Can't help you. Wasn't there until *after* the guy was smooshed, remember?'

'You can at least listen to me.'

'I have been. You've been saying the same thing over and over. You don't remember the sound of the garbage truck-cum-snowplow. But I will point out there was a howling blizzard going on.'

She went to the condiment cart and snagged a newspaper, holding up the front page. '"Alberta Clipper Brings 18 inches of Snow", remember?'

'I'm well aware of that, but—'

'See?' Sarah said, throwing down the paper and tilting the lid of the cream pitcher up to peek in. 'When I *do* contribute a thought, you argue with me.'

'But the argument adds value,' I said, taking the pitcher from her to fill. 'You help me to talk it through.'

'Argue it through, you mean.' She opened the door of the condiment cabinet and pulled out a box of sweetener packets.

I set the pitcher on the counter of the service window. 'You see, I assumed I became aware of the snowplow again because it was coming closer. That maybe it had come around the corner to clear this side of the street.'

'Then maybe you should have warned the poor dead guy,' Sarah said, as footsteps sounded on the porch steps.

'I told you that I tried. Belatedly.'

'For the now permanently be-late Barry Margraves,' Sarah said, as the chimes on the door sounded.

'Yes.' I leaned across the counter to snag the carton of cream. 'Thing is, if the truck was parked half a block away, idling the whole time, why didn't I hear it? I wonder if Christy was aware of it.'

'I'd advise you not to ask her for a while,' Rebecca Penn said, pulling off her gloves as she closed the door behind her. 'I'm afraid I told her about Barry being a married man this morning.'

'Oh dear.' I straightened with the cream carton in my hand and turned to her. 'But she has to know, right?'

She slumped into a chair at the nearest table. 'I suppose. I just . . . just feel so responsible for this whole awful thing.'

'Please tell me you ran down Margraves with the plow,' Sarah said. 'Maggy's been picking at scabs trying to make something bleed all morning. You could be it.'

'I have no idea what that means,' Rebecca said, looking confused.

'Join the club,' I said, pouring cream into the pitcher and letting the lid drop with a clink. 'But I assume what *you* mean is that you feel responsible for suggesting Christy use the dating site in the first place.'

'Well, yes.' Rebecca removed her knitted beret and set it on the table, shaking out her dark hair. Snow was melting off her boots creating a puddle under the table, but I let it pass. 'That, and I encouraged her to answer Barry's ping or ding, or whatever they call it, from the dating app when it first came in.'

I went to set the pitcher on the condiment cart and then came back to her table. 'Can I get you something?'

'Flat white, please.'

Sarah lifted her eyebrows at me. 'See? I'm not the only one.'

'I'm not judging even you,' I told her. 'We ordered pad thai last night.'

'I'm starting to remember why I stopped coming in here,' Rebecca said, her eyes shifting between the two of us. 'I'm never quite sure what you're talking about.'

'And let's keep it that way.' Sarah went in the service door and reappeared behind the service window. 'One very flat, very white coming up.'

'See?' Rebecca appealed to me.

'I do. More than you can possibly imagine.' I pulled out a chair and sat down across from her. 'What brought you back anyway?'

'Here?' She looked around. 'I wanted a cup of coffee. So sue me.'

I ignored the hostility. Rebecca had taken Christy off our hands yesterday. I was grateful, which was why I was pretending to care about her life. 'I meant why did you come back to town. You went to New York to paint, right?'

'That was the plan, such as it was.'

'It didn't work out?' I asked.

'Small fish, big pond,' Sarah, ever sensitive to other's feelings, suggested above the steamer noise.

Rebecca didn't seem to mind. 'More like I was an amoeba in the ocean. When Michael and I were together, I convinced myself that he was the only thing holding me back from reaching my potential as an artist.' She pronounced it 'arteest'. 'That all I needed to do was pack up my watercolors and go to New York, where they'd recognize my talent.'

'You were only gone for a year or so,' I said. 'Do you think you gave it a fair chance?'

'I gave it all the chance I could afford. Expensive place, New York.' She tried to smile. 'Apparently it wasn't Michael preventing me from reaching my true potential. I just plain didn't have any.'

I frowned. 'That's nonsense – I've seen your work. You're good.'

'Good's not enough. At the very least, a little luck helps in the art world. And being dead wouldn't hurt at all.' She laughed a little bitterly.

'I don't recommend the latter,' I said.

'No.' She was gazing out the window. The sun had come out today, starting to melt the snow. In the center of the road, where Barry Margraves had been struck, a rusty red tone was mixed with the gray packed-down snow now turned to ice. 'Poor Christy. Maybe I should have let her believe that Margraves loved her. At least she could mourn . . . uncomplicatedly, you know?'

'Just because he was married to somebody else,' I said, 'doesn't mean he didn't love her.'

Rebecca seemed surprised. 'That's very generous of you, Maggy.'

Given my cheated-upon and dumped status, I was surprised, too. But the truth was that Ted had genuinely loved Rachel Slattery, the woman he had left me for. It had gone badly, and he'd paid, but there it was.

'Bullshit.' A flat white thudded on the table; Sarah's contribution. 'The guy was married and went cruising on a dating site. This wasn't a chance romance.'

'Well, regardless. Eventually somebody had to tell her.' And I was eternally grateful it hadn't been me. 'Did Christy stay with you last night, Rebecca?'

'No, I stayed at her house, thinking she'd sleep better. I was wrong about that, too.'

'Her married lover was just mowed down by a snowplow,' I told her. 'Doesn't really make for sweet dreams.'

'I didn't tell Christy that Barry was married until this morning, but the rest of yesterday's events were enough to give her nightmares.'

'Did you get any sleep?' I asked as Sarah plopped into the third chair.

'Not once she climbed into bed with me. That was after she checked every door and window against imaginary intruders and cleaned the kitchen. Again.'

I was trying to imagine what Christy wore to bed. A hypo-allergenic onesie? 'And this morning you broke the news?'

'Yes.' Rebecca looked miserable. 'She was about to call the morgue to claim the body. I kind of blurted it out.'

Sarah nodded. 'Good thing. It would suck to have the current Mrs Margraves and unofficial future Mrs Margraves meet over the body.'

'Hopefully the twain will never meet,' I said, mindful of my promise to Pavlik.

'Christy was scheduled to work today,' Sarah said. 'Might be good for her to get out of the house.'

Rebecca glanced out the window. 'There she is now.'

Christy had stepped out onto the porch to get the newspaper. As the carrier returned to his truck, Christy seemed to sense us watching and shielded her eyes to see across the street.

I went to wave and then realized she was staring at the bloodstain.

'I should probably go,' Rebecca said, getting up. 'I told her I was just coming over to get coffee for us.'

'I'll put that in a to-go cup, shall I?' I stood up and took her untouched drink. 'And one for Christy?'

'Please.'

Christy had disappeared inside as Rebecca avoided the brownish stain by going to the corner by the train tracks to cross with the two drinks.

'I've never been that fond of Rebecca,' I said, watching, 'but it is good of her to take care of Christy like this.'

'So we don't have to, you mean?'

'Well, yes. Neither of us is particularly good with this stuff.'

'You mean sensitivity?' Sarah asked, joining me at the window. 'Think she took the hint about Christy coming to work today for her own good?'

I rest my case. 'You mean *your* own good.'

'I had to open. On my day off.'

'Yes, I know. You have whined about it all morning. I was here by seven.'

'And I was here at six. That means getting up at quarter to.'

'Wait. You get out of bed fifteen minutes before you start work?' I asked.

'Sure. Five-minute drive here. That leaves me ten to shower and dress.'

I was happy to hear about the shower part. And I had to admit that choosing a wardrobe of Uncommon Grounds T-shirt and jeans didn't take long.

'Will you look at that?' A tall blond man had paused by the mailbox across the way to wait for Rebecca. 'Michael Inkel.'

'What about him?' Sarah asked as I watched Rebecca hand Michael the to-go cups to hold as she went to pull something out of her purse to mail.

I shrugged. 'The two seem civil.'

'Christy said they're off and on.' Sarah flung open the door and leaned out. 'Hey, Rebecca?'

'Yes?' she said, twisting around.

Sarah cupped her hands: 'Tell Christy she starts work at three.'

Rebecca cocked her head like she hadn't heard.

I took the opportunity to elbow Sarah aside. 'She said, tell Christy love from Sarah and me.'

I got a nod from Rebecca and a grin from Michael as he handed Rebecca back the to-go cups.

SEVEN

'"Tell Christy love from Sarah and me"?' Sarah repeated, ducking back into the shop.

'"Tell Christy she starts work at three" is so much better? How uncaring can you be?'

'But it doesn't even make sense,' Sarah said, waiting for me to get in and slamming the door behind me. 'If you're repeating what I supposedly said, wouldn't it be, "Tell Christy love from *Maggy* and me"?'

'Well, yes. I guess so.' Damn.

'Unless I, Sarah, am a complete idiot, that is.'

I know when to keep my mouth shut.

'Besides,' she continued, 'you're just as uncaring as me. You just repress it. Which isn't good for you.'

'Really?' I picked up a used plate from a deuce table and swept errant crumbs onto it. 'The way I see it, I close my mouth and whatever I'm repressing shoots out yours.'

'Then you admit it. You don't want to be here at the shop any more than I do.'

'If it means having this conversation with you? Hell, no.'

'I can always leave—'

'Trouble in paradise?' Caron stuck her head around the corner. She must have come in the door from the train platform.

'You don't know the half of it,' Sarah grumbled. 'Want your partner back?'

'Not on a bet.' She grinned at me.

'Did Bernie make it back yesterday?' I asked.

'Nope, but he caught an early flight into Milwaukee today. I'm here to pick him up from the train.'

'What train?' I frowned at the Brookhills clock overhead. Just past ten and it was a Wednesday. The commuter train did two round-trip circuits into Milwaukee and back each morning and evening. Weekends and holidays, the trains started later and ran throughout the day.

'They added a ten thirty today, because of yesterday's cancellations. People were left stranded.' Caron sat down at the table I had just cleared. 'I guess I missed all the action yesterday. Is it true what I'm hearing?'

'The man was hit and killed by a county snowplow,' I said, setting down the crumby plate and picking up a rag to wipe the table. 'Though I think it's strange that—'

'Here we go,' Caron said.

'I've had to listen to it all day.' Sarah's voice pitched higher in what I assume was supposed to be mimicry of me: '"But *why* didn't I hear it, Sarah? Why?"' She held her hand to her heart dramatically.

'I just said that if the plow was sitting in front of Clare's shop idling, I should have been aware of it when Christy and I stepped out on the porch. But I wasn't.'

'Clare's shop is close by,' Caron admitted.

'I want *her* back,' I told Sarah, pointing at Caron.

'She's missed the last three or four murders,' Sarah said. 'She comes back, she'll find you tedious, too.'

'Been there and done that,' Caron said. 'But I have to admit I'm intrigued. The man who was hit was the boyfriend you said Christy was so excited about?'

'Yes,' I said, sitting down on the chair across from her. 'Barry Margraves from Denver.'

Caron leaned forward, as if relaying a confidence. 'Margraves stayed at the Morrison the night before.'

Monday. Now there was news.

I frowned. 'But Christy saw him being dropped off by a car. Why would that be? The Morrison is maybe five blocks away.'

'Oh, people do that all the time,' Caron said, waving her hand. 'They just automatically call a cab or punch up a ride-share, not realizing how small Brookhills is.'

'And it was snowing,' Sarah reminded me.

'That's right.' Caron was nodding. 'I made that walk in the snow yesterday. It wasn't fun.'

'Did you see Margraves before you left?' I asked.

'No, I didn't meet him at all. But apparently, he was nice enough. Left a housekeeping tip in the room. Which goes to show you can never tell.'

'Because Margraves was cheating on his spouse?' I asked.
'I seem to recall you had a bout of that yourself.'

Why was it I couldn't help but point out the other side of
the argument, whatever that argument might be?

Caron's freckled nose pinked up. 'That was a long time
ago, Maggy. And Bernie forgave me.'

Much like I had forgiven Ted. But I had divorced him first.
Bernie and Caron had stayed together, and I was glad they
had. I loved them both.

So I shut up about it. 'Margraves flew in on Monday then,
which makes sense given the conditions on Tuesday. How
many nights did he book?'

'Two. Though the room wasn't slept in last night, obviously.'
She frowned. 'Think I should refund it on his credit card?'

'Why?' Sarah asked. 'It's not like he's going to know one
way or the other.'

'No, but his wife might appreciate it. She's expected in
tonight.'

'And staying at the Morrison, too?' I asked.

'Yes.' She wrinkled her nose. 'Did Christy know?'

Sarah pulled a chair over. 'That Margraves was
married? No.'

'She's devastated,' I told Caron. 'For more reasons than
one. Does the wife – Helena – know Barry had a room there?'

'I don't know. She booked her stay on the Internet.'

'You should probably tell her when she checks in,' I said.
'She may want to take his things back.'

'Or burn them,' Sarah suggested as a train whistle blasted,
signally it was pulling into the station. 'Have you thought
about what she'll find?'

'What do you mean?' Caron asked.

'The guy packed for an affair. He'd have . . . things.' She
wiggled her eyebrows.

'You mean like candles? Massage oil? Edible underwear?'

'At best. At worst—'

I held up a hand. Even the 'best' seemed incongruous when
paired with Christy. 'The thing is, Helena doesn't know
about Christy. According to Pavlik, it's not in their purview
to speculate on what – or who – Margraves was doing here.'

'Nice turn of phrase,' Sarah said approvingly.

'Thanks. Just one of those things I'd normally repress and leave for you to say.'

Sarah dipped her head. 'It would have been an honor.'

'But that's the thing,' Caron said, motioning us closer as the chatter of people alighting from the train reached us. 'I checked the room this morning. There is nothing in it. No suitcase, no nothing.'

I frowned. 'He certainly didn't have a suitcase with him yesterday. Are you sure he didn't leave it with the bellman?'

She nodded. 'Positive. The room was slept in Monday night and housekeeping made it up the next morning. Towels were hung up and sheets were not changed because it was a two-night booking. We're eco-friendly, you know.'

I knew.

'Like I said,' Caron continued, 'the bed was still made from Tuesday night, since he was—'

'Dead,' Sarah supplied. 'But then what happened to his luggage?'

'I wonder.' I stood up to serve the incoming commuters. 'And I'm also starting to wonder what else we don't know about the dead guy, himself.'

'Dramatic cliffhanger,' was Sarah's assessment after Caron left to run her husband Bernie home. '"What else we don't know about the dead guy, himself." *Dun, dun dunnnn!*'

'I know.' I was wiping tables after the unusual noontime rush. People had actually wanted to buy lunch. Go figure. 'I like to give Caron a little something. Make her miss me.'

'She does seem to want in on this one.'

'This one what?'

'Your investigation of whatever this is.' Her eyes narrowed. 'You miss her?'

'Of course I do. Caron is all the things you're not.'

'That I'm not, huh?' Sarah's lips tightened. 'Like what?'

'Hopelessly naïve, for one thing,' I said. 'You look on the dark side, so you don't shock as easily.'

'Sorry.'

'That's OK. Variety is good.' I set down my cleaning cloth

and picked up my phone to check the notifications. 'No answer from Pavlik.'

'What did you ask him?'

'If Kelly Anthony talked to the ride-share driver. I'm not sure she would have, given they think it was an accident or negligence on Harold's part.'

'Which you don't agree with.'

'I don't know.' I shrugged. 'I just have a feeling there's more to it. Where is his suitcase, for one thing?'

'In the car?'

'Maybe. It's not at the hotel and he sure didn't have it with him when he crossed the road.'

'Maybe he left it on Christy's porch? I mean, he was coming to see her.'

'But Christy seemed a little affronted when Kelly Anthony asked if Barry was staying at her place.'

'Doesn't mean he didn't have that intention.'

I considered that. 'I suppose. But she would have told us if she found his suitcase or duffel or whatever.'

Sarah's head tick-tocked side to side. 'Probably. She doesn't keep much to herself.'

'But,' I said, remembering, 'Christy couldn't have seen it until she and Rebecca went back to her house after the accident. We haven't spoken to Christy since then.'

'We have spoken to Rebecca, though,' Sarah pointed out. 'She didn't say anything.'

'And I watched them go into the house. Christy stopped for the mail, but I didn't see her react to a suitcase or something unexpected on the porch. I should text and ask.'

'Good idea,' Sarah said. 'Probably best to have her come here.'

I groaned. 'I am not going to ask Christy to come to the shop so you can disappear out the back.'

'Oh, Maggy.' Sarah took the rag from me. 'You do know I can escape out the back door anytime I want. I don't have to wait for relief.'

'But you will, because you're a good person.'

'I'm not, you know.' She was heading for the back.

'I know. But don't leave me this way.'

Sarah stopped. 'Thelma Houston. Disco. I'm surprised you didn't sing it.'

'I thought that might be too much.'

'You'd be right.' She threw the cleaning cloth in the dirty towel pile. 'Are you ever going to take these home to wash?'

'Tonight,' I promised, digging my phone out of my apron pocket. 'I'm going to call Kelly and ask her about the ride-share. And maybe text Christy about the suitcase.'

'You're really going to ask the bereaved other woman whether she has the dead guy's suitcase?'

'You're right,' I said, looking up from my phone. 'That would be insensitive.'

I punched up 'recent calls'. 'I'll text Rebecca instead.'

But nobody texted me back.

'Sometimes I feel like my texts are disappearing into a black hole,' I told Pavlik when he got home. 'And don't even get me started about emails.'

'What—'

'Or, God forbid, an actual phone call.' I pulled the cork out of a Pinot Noir. 'I don't even bother leaving a voicemail for Eric. He never listens to them. Just calls me back when he sees a "missed call" from me and feels like it. I'm his mother. What if I were dead?'

'You wouldn't answer?' Pavlik set two glasses on the table.

'Yes, but at least I'd have an excuse for behaving like everybody else does,' I said. 'Case in point: Kelly Anthony didn't call me back today.'

'That's not Deputy Anthony's job,' Pavlik said, reaching for the glass of Pinot I had just poured for him.

'You told her not to,' I accused him, withholding the Pinot.

'Yes.' He took it anyway. 'I'd prefer you ask me what you want to know instead of calling my deputies.'

'That's not very efficient,' I said, leaning back against the kitchen counter. 'You have more important things to do.'

He grinned and pulled out a kitchen chair to sink into. 'Those important things are now done. Ask away.'

Obviously, Pavlik didn't think my pumping his deputies for information was a good look. And he was probably right.

'I'm sorry.' I sat down across from him. 'It's just that Caron stopped by today.'

'It's been a while since I've seen her and Bernie. How are they doing?'

'Just fine.' I allowed the detour, knowing I would bring us right back on the main track. 'They bought the Hotel Morrison, you know.'

'Yes.' Pavlik took a sip and waited.

'Caron said Barry Margraves stayed there Monday night.'

'Yes.'

I cocked my head. 'You knew that, too?'

'I'm not surprised. It's the logical place to stay in Brookhills.'

Actually, it was the only place to stay in Brookhills. Most people visiting flew into Milwaukee and were likely to stay at one of the hotels downtown, like the luxe Slattery Arms, owned by my ex's in-laws, or an airport hotel.

'Margraves booked two nights,' I told him.

'Monday and Tuesday?'

'Yes.' I leaned forward. 'Though the room went unused Tuesday night, obviously.'

'Obviously.'

'Helena Margraves is booked for tonight – oh, I assume she made it in?'

'To identify her husband's body? Yes. And she confirmed it is Barry Margraves, before you ask.'

'I had no doubt.' I leaned forward, my fingers playing with the stem of the wine glass. 'Thing is, when Caron told me Helena was staying, I suggested that she could take her husband's belongings home.'

'She will have gotten his personal effects after identifying his body.'

'What was on him, yes. But I was talking about what he left in his room.'

'Oh, good thought.' Pavlik had been swirling his wine and now set it down. 'What did you have for dinner?'

'Toast.' Bread was pretty much all we had in the house, which explained why the dogs were not hovering. The two of them would be eating better than the two of us until I got to the store for human food tomorrow. 'Want some?'

'Got peanut butter?'

'Of course.' I stood up. 'Chunky or creamy?'

'Doesn't matter.'

Good thing, because when I opened the chunky, it was nearly gone. As was the creamy, but between the two, I patched together enough to feed my man.

'I'll get some more tomorrow,' I told him as I put the plate in front of him and sat down again.

'Thank you,' he said. 'And maybe some other protein. And vegetables.'

'You got it.' I picked up my wine. 'But back to Margraves' hotel room. Caron told me it was empty.'

'We've already established that he's dead.' Pavlik crunched into his toast with peanut butter all the way to the edges just as he likes it. Can't say I'm not a good fiancée.

'But she said the room was totally empty. No luggage, no toiletries. Which is why I called Kelly. I thought she might have contacted the taxi or ride-share and knew if he'd left his luggage in the car somehow. Or maybe dropped it off at the airport.'

Now I seemed to have piqued Pavlik's interest. 'That *is* odd. Unless he didn't have luggage.'

That had not occurred to me. I sat back. 'I suppose that's possible. But why?'

Pavlik shrugged. 'Quick trip in and out?'

'But he booked the hotel for two nights.'

'Caron is sure of that? And that he didn't leave bags with the bell clerk?'

'She says so,' I said, gnawing at my thumbnail as I thought. 'Maybe I'll stop by and see her at the hotel tomorrow. Just to confirm.'

'Helena Margraves is flying out tomorrow. Better go early if you hope to catch a glimpse.'

He knew me too well. 'I am kind of curious.'

'Probably late thirties. Nice, normal woman.'

Normal was one-up on Christy. 'You didn't answer about whether Kelly contacted Barry Margraves' driver.'

'I don't know the answer.' He held up his plate. 'Scare up enough peanut butter for a second slice and I'll ask Kelly tomorrow?'

'Deal.'

The heel of the bread loaf was toasting, and I was using a rubber scraper to clean out the peanut butter jars when my phone rang.

'Maggy!'

'Christy?' I popped up the toast. 'Are you OK?'

'*I* am, but I'm staying with Rebecca tonight.'

'And there's something wrong with her?'

'No, no, no,' Christy said irritably. 'Is the sheriff there?'

'Pavlik?' I shrugged and put her on speaker phone as Pavlik waved me off. 'He's in the bathroom. It may be a while.'

Pavlik rolled his eyes, but I knew he was grateful.

'Tell me what's wrong,' I said.

'I told you I'm staying with Rebecca. We finished up a jigsaw puzzle and I went back to my house to get my sheets and pack—'

'You brought your own sheets?'

'And pillow. I can't believe you're surprised at that.'

I wasn't. Not really. 'Go on.'

'I went to get my tennis bracelet because I forgot to put it on this morning and you'll never believe it. It's gone.'

'Gone?' I raised my eyebrows at Pavlik. 'Are you sure?'

'Of course I'm sure.' Then, presumably to Rebecca: 'I told you someone was skulking around the house last night.'

'I don't think they got in then,' Rebecca said, getting on the line. 'But the lock on Christy's back door has been forced.'

Pavlik picked up my phone. 'Christy, have you called the police?'

'Yes, I called you,' Christy said, seeming surprised. 'Are you still in the bathroom?'

'No.' Pavlik scowled at me. 'We'll be there in ten.'

'Wash your hands,' I heard Christy say as I went to end the call.

By the time we got to Christy's, the squad that Pavlik had called en route was already parked in front. Kelly Anthony was standing on the porch with Christy and Rebecca.

'A diamond tennis bracelet,' she said, writing it down. 'Anything else?'

I mounted the steps in time to see Christy's face redden in the porch light. 'Yes, umm, a manila envelope.'

'Containing . . .' Anthony led her.

'Containing . . . I'm not sure. I didn't open it.'

Kelly Anthony glanced at me and then back at Christy. 'Was this the envelope we saw you retrieve from your mailbox yesterday after Mr Margraves was killed?'

It was Rebecca who nodded. 'It had Margraves' return address. She didn't open it.'

'I couldn't.' Christy faltered, steadying herself by grasping the porch rail. 'Just seeing his handwriting on the envelope, knowing he'd licked the flap himself. I . . . I just wanted to preserve it. I'd promised him we would open it together.'

That was all well and good, but: 'You said he was sending a diamond. Didn't you want to see it?'

'What for?' Christy was sniffling. 'The promise it represented is gone. Everything is gone. Ruined.'

I wasn't sure if that was because Barry Margraves was married or dead. Or both. But it reminded me. 'Did you see anything else here on the porch yesterday?'

Her hand tightened on the railing. 'Like what?'

I glanced over at Pavlik and he nodded. 'A bag maybe? A suitcase or duffel Barry might have left before he crossed the street to the shop.'

'No.' Christy's forehead was wrinkled. 'I told you he wouldn't arrive expecting to stay at my house. He wasn't like that.'

Or married, she had believed. The truth was, Christy didn't know anything about Barry Margraves. Not that I said that.

'Back to the missing envelope,' Anthony took up. 'Not knowing what was in it, we can't very well put a value on it. Was the bracelet, at least, insured?'

'Insured?' Christy ran her hand over her wrist like the bracelet was still there. 'I'd only had it for a few days.' Her voice broke.

'Rebecca, you said a door was forced. Can you show us?' Pavlik asked.

She ushered Pavlik around to the back, the rest of us trailing. 'Here.'

Pavlik inspected the splintered wood of the back door. The lock was the type built into the doorknob. A tab you twist before closing the door to lock it. 'You believe this happened last night?'

'No.' Christy shook her head positively. 'The door was fine when I locked up to go to Rebecca's this morning. But I am certain somebody was lurking last night. I think we must have scared away the thief and they came back after we'd left.'

'You think they were watching you then?' Anthony asked. She was keeping her voice even but seemed skeptical.

'Could be,' Christy said, nodding this time.

'We were up practically all night with the vacuum going and the lights blazing,' Rebecca said. 'I can't imagine anybody deciding to break in. I think Christy's right that whoever it was came back after we'd gone to my place.'

'Which was when?' Anthony asked.

'This morning after I got the drinks from Uncommon Grounds,' Rebecca said. 'When was that, Maggy?'

'Maybe nine thirty,' I guessed.

'That sounds right,' Rebecca, said. 'Christy was taking a shower when I returned.'

Christy shuddered. 'I could have been stabbed in the shower. Like Janet Leigh in *Psycho*.'

If Sarah was there, she'd have muttered, 'I'll tell you who's the psycho.' Me, I was gratified by Christy's knowledge of the classics.

'Where were the bracelet and the envelope?' Pavlik asked, stepping past the splintered door jamb into the kitchen.

'In my bedroom,' Christy said, her face flaming red again. 'I can show Detective Anthony.'

Kelly Anthony glanced at Pavlik and he nodded, turning to me as the other three disappeared down the hall. 'Something I'm not allowed to see?'

'Her underwear drawer,' I explained. 'I heard her tell Margraves that's where she'd keep the gift when it arrived.'

'First place a thief looks for jewelry,' Pavlik said dryly. 'I've seen inside a few drawers in my time.'

'I'm sure you have,' I said, with a grin. 'But not Christy's and if I were you, I'd be grateful Anthony is taking one for the team.'

'But now I'm curious.'

'I know,' I said. 'Christy has said she's quite adventurous. I'm just not sure what that would look like, given her hygiene penchant.'

'You're right,' he said, as the others reappeared in the hall. 'Best not to know.'

'But you will see Anthony's report,' I said, putting my hand on his shoulder. 'And tell me, right?'

'Wrong.' He turned to Christy. 'Nothing was taken besides the bracelet and envelope?'

'Nothing,' Christy said.

Looking around, I could not see much to steal. Christy took minimalism to the extreme. The counters and table were empty. Probably easier to clean.

'Do you keep any money or firearms in the house?' Anthony asked.

'Money, just what's in my purse,' she said, moving to a kitchen drawer. 'But I do have a gun in this—'

'No!' The shouts of both Pavlik and Kelly Anthony stopped her as she opened the drawer.

'Oh. Sorry,' she said, holding up her hands. 'It's in there.'

Anthony reached in and carefully slid out a small pistol, removing the magazine and clearing the remaining round. 'You have a permit for this?'

'Of course,' Christy said. 'It's there in the drawer under the bullets.'

Anthony slipped the permit out and unfolded it. 'All in order.'

'You can put it back,' Pavlik told her. 'Unloaded.'

'Why do you have a gun in the kitchen?' I asked.

'You of all people can ask that?' Christy asked. 'After what happened to us in my kitchen?'

That was another story.

'She took it out and loaded it last night,' Rebecca said. 'I told her she was more likely to shoot me than an intruder.'

'Better to call the police if you hear something suspicious,' Pavlik told Christy and went to confer with Deputy Anthony.

'Are you OK?' I asked Christy. 'Not only about the bracelet and diamond, but also about Barry being—'

'Married? Yes.' Another sniffle. 'I'm just sorry he felt he couldn't tell me.'

Now that was a reaction I had not expected. 'You wouldn't have cared?' I think there was accusation in my tone.

'Obviously, Barry was unhappy. His wife is probably a shrew.'

OK, so this got my back up. 'That's what all cheaters say. If Barry was unhappy, he should have gotten a divorce before he started to "date".'

'You were more charitable about him this morning,' Rebecca said, with a bit of a smirk. 'Could still be love and all that.'

'I know. I can only sustain charity and understanding for so long,' I admitted. 'Besides, Helena Margraves is a perfectly nice woman.'

'You've met her?' Christy asked.

'Well, no.' But I decided there and then that I would.

EIGHT

AND so it was, that bright and early on Thursday, I was
waiting for Caron Egan in the lobby of the Hotel
Morrison.

Before we'd left her the night before, Christy had insisted
she wanted to keep busy to take her mind off her loss. I
assumed she meant Barry, not the bracelet and presumed
diamond, but either way I took pity on her and suggested she
open with Sarah the next morning, thereby freeing myself.

'Coffee here in the lobby, Maggy?' Caron asked, bustling
out the door behind the registration desk. 'Or do you prefer
a full-on breakfast in the restaurant?'

'Lobby,' I said, debating between one of the brocade-
upholstered chairs facing the door or the matching couch with
a sight line to the front desk. 'You have in-room checkout?'

Caron looked offended. 'Of course. We slip the bill under
the door. If there is a problem, the guest can call or come
to the desk. Otherwise, they can check out via the television
or just leave.'

'Great.' I chose a chair. 'I'm hoping to catch Helena
Margraves on the way out.'

'Please don't make the woman cry in my lobby,' Caron
said, settling onto the sofa. 'We have a nice establishment
here.'

'Unlike my coffeehouse?' I asked, glancing around. It was
a pretty lobby, if a bit fussy for my taste.

'Nary a body to be found here,' Caron said, signaling a
waiter. 'French press all right? We specialize in it.'

'Fine,' I said. 'And you know full well that we've never had
a body in Uncommon Grounds.' Under Uncommon Grounds.
Next to Uncommon Grounds. In front of Uncommon
Grounds. But never in.

I waited for the waiter to bring the plunger pot filled with
hot water and ground coffee to the table, press and pour. We

stocked French press pots for retail sale at Uncommon Grounds and made plunger coffee on request, though the majority of our business was espresso-based drinks.

Caron was smart to feature something that still entailed a ceremony – measuring the ground coffee into the pot and adding the hot water, waiting for the prescribed three to four minutes before pressing the mesh piston to force the grounds to the bottom and, finally, pouring the strong, rich brew – but could be done with minimal equipment and in front of the customer.

I took a sip. 'Delicious. Maybe we should do more press coffee.'

'Maybe you shouldn't,' Caron said. 'It's our shtick.'

I grinned. 'Fine.'

Caron set down her cup. 'So what did you want to talk about?'

Talk? 'I told you. I want to see Helena Margraves.'

A sigh, as Caron sat back on the couch and folded her arms across her chest. 'And you couldn't have done that without taking up my valuable time?'

Valuable, shmaluable. However you spell it. 'Of course not. I need you.'

She rolled her eyes. 'You don't know what the woman looks like, do you?'

'Of course not.'

'Of course not.' Another sigh. 'Fine. I checked her in. Short with dark hair. Seemed very nice.'

'Nice was the word Pavlik used, too.' My head swiveled as an elevator dinged. A man emerged. 'He asked me if you were sure Margraves hadn't left his luggage with the desk. Which is another reason why I wanted to talk to you in person.'

'Sure it is.' Caron picked up a delicate pitcher and dumped a little cream in her coffee. 'I told you no. No luggage at the front desk, the bell stand or in storage.'

'Is it possible he didn't have any?' I asked, as the revolving door whirled and spit in an older woman with a young boy.

Caron cocked her head and looked skyward, thinking. 'I suppose it's possible. But for two nights?'

'That was my thought, too. At least the man would need a toothbrush.'

'We have complimentary toothbrushes and razors.'

'Underwear, too?'

'We're not that full-service.' She smiled now. 'Could he have dropped his baggage off at the airport?'

'I thought about the airport, but you told me he had a room booked for that night.'

'Meaning Margraves had no intention of flying out, so why would he take his things with him. Unless' – she tapped her fingernail on the edge of the saucer – 'he changed his mind.'

If so, he'd made that decision before meeting Christy. 'I don't suppose you keep track of the toothbrushes and razors you hand out.'

'Not formally, but I can check with the desk and house-keeping. Somebody may remember. What about the cab driver?"

'Ride-share. Pavlik is checking,' I told her. 'If I'd thought about it, I would have asked Deputy Anthony last night.'

'Why? What was last night?'

'Christy was robbed. Her tennis bracelet was taken, as well as a package from Margraves that she hadn't opened.'

Caron's nose wrinkled, connecting the freckles normally sprinkled across it into a pert brown mass. 'That's odd, don't you think?'

'The fact she hadn't opened it or the fact they were stolen?'

'Both, I guess.'

'Agreed.'

'What are you going to ask Helena Margraves? Whether after identifying her husband's body she snuck into his lover's house and stole the gifts he gave her?'

I set my cup back into its saucer and sat back. 'I hadn't thought about it, but that's an idea. Thing is Helena apparently doesn't know about the affair.'

'You always know about the affair,' Caron said. 'Even if you don't admit it to yourself.'

Let's be clear. It wasn't Bernie Egan who had the affair, it was Caron. So I wasn't sure what she knew about being on the short end of that particular stick. 'I didn't.'

'Search your heart. I think you'll find differently.'

I closed my eyes, remembering why Caron occasionally

had driven me crazy as a partner. Sarah might be a pain in
the ass, but she was seldom a sanctimonious pain in the ass.

I was saved from answering by another whirl of the revolving
door. This time it burped up somebody vaguely familiar. As
she approached, I realized it was the woman who had stopped
by the coffeehouse Monday, only to be scared off by Sarah
and Christy.

'Hello again,' I called, as she passed. 'Enjoying your new
home even with the snow?'

'Oh, yes,' she said, hesitating. 'Thanks.'

'Well, stop into Uncommon Grounds again.' I was trying
to cue her to where we had met, since she was obviously
confused. 'Have you met Caron Egan? She owns the Morrison.
And Caron, this is . . .' I swiveled my head toward Caron.

She was looking at me like I was crazy. 'Helena Margraves.'

I glanced around the lobby. 'Where?'

Caron leaned forward. 'You're talking to her.'

I pointed to the other chair and practically ordered Helena
Margraves to sit in it.

She did. 'I knew I should have taken the earlier flight.'

Not so 'nice' now. 'You were here in Brookhills on Monday.
That was the day before your husband was killed.'

'Yes.' She took off her hat and shook out the dark bangs
as she had done in the shop.

'When you came here,' I continued, 'did you know about—'

'The affair?' She nodded, her eyes welling. 'I mean, I
suspected. There were charge card bills. Gifts he bought that'
– she held out her hands, palms facing down – 'I never got.'

'Like the tennis bracelet.'

'Yes.' A single tear escaped, and she swiped at it. 'I thought
my heart was literally going to break when I saw it on her
wrist. You even said Barry's name. I couldn't get my breath.
I had to get out.'

She tugged the purse next to her onto her lap. 'I think I
owe you for a latte.'

Wow. She was nice. 'On me,' I said.

Caron snagged a cup from the next table and went to pour
Helena a cup from the press pot before realizing it had gone

cold. She signaled the waiter and sat back down. 'We'll get you some hot coffee.'

'Thank you,' Helena said.

'How did you trace Christy?' I asked. 'Phone records?' A wealth of information, in my experience.

'No,' she said. 'I looked on the statement for our iPhones, but Barry must have had a separate cell phone. What do they call it? A burner?'

I nodded. 'But you did find her somehow.'

She nodded her thanks as the waiter took away the cold coffee and brought a clean cup and saucer. 'Her name and address were on a bill. Something Barry had ordered.'

'And you decided to come looking for a piano teacher.'

'It was a lame excuse, I know.' A smile threatened but then disappeared. 'I honestly didn't think about what I'd do when I got here. I just had to do something. I had to know.'

'Of course you did.' Caron took the press pot from the waiter and indicated she would take care of it from there. He moved off.

'It took all my courage to climb the porch steps to her door,' Helena continued, 'only to see the note saying she was at the coffeehouse. I made myself cross the street and go in, but then I kind of freaked.' She nodded to me. 'As you saw.'

'I did. But it took a lot of courage to get that far.'

'More adrenaline than courage,' she said. 'I felt so angry, so betrayed. Now, I think I'd forgive anything to have him back.'

'You poor thing,' Caron said, as she pushed the plunger down and poured the fresh coffee. 'When did you find out that your husband was dead?'

Helena didn't seem to notice the cup Caron slid to her. 'That afternoon. I was here at the hotel when I picked up the message from the Brookhills sheriff. She said there had been an accident and Barry was dead.'

I frowned. Kelly Anthony said she had left a voicemail, but I had assumed she'd waited until the woman had called her back to break the news.

'I . . . well, I panicked. It was like I was in some horrible old movie. I was embarrassed that I had come snooping and suddenly Barry was dead. Right here in Brookhills.'

'How did you know he would be here?' I asked, moving the cup toward her. 'Or didn't you?'

She took a sip. 'I assumed. Barry said he was going to San Diego, but the plane ticket was booked through Milwaukee. It didn't make sense.'

Especially since Milwaukee was not really a hub. If people were connecting to west or east coast flights, they would typically fly through Chicago. 'His ticket was Denver-Milwaukee-San Diego?'

'Smart, right?' She attempted a smile. 'You carry-on your luggage and simply don't take the last leg.'

So Margraves had been traveling light. Which might explain the lack of . . . I smacked myself in the forehead as the light dawned.

Helena glanced over at me but continued what she was saying. '. . . Afraid I'd somehow be blamed for Barry's death.' She pulled out a tissue and blew her nose. 'That was before I realized it had been this horrible, freak snowplow accident.'

'What did you do?' Caron asked.

'Packed and left. Got the first flight out when the snow let up and then called the deputy when I landed back in Denver.'

Milwaukee to Denver direct would be a fairly short flight. Maybe two and a half hours. 'You arrived here on Monday, flew home on Tuesday night and then turned around and flew back yesterday, Wednesday.'

'Exactly.'

'The reservation for Monday and Tuesday nights,' I said, turning to Caron, 'was it for Barry or Helena Margraves?'

Caron closed one eye and thought. 'I'm sure it said Barry Margraves.'

'We make all our hotel reservations under Barry's name and number,' Helena said. 'Points, you know.'

'You give points?' I asked Caron.

She nodded. 'Of course. We've joined—'

'If you'll excuse me,' Helena said, rising. 'I have to pack and catch an eleven o'clock flight.'

Before I could answer, she had stepped into an open elevator and the door had closed.

'I guess I could wait and corner her on the way out,' I said.

'I'd prefer you didn't,' Caron said.

'She'll probably duck out a different door anyway,' I said, chewing on what Helena had told us. 'Do you realize what we've learned?'

'No, but I'm sure you'll tell me.' She got up and stole another clean cup and saucer, sitting down to pour herself a fresh cup from the press pot.

She didn't pour one for me. 'It was Helena Margraves, not Barry, who made the reservation for Monday and Tuesday night.'

'Yes, that much I got.' Caron managed to look bored. 'So?'

What did she have to do that was more exciting? Paperwork? Making sure the sheets were clean, the towels dry?

Which reminded me I had forgotten to take the rags home to wash. Again. 'So Helena arrives here on Monday and finds out her husband gave Christy a diamond bracelet. On Tuesday, while she is still in town, her husband is killed.'

'By a snowplow, don't forget.'

'A snowplow that had been left unattended and was pointed in the right direction,' I reminded her. 'Warmed up, even.'

'A smoking gun waiting for somebody to be smoked?'

I glanced sideways at her. 'Well, yeah. I guess.'

'But what are the odds of Helena just happening to be there – with the running plow within reach – when Barry Margraves stepped into the street? That would be quite a coincidence, don't you think?'

'Not if she was following her husband. Or, more likely, following Christy.'

'Helena didn't even know for sure that Barry was there,' Caron offered. 'She was just surmising.'

Naïve, like I said. 'I'm not suggesting Barry's death was premeditated. But if you knew your husband was in town somewhere and wanted to catch him cheating, wouldn't you stake out his mistress' house?'

'I suppose.' Caron was stirring her coffee. *Clink, clink, clink.* 'Then she hopped into the garbage truck and ran over her husband with the plow? How? She's too short.'

I didn't realize short was a defense or I would have used it when I was a suspect. 'What in the world does her height have to do with it?'

'Have you ever tried to climb up into one of those county garbage trucks? You need a stepladder.'

'Honestly, Caron.' I put my hand on hers to stop the stirring. 'Do you have no imagination? Maybe the woman has terrific upper body strength and hoisted herself up.'

'Maybe.' She set the spoon in the saucer with a clink.

'Besides, what do you know about climbing into a garbage truck?' I asked, eyeing her.

She sniffed. 'I'd prefer not to talk about it.'

I considered worming the story out of her, but it was probably something exciting like her third-grade class had gone on a field trip to Waste Disposal.

'Anyway,' I said, standing up. 'I need to see Pavlik.'

Caron put her hand out. 'You're not going to tell him Helena was here.'

'When her husband was killed?' I shook her off. 'Of course I am.'

'But you've met the woman. She's a nice person.'

Yeah, yeah, yeah. 'So are you, but you can't tell me that if Bernie cheated on you and you saw a snowplow sitting there just waiting to run him over, you wouldn't think about it.'

'Think about it is one thing, doing it is another. You're fulfilling Helena's self-fulfilling prophecy, you know.'

I frowned. 'I believe she's the only one who can do that.'

'Helena left town because she was afraid she'd be unfairly suspected of killing Barry.'

'Or Helena left town because she did kill Barry.' I stood up.

Caron stood up, too, lifting her chin. 'And as for your question, I couldn't run Bernie down with a snowplow under any circumstances.'

'No matter how angry you were.'

'No matter.' She wrinkled her nose again. 'I can't drive a manual transmission.'

*   *   *

The manual transmission was an interesting wrinkle, I thought as I sat in the sheriff's outer office, waiting for him to finish a meeting. I had not driven a stick shift since I was a teenager, but I assumed it came back to you like riding a bike did.

But the other consideration was the manual transmission itself. Caron was correct that this particular truck was manual, even though others in the county fleet might be automatic. Pavlik had not committed to whether the parking brake was engaged or not. But even if it had been and somebody simply released it, would that have been enough to send the plow rolling down the street and over Margraves?

I thought about our block of Junction Road. Was there a hill between Clare's shop and ours?

Not much of one. And I did remember hearing the roar of the truck's engine as Margraves was hit. Unless Sarah was right, and it was the roar of the storm I—

'Maggy?' Pavlik's door had opened and two deputies came out, followed by the sheriff. 'Did you need to see me?'

'Always,' I said, following him back in and closing the door behind me.

'Whoa,' he said, turning at the desk. 'Is this where you throw your coat open, displaying little or no clothes and have your way with me on the desk?'

'Sadly, this is where I throw my coat open displaying jeans and a T-shirt,' I said, taking off said coat to expose said garments. 'I'll do you tonight.'

'Deal.' He waved me into the guest chair and went to sit in his chair on the opposite side. 'Should I get a pad out? Am I going to want to take notes?'

'Maybe,' I said. 'I went to the Morrison this morning and met Helena Margraves. Turns out I already knew her though.'

'Really?' Pavlik cocked his head, frowning. 'That's quite a coincidence.'

'Not really. She stopped in the shop on Monday morning.'

'This past Monday?' If I had not garnered the sheriff's full attention before, I had it now.

'Yes. Turns out the hotel reservation at the Morrison that Caron told me about was for Helena, not Barry.'

'What was Helena doing here on Monday?'

'She says she found some odd charge purchases on Barry's card and suspected an affair. When she came across Christy's name and address, she flew here to find out.'

Pavlik's chair squeaked as he leaned forward. 'Then she lied to Anthony when she said she didn't know Barry Margraves was here. That he was supposed to be in San Diego.'

'Margraves did have a plane ticket to San Diego. With a stop-off here.'

'Funny way to get to San Diego from Denver.'

'Fly a thousand miles the opposite direction first? Exactly.'

'Did she see him?'

'Did Helena see Barry? She says not. But she did find Christy. In fact, she came into the shop to ask about her.'

'About Christy.' He had his trusty notepad out.

'Yes, on Monday when Christy was working. Helena said she'd just moved here and was looking for a piano teacher.'

'She certainly couldn't have expected to find Christy and her husband *in flagrante* in the coffee shop.'

'No, but Christy had tacked up a note on her studio saying she was across the street at Uncommon Grounds. Helena had Christy's address and had worked up enough courage, according to her, to go up to her door.'

'And when she wasn't there, track her to your place via the note?'

'Yes, but she was already having second thoughts, I think. She seemed very unsure of herself, skittish. She managed to order a drink but disappeared before she got it. Though she did offer to pay for it this morning.'

'High marks for that,' Pavlik said, a bit dryly. 'What did she say when she came in?'

'She asked for Christy by name, as I recall, so I introduced the two.'

'What was Mrs Margraves' reaction?'

'To Christy and her yellow rubber gloves? Surprise, I think. But then she saw the tennis bracelet.'

'Which Margraves had bought.'

'And had sent. Which may account for the address Helena found.'

'Margraves was careless to leave it lying around,' Pavlik said.

'Or Helena was resourceful to find it,' I countered. 'It takes balls to track down your husband's mistress and fly halfway across the country to confront her.'

'And did she confront her?'

'No. Helena says adrenaline got her that far, and I think I believe it. Once face-to-face with Christy, though, she didn't seem to know what to do.'

'You said she saw the tennis bracelet. What did she say?'

I thought back. 'That it was pretty, I think. Christy kind of preened and I asked if it was a gift from Barry.'

'Which pretty much clinched it.'

'Pretty much. Helena was out the door within a minute or two, sans latte.' I leaned forward. 'Is it possible that Barry Margraves' death was more than an accident?'

'Something beyond negligent homicide, you mean?' I could tell he was irritated, but not at me. 'Maybe. The initial assumption that it was the driver who was killed cost us time and therefore evidence.'

'Because of the falling snow.'

'Exactly. It's not like we can go back to look for footprints or other physical evidence now. Even a half hour after the accident it was too late.'

'I know that sometimes I look for trouble when there is none, but—'

'Could Barry Margraves' death be murder, you mean?'

I nodded. 'Is it just coincidence that Helena was here in Brookhills when her husband was killed? And that she suspected he was cheating and had just met his cheatee?'

He glanced up from a note he was making. 'You say Helena Margraves already was in Brookhills on Monday. But she flew in yesterday. Anthony picked her up at the airport.'

'She left and came back.'

'Because?'

'Because she picked up a voice message on Tuesday after-noon from Kelly Anthony saying Barry had been killed—' I interrupted myself. 'By the way, Kelly told me she'd left a message for Helena to call back. Helena says the voicemail said her husband had been in an accident and was dead. Isn't that kind of cold, leaving a voicemail with that kind of news? I mean, some people don't even listen to their voicemails.'

I was getting a 'focus, please' stare from Pavlik. 'I'll speak to her. But you were saying?'

'That Kelly, who I assume identified herself as a Brookhills sheriff's deputy, left a message saying that Barry was dead.'

'Then Helena would have known Barry's accident was here in Brookhills.'

'Exactly. So she panicked. Flew back to Denver as soon as she could get out on Tuesday night and then called Anthony back from there.'

'Resourceful is right,' Pavlik said, tapping his pen on the desk. 'She pretends to Anthony that she's just found out and then turns around and flies back the next day, the bereaved wife.'

'Which she is, to be fair.'

'Why all the machinations then?'

'Put yourself in her place,' I said, trying to do just that. 'You suspect your husband is cheating and pull together the courage to find out for sure. You follow him out here and confront the woman he's seeing—'

'But not him, according to her.'

'Yes.' I hate being interrupted when I'm roleplaying. 'You're traumatized because the woman is not exactly what you expected—'

'But is wearing a diamond bracelet your husband charged to his card.'

'You go back to your hotel room, trying to figure out what to do—'

'Do you know this or are you just making it up now?'

'Helena said she was at the Morrison. But wherever it was, she picked up a voicemail saying her husband was, indeed, in the same town and had met an unfortunate end.' I held out both hands, palm up. 'Wouldn't you be confused and frightened?'

'Because I watch too many movies?'

I had to give him that one. 'Maybe.'

'I might also have wondered how he had died and whether this mysterious new woman had anything to do with it.'

That stopped me. 'Christy?'

'In this scenario you're weaving, Helena Margraves knew full well that she didn't kill her husband. Wouldn't she want to know who did, rather than run away afraid she would be implicated?'

'If she were a superhero. But resourceful or not, Helena is a regular human being, afraid of being caught spying on her now-dead husband. She was not thinking clearly. But once she got home and realized he had been run over by a snowplow, she—'

'Could relax. Knowing, at least, that her husband's death was an accident not anything more sinister?'

'Wouldn't you be a little relieved?' I asked.

'I guess I would.' Pavlik picked up the phone. 'Where is Helena Margraves now?'

I glanced down at the time on my own phone. 'The airport, presumably. She said she had an eleven o'clock flight to Denver.'

'It's just past ten. I'll have Anthony get over there.'

NINE

'Helena is going to freak,' I said, more than a little regretful about running in to Pavlik to tattle. This was one of the drawbacks of being engaged to the sheriff.

'Are they going to arrest her?' Christy asked. The little redhead had stayed on when I had arrived back at the shop. Sarah had bailed before I had my coat off.

'Pavlik says they just want to talk to her,' I told her as I unloaded cups from the dishwasher and handed them to Christy to put on the shelf.

'That's what they always say.' Christy's eyes were wide. 'Then, clang! You're in the slammer.'

I guessed she should know. 'I was thinking about your bracelet.'

'The one that was stolen, you mean?' She put her hand up to her mouth. 'Oh! You think Helena stole it?'

Sure, why not pile on the widow? 'You were wearing it when you met on Monday. She commented on it, remember?'

Christy's face dropped. 'And I showed it to her all happy. She must have been devastated.'

Devastated enough to run over her husband with a snowplow the next day?

'And jealous, of course,' Christy added.

'Helena took the first flight she could get home on Tuesday after she heard about Barry's death.'

'Proving she didn't love the man,' Christy said. 'How do you just leave him lying there like that? It was awful for me, when you wouldn't let me go to him.' She put her hand to her heart. 'Though I know you had the best of intentions.'

'You wouldn't want to remember him like that.' Or mess up a possible crime scene even more than it had been, as it turned out.

I held a latte mug up to the light. 'Is that lipstick?'

'Yes,' Christy said. 'Put it back.'

I obeyed.

'But for his own wife, just to up and leave like that. Only to have to come back and identify his poor broken body.'

'Panic, I guess.' I passed her another cup.

'More like guilt.' She frowned, thinking. 'I was wearing the bracelet Tuesday, wasn't I? And the package arrived Tuesday, too, and they were both taken.'

'They were together – the bracelet and the package – when they were stolen, right?'

'Oh, yes.' Christy's head was bobbing up and down.

'In your underwear drawer.'

Christy's eyes narrowed. 'How did you know that?'

'When you were on the phone to Barry, you said that's where you were going to put the envelope until he arrived.'

'Oh, yes,' she said. 'Dear Barry. It had his writing and return address and now I'll never see it again.'

A package with her own return address on it would have been hard for Helena to resist if she'd seen it. But when did she have the opportunity? Tuesday before she caught the flight back to Denver seemed a real stretch. 'Pavlik says the under-wear drawer is the first place that thieves look.'

'But why look at all?' Christy asked, leaning past me to take another mug out of the dishwasher. 'I don't have much of anything to steal.'

As witnessed by her stripped to the barebones house. 'Somebody saw you with the bracelet. The envelope was just a bonus.'

'Maybe Helena didn't leave after all,' Christy said.

'Pavlik said Kelly Anthony met her at the airport yesterday, though. Returning.' Can't return, if you never leave. Which should be a country song, if it wasn't already.

'Please,' Christy said disdainfully. 'If you walk out of an airport, people just assume you've come off a plane. Easy peasy.'

More personal experience? 'But—'

My phone rang. I glanced over intending to silence it, but saw it was Caron. I picked up as Christy closed the dishwasher and disappeared into the office.

'She's back!' Caron's voice said. And roaring mad. 'You didn't steal her passport, did you?'

'Wait, wait, wait,' I said, putting up my hand in a stop sign like she could see me. 'You're talking about Helena Margraves?'

'Yes, she couldn't get through security because her passport is missing. She's rifling through her dirty room as we speak.'

I checked the time. Ten after eleven. 'Is Kelly Anthony there?'

'The sheriff's deputy? No, why would she be?'

'Because . . . No, forget it,' I said, changing my mind. 'I'll be right over.'

Hanging up, I hesitated. I didn't have time to get Sarah back to the shop. That meant leaving Christy to man the store. And I couldn't tell her where I was going, or she'd want to go with me.

So I fibbed. 'Be right back,' I called. 'Sheriff's business.' And I was out the door.

Caron was at the desk when I got there, as was Helena Margraves, purse clutched in her hands, parka draped over the roller suitcase at her side. I hung back by the sofa, the better to listen.

'. . . And don't have another ID with me,' Helena was saying.

'I'm sorry,' Caron said. 'Are you sure that your passport isn't in your purse? Sometimes a fresh eye helps. My husband finds things where I swear I have searched a hundred times. I could take a peek if you—' She was reaching for the bag as she said it.

'Please.' Helena pulled the purse away and set it on her suitcase. 'Don't you think I looked?'

'What about the cab?'

'Ride-share. And I've already checked with the driver.' Helena's jaw was tight as she picked up her parka.

'Did you check your coat pockets? I always slip my passport in my right one, so I can get it out easily at secur—'

'I'm not an idiot,' Helena snapped. 'It's not in my purse or my pocket. Which is why I must have left it in the room.'

'But you've checked and it's not there,' Caron said, reasonably.

'Not anymore. For all I know I left it on the dresser and your maid took it.'

'Your room hasn't been made up yet. Besides, our *house-keepers* are not thieves.'

'Speaking of thieves,' a voice said from behind me. 'Did you steal my bracelet?'

I closed my eyes, counted to three and turned. 'You're supposed to be manning the store, Christy.'

The redhead's arms were folded across her chest. 'You lied to me, Maggy.' Her foot was tapping.

Helena Margraves slipped on her jacket and faced Christy, hands in her pockets. 'How dare you accuse *me* of stealing? You're the one who is a thief. A husband-stealer.'

The widow launched herself at the wannabe-wife. Christy staggered back, gravity and her heavy wool coat pulling her down backwards as the corner of the coffee table caught her at the back of the knees. The two women landed on the sofa, one on top of each other.

'Oh dear, oh dear, oh dear,' was all Caron could say.

She had been equally helpful when we found our other partner Patricia face-up in a pool of skim milk some three years back.

For me, on the other hand, this was small stuff. Nobody had died. At least, today.

I hauled Helena off Christy so the redhead could sit up. 'Enough. Caron – call the sheriff.'

She just stared at me.

I sighed.

'The sheriff?' Helena Margraves repeated.' I didn't even hurt her.'

'Says you,' Christy said, rubbing her arm. 'I think I have a bruise.'

'And I have a dead husband,' Margraves countered.

Christy lifted her chin. 'Not my fault. And I have an alibi. What's yours?'

'My alibi?' Helena repeated. 'Why would I need an alibi? My husband was killed in an accident. With a snowplow.'

I had let go of her and now she snagged her purse, pulling up the handle of her roller bag. 'I'm getting out of this insane asylum.'

'You don't have a passport,' I reminded her, wondering how Kelly Anthony had missed her at the airport. 'Did you get all the way to Mitchell International?'

'Yes. I was at the front of the security line and had to catch a ride back when I realized I'd left my passport.' She checked her watch. 'I've missed my plane now.'

'Need a room for tonight?' Caron wasn't much help in an emergency, but she was an efficient hotelier.

'This hotel is the last place . . .' She stopped and took a deep, shuddering breath. 'I am so sorry. This is not who I am.'

She sat down, Christy scooting over to make room on the couch.

'I'm sorry, too,' Christy said. 'I didn't mean to steal your husband. I didn't know he *was* a husband.'

'I know,' Helena Margraves said. 'I guess I knew that the moment I saw you. But that meant Barry lied to us both and it . . . it . . .' She burst into tears.

Christy had her arm around Helena and the two women were sobbing on each other's shoulders as Deputy Kelly Anthony burst into the main lobby.

'What on earth do you make of all this?' Anthony muttered, stopping short to take in the scene.

'You didn't catch Helena at the airport, because she lost her passport,' I told her.

'And her husband.' Caron had joined us. 'Christy, her married lover.'

'Not quite lover,' I said. 'But I suppose that doesn't make it any easier from her standpoint.'

'So they're . . . bonding?' The deputy was still staring at the woman.

I just shrugged.

Caron turned to Anthony, nose wrinkled. 'Why are you here?'

'You called me.'

'Maggy told me to,' Caron said. 'But I'm not sure why. Are you going to arrest one of them?'

Anthony glanced over at me and then shook her head. 'I need to ask Mrs Margraves some questions.'

'Oh, yes. Because she told you she wasn't in Brookhills when her husband died and she was,' Caron said, head bobbing. 'We wondered about that, didn't we, Maggy.'

'We did,' I confirmed, then checked the time. 'Umm, Christy?'

The redhead lifted her tearful face. 'Yes, Maggy?'

'Did you lock the store?'

'Uh-huh,' she said, swiping at her nose. 'And I texted Sarah to come back.'

That was not going to go over well with my partner. Though Sarah had bailed on me, if truth be told.

'Do you want me to go back?' Christy asked, patting Helena on the shoulder before standing up.

'That would be . . . lovely,' I said, a little surprised.

Kelly Anthony was visibly relieved. 'Yes, I . . . um, yes, I need to talk to Mrs Margraves alone, so that probably would be best.'

'Maybe call Sarah and tell her she doesn't need to come back?' I called after Christy as she went through the revolving door.

To my disappointment, Deputy Anthony did not think the hotel lobby made a good interrogation room and took a still distraught Helena Margraves to the station.

Which meant I had no reason not to go back to Uncommon Grounds. Unfortunately, Sarah was already there.

'Christy was supposed to call you off,' I said, kicking my boots off on the mat.

'And you were supposed to keep the shop open and functioning,' Sarah said sourly.

Noonish and there was no one there anyway. Though the locked door and closed sign might have had something to do with that.

'I'm sorry, but there were new developments. Kelly Anthony has taken Helena Margraves back to the station. She's . . .' I stuck my head around the corner. 'Where's Christy?'

'I sent her home. She's less than useless in this state.'

'Besides, admit it,' I said, sitting down at a table by the window, 'you want a full update, unredacted.'

'Redacted for Christy's sake, you mean?' she asked, joining

me. 'Yeah, pretty much. Besides, I am getting tired of being nice to her, just because of . . . you know.'

'The death of her imagined love of her life?'

'Right. Spill.'

I did.

'Seems to me,' Sarah said after I had finished, 'that the gigolo was run down by a truck left unattended by somebody with bowel issues. The fact that the suspicious wife—'

'Rightfully suspicious.'

'Yes, yes,' she said, waving me off. 'The fact that the rightfully suspicious wife was here or not, doesn't change that.'

'But Helena lied.'

'Wouldn't you?' Sarah asked, pushing her chair back and crossing one trousered leg over the other. 'She snooped on her husband's charge card and phone bills—'

'Not the phone. He must have had a burner because there was nothing on their bill.'

'Smart man,' Sarah said. 'Anyway, you've had a cheating husband. You snoop around—'

'Justifiably, as it turned out. And after the fact. Ted had already left.'

A groan. 'Yes, but you still felt guilty, didn't you? That's why you keep with this "rightfully, justifiably" shit.'

'Well, yes, I suppose.'

'So Helena invaded Barry's privacy' – she held up a finger to prevent an interruption – 'and then flew halfway across the country to see the woman he was corresponding with and maybe even catch her and the slimeball in the act.' She shrugged and held up both hands. 'And then?'

'Slimeball dies horribly,' I said.

'Horribly, really?' Sarah asked. 'I thought you said it was quick.'

'Well, yes,' I said. 'I think he probably died when the plow hit him, but then the tires, at least one maybe two, caught him . . .'

'Yeah, see what you mean.' She got up. 'Want something?'

'Not a flat white.'

She turned back. 'I was thinking sticky bun.'

Hmm. 'Fine. And maybe just pour me a cup of brewed?'

'Got a broken leg? Get it yourself.'

I did, as she retrieved the pastry.

'We're sharing?' I asked as she set the plate with one bun on it between the two of us. Sarah usually wasn't a sharer. Nor was I, really.

'Only one left,' she said as she cut it into four pieces.

'Gotcha.' I took one piece and popped it into my mouth.

We were lucky to have any of Tien's sticky buns left, though if I said that to Sarah, she would point out – again – that the store had been closed smack dab in the middle of the day.

Sarah ate one piece and then picked up a second. 'The person who is really in trouble in all this is Harold. I heard the county wants to fire him.'

'Oh, no,' I said, leaning forward. 'If it was his fault, it was an accident.'

'Thing is, he can't prove that he locked the truck. Or even turned off the ignition. The engine was on when it finally came to a stop, I'm told.'

'Like I said. I never should have doubted myself.' The roaring wind, my butt.

But poor Harold. It would be a tough thing to live with, accident or not. 'I can still see Margrave's face, illuminated as . . .' I stopped.

'What?'

'The headlight from the snowplow. It illuminated his face.'

'You said that. So?'

'So it was dark and then it wasn't.'

'You're saying somebody turned on the headlights before mowing him down.'

'I don't know what I'm saying.' I reached to take the last piece. It was gone. 'I just remember thinking at the time that the plow must have come around the corner. That's why I suddenly heard the sound and saw the light.'

'But you know that doesn't make sense. It had been sitting there not half a block away the whole time.'

'But turned off,' I said. 'No engine, no lights.'

Sarah used her finger to collect sticky crumbs. 'If you're right, that gets Harold off the hook.'

'But somebody else on.'

TEN

'You have your cell phone?' I asked Sarah.

'In the office. Why? Where's yours?'

'Get it.'

'Yes, ma'am.' Pulling a face, she carried the empty plate to the back and returned with the phone.

I took it. 'You were taking photos that day, remember? Do you have any of the . . . Damn! What's your passcode?'

'How should I know?'

I looked up. 'How do you get into your phone?'

'My face.' She snagged the phone and held it up in front of her. 'See?'

It opened. 'Of course, I see. But you still need the passcode when you restart your phone.'

'Who restarts their phone?'

'Me,' I said, taking the phone back to punch up her photos. 'When things start acting funny. Or slowing down.' I tapped the photo icon again. Nothing. 'Like now.'

'I don't even know how to turn this one off,' she said. 'Or on. That button at the top is missing. I wish they'd stop changing things.'

I sighed and handed her back the mobile. 'Can you pull up your photos?'

She diddled around with it and then finally: 'There.'

Sure enough. I did not know or care how she did it. I scrolled through recent photos. Most of them were of her car, a vintage 1975 Firebird, then a couple frames of the EMTs around Margraves' body. But one . . . 'See?'

'See what?' Sarah asked, sliding her chair around so we both could, indeed, see. 'The garbage truck stuck in our snow pile?'

I squinted. 'The plow was traveling at a good pace. Do you think that pile of snow was big enough to stop it without somebody inside braking?'

'It's all the snow from the parking lot from the first snowfall up until that day.' She got up. 'Let's go see.'

I didn't quite understand why we had to go outside in the cold to see a mound of plowed snow that was perfectly visible on a picture. I followed her out onto the train platform, though.

'Brrr,' I said, folding my arms against the cold. 'Let me go get my coat.'

'Don't be a wuss,' she said, pointing. 'There's the pile.'

I surveyed the dirty gray pile, a mix of snow and salt and sand put down to both melt the snow and provide traction. It stood about six feet high, maybe eight feet across. There was an impression where the wheels went in. 'Snow has been added since Tuesday.'

'When they plowed out the lot after the storm that night.'

'And anything that fell on top of the pile throughout,' I said. 'Still, even in the pictures it looks substantial enough. Plus' – I pointed – 'there's the light pole in the middle of it.'

'True,' Sarah said. 'To keep going it would have had to plow through the pile, the pole and back out the other side.'

'Let's go in.' I was rubbing my hands together to keep circulation going. 'I want to see something.'

Back inside, I peered at the photo. 'Obviously it's sitting with the headlights in the snow, but the taillights are visible and they're on.'

'Then you were right,' Sarah said. 'The lights were switched on. Unless Harold left them that way and you just think they flashed on because the truck was getting closer. Same with the noise.'

'Hmm,' I mumbled, not really paying attention. I pinched to expand the photo more. 'What's . . .?'

'What's what?' Sarah said impatiently, shouldering in.

'That.' I pointed to the snow next to the passenger door. 'Is that a footprint?'

She squinted. 'Pretty small.'

'But the snow was still falling. It might have filled in the print or prints. Yes! Look.' I slid my finger down. 'There's another and another.'

Sarah peered closer and then stood back. 'Somebody got out of the truck. But from the passenger side.'

I tick-tocked my head, thinking. 'Harold had a passenger with him? Is that possible?'

'It would explain why he left the thing running,' Sarah said. 'To keep his passenger warm.'

'But why not say so?' I asked.

'Because it was against the rules to have somebody ride with him, presumably. He didn't want to get fired.'

'But he's been fired,' I said. 'Why not come clean now?'

Sarah shrugged. 'Maybe he has, for all we know. He seems to have gone underground.'

I frowned. 'Can you send me the photo?'

'You've seen how well my phone works,' Sarah said.

'Well then, can I borrow it?'

'So you can run to Pavlik? With my evidence?' Sarah was untying her apron. 'I'm going, too.'

'Somebody has to stay here.'

'Why?' Sarah chin gestured. 'The closed sign is still up.'

From when Christy closed the shop. No wonder nobody had come in since we had been back.

'Fine,' I said, untying my apron as well. 'Let's blow this joint.'

Brookhills County Sheriff Jake Pavlik was behind his desk, Deputy Kelly Anthony hunched over his shoulder. Sarah and I sat in the sheriff's guest chairs.

'I see what you mean.' He handed the phone to Anthony. 'Send those to yourself.'

'All of them?'

'All of them,' Pavlik said a little shortly. 'Who knows what else we missed in those early minutes.'

Anthony wisely kept her head down.

'Has the truck cab been fingerprinted?' I asked.

Pavlik swung his head a millimeter toward Anthony.

'No, sir,' she said. 'We had no way of knowing—'

He held up his hand. 'Then do it.'

'Yes, sir.' She was still fiddling. 'I cannot get these to send. I'm going to shut it down and re—'

'No!' both Sarah and I shouted.

Anthony lifted her head. 'Why?'

'Because Sarah doesn't know her passcode,' I told her. 'You won't be able to start it up again.'

But Pavlik just shook his head. 'Take care of it, will you, Anthony?'

'Yes, sir.' She departed the office.

'My phone,' Sarah wailed, as the door closed.

'Big deal,' I said. 'It was barely working.'

'Working well enough to solve the crime for you all,' she said, settling sullenly back in her seat.

'Is Helena Margraves still here?' I asked Pavlik.

'Yes. When you called, I told Anthony to hang onto her in case we had more questions.'

'Which you do,' Sarah said. 'Thanks to me and my crappy phone.'

'Which you will get back,' Pavlik said, with a little grin. 'But, yes. Thank you.'

'It seems to me that there are two possibilities,' I said. 'Or maybe one certainty that's caused by the two possibilities.'

'Spit it out, dammit,' from a grumpy Sarah.

'We know somebody was in that truck.'

'That's the certainty,' Pavlik said. 'The possibilities?'

'We don't know who. It's possible Harold had a passenger. But Helena Margraves was in town. If I were her and had tracked down the woman that my husband was cheating with—'

'You'd be staking out that woman and waiting for him to make an appearance.' Sarah had absolutely no patience today.

'Not to kill him, I hope.' Pavlik held up his hands. 'Not that I'm asking for personal reasons.'

I smiled. 'My point is that it's very possible Helena was in the immediate area. She wasn't scheduled to leave until the next day. What else was she going to do until then?'

'That's true,' Pavlik said, seeming a little surprised. 'I don't know that Anthony has asked her that question. But what's your theory?'

'I know it's a long shot, but maybe she saw the empty truck—'

'If she was there, she couldn't have missed it,' Sarah said, perking up. 'Maybe she climbed in to keep from freezing to death.'

'Exactly. Even if she did not start the engine, it would be warmer than out in the wind and the snow.'

'But Harold could have come back at any minute,' Sarah pointed out.

'So? Sitting high up in that truck gave her a good line of sight,' I said. 'She could have hopped out the driver's side door and disappeared into the storm. Harold would never have known.'

'It would also provide a good vantage point for seeing her husband with Christy,' Pavlik said. 'Then what? She puts the truck in gear, switches the lights on so as not to miss and floors it?'

'Sounds pretty callous when you say it like that,' I said.

'Running somebody down with a snowplow *is* pretty callous.' Pavlik steepled his hands. 'Assuming it was deliberate.'

'The evidence of the footprints isn't enough to prove anything, is it?' I asked.

'No. If it wasn't just a photo—'

'Time and location stamped,' Sarah reminded him.

'True, but still a photo and still with snow actively falling at the time. Measuring footprints from a photo like that?' He shrugged. 'Not that we won't try.'

'Fingerprints in the cab?' I suggested.

'Also a good thought. But given it was the middle of a blizzard in Wisconsin, it's likely whoever was in there had gloves on.'

Ugh. 'True.'

'Unless Harold did have a ride-along,' Sarah suggested. 'If so, he or she had been in there the entire time and might have taken them off.'

'We'll check,' Pavlik said. 'Or Anthony will.'

'Don't be too hard on Kelly,' I said. 'It was a confusing scene.'

'Even so,' Pavlik said. 'Taking photos immediately to preserve a changing crime scene would have been good, as evidenced by Sarah.'

'You're welcome,' she said, self-satisfied.

'Anthony also should have noticed those footprints. The truck was the cause of death.'

I had a thought. 'Those footprints couldn't have been from

Kelly, could they? Maybe she did climb up to check out the truck.'

'She would have said so,' Pavlik said.

Given how ticked he had been, I wasn't so sure.

'There was only one set,' I said, effectively submarining my own theory. 'Presumably leaving the truck.'

'Unless somebody climbed up and hid in it after the fact,' Pavlik said, markedly exasperated. 'I wouldn't rule out anything at this point.'

'The other strange thing is the footprints are on the passenger side,' Sarah pointed out. 'Wouldn't a driver get out his or her own side?'

'They were trying to throw us off?' I guessed.

The 'us' got a ghost of a grin from the sheriff. 'If there were no prints on the driver's side. Unfortunately, nobody checked at the time – at least before the snow had obliterated everything – and Sarah's photo doesn't show that side.'

'What screwed things up,' I mused, 'was the assumption that the driver had gotten out farther up the street and then been run over by his own plow. There was no reason to look for footprints where the' – finger quotes – '"runaway" plow had come to a stop.'

Pavlik shook his head crossly. 'But that *was* the theory only because the truck was empty.'

'Then maybe Maggy is right,' Sarah said, 'and the foot-prints are one of the first responders'. I saw somewhere that investigators try to step in their own footprints.'

'Literally retracing their steps,' I said. 'Maybe that's why there is only one set. Or someone went in on the passenger side and out on the driver side, where we can't see them in this photo. Or vice versa.'

'Maybe.' Pavlik was done talking about what he saw as a myriad of mistakes by his people. He would likely worry that bone at home tonight.

And he did. 'No luck on the fingerprints,' he told me that night. 'At least no matches to Helena Margraves.'

'But there were other prints in the cab besides Harold's?' I asked, passing him a piece of peperoni pizza.

'Tons. It is a garbage truck.'

On cue, our own canine garbage truck wandered in, followed by his clean-up act, Mocha. I cut up a slice to divide between the two of them and sat down with mine as they made quick work of theirs. 'What are you doing with Helena? Can you keep her here?'

'Her missing passport is effectively doing that, at least until she can get another form of ID sent to her. You didn't steal it, did you?'

'Her passport?' I was practically speechless. 'That would have taken real skill on my part.' So thank you.

'Or you could have had Caron instruct her housekeepers to lift it.'

'Didn't think of it,' I said ruefully. 'Caron probably wouldn't have done it anyway. Too ethical.'

'Good thing you have Sarah now,' Pavlik said with a grin.

'Sometimes it is,' I said, taking a second piece of the pie. 'I wonder what did happen to the passport.'

'Probably fell down next to the seat in her taxi,' Pavlik said, scoring the last slice. 'Passports, charge cards, cell phones, they all seem to go that way.'

'But the driver would turn it in, wouldn't he?'

'If he or she is honest. But these things also can be sold.'

'Do you honestly think Helena killed her husband?'

Pavlik stopped mid-bite. 'Not necessarily. But I am surprised you have doubts. You're the one who has been passing on all this information.'

I shifted uncomfortably. 'I just thought you needed to know she was here when he died. And why.'

'And you were right.' He set down his slice. 'There's more to this than meets the eye. Helena says her husband has been siphoning money from their accounts.'

Now that was interesting. 'More reason for her to want him dead? Maybe Barry really was going to leave her for Christy and then got cold feet.' Literally, figuratively and forever.

'Possibly. Or maybe he was using Christy. I'm curious about this package – this diamond, she thinks – that he sent.'

'Which is now missing, along with the diamond bracelet.

I'm curious about that, too.' I eyed the piece of pizza he had set down as I finished my own. 'Helena is the logical thief.'

Pavlik shook his head. 'Christy reported the loss on Wednesday evening. She believes she heard somebody Tuesday night, but the door wasn't broken in until Wednesday.'

'When she was at Rebecca's.'

'Correct. But the bulk of that time, Helena Margraves was in Denver. She flew out Tuesday evening and then returned Wednesday afternoon. Anthony picked her up at the airport, brought her to the morgue to identify her husband's body and then dropped her off at the Morrison. It doesn't leave much time for breaking and entering.'

'Christy thinks Helena may have faked leaving. And coming back.'

'But like I said, Anthony picked her up at the airport.'

'Christy says, you walk out of an airport with your bags, people just assume you flew in.' I shrugged. 'And before you ask, I don't know how she would know that.'

'It sounds a little out there, but I'm starting to think anything is possible in this case.' Pavlik frowned and pulled out his phone to make a note. 'I'll have Anthony double-check that she was on the flight.'

'Both flights. To and from.' I cherry-picked a piece of peperoni from Pavlik's slice, eliciting a whimper from Mocha. 'Are you thinking that you and Frank are getting that piece?'

'It's a fairly good bet,' Pavlik said. 'Especially now that you've denuded it.'

'Sorry.' Though I wasn't. 'Do we know where Barry stayed the night he flew in? Obviously not at the Morrison since the booking there was for Helena.'

'We checked recent purchases on his credit card. Apparently he booked the Slattery Arms in Milwaukee.'

'The man had good taste,' I said, as I divvied up the puppies' second slice. 'Or at least expensive taste.'

Pavlik raised his eyebrows. 'I have an idea. Why don't you call your old boyfriend and pump him for information?'

Stephen Slattery was the brother of my ex-husband Ted's wife Rachel. It's messier than it sounds.

'Stephen and I never really dated, and I keep as far away from the Slattery family as possible these days.'

'And yet you turned pink when I mentioned his name.'

'Did not.' I stood up. 'Anything else I can get you?'

'Nope. Making you blush was enough for me.'

ELEVEN

'It's not surprising that Barry Margraves stayed at the Slattery Arms,' Sarah said on Friday morning. 'It's the best hotel in town.'

The morning had been remarkably busy. Probably helped that we had flipped the sign to 'Open'.

'Best in downtown Milwaukee,' I agreed. 'But not really convenient if he was coming to the 'burbs. We're a full fifteen miles away.' Hence the commuter train that ran between Brookhills and Milwaukee.

'I assume he flew into Mitchell International. It would figure he'd stay in Milwaukee rather than search for hotels in Brookhills, where the pickings are slim.' As in one: the Morrison.

I was placing the cups Sarah was handing me into the dishwasher. 'Pavlik found the charge in Margraves' recent transactions – things that hadn't posted to his bill yet so even Helena didn't know.'

'Or so she says.' Sarah paused, cappuccino cup in hand. 'Between our phones and our credit cards it's hard to keep anything secret.'

'True. Unusual spending is what caught Helena's attention and brought her here in the first place. But Pavlik said . . .' I stopped.

'Pavlik said what?' She passed me the cup.

I put it in the dishwasher and closed the door to gain time. 'I'm not sure if this is one of the things Pavlik would expect me to keep confidential.'

'Or not. Come on, don't be a wimp. Err on the side of throwing caution to the wind.'

I grimaced. 'If I do, you can't tell anybody.'

'Do I ever?' She reached past me to push the start button on the dishwasher.

'Yes.' I leaned my butt against the dishwasher and sighed. 'He said that Helena told them that money had been transferred – siphoned, was his word – out of their family's accounts.'

'*Now* she's saying that? What happened to "I'd forgive anything to have him back". Isn't that what she told you and Caron?'

'Maybe she meant "him and our money",' I said.

'If this is true,' Sarah said, 'and I assume Pavlik has confirmed it . . .' She looked at me.

I shrugged.

A roll of the eyes. 'Anyway, if Barry was hiding assets, it sounds like he was preparing to leave Helena. Or fake his death. I don't suppose there's any chance he's still alive?'

'Afraid not. He might have been flat, but he was identifiable.'

'By his wife and the contents of his wallet,' Sarah pointed out. 'Helena could be lying and the wallet planted on some unsuspecting patsy.'

'A patsy who identified himself as Margraves and then got mowed down by a truck nobody knew was coming?' I asked. 'That's dedication.'

'The very definition of the word "patsy",' Sarah said stubbornly. 'And the reason Helena ran him down. Get rid of the loose ends.'

It was a fun theory, but: 'Why would Helena help her husband disappear with their money?'

'Because there's obviously something in his past we don't know,' Sarah said, folding her arms.

'There's a lot we don't know,' I said. 'But can we get back to what we do know? Barry Margraves was hiding assets and fooling around – at least virtually.'

'Are you going to ask Pavlik about Barry?' Sarah's arms were still folded.

'Whether they're sure it's him who is dead? Of course I will,' I promised, knowing we wouldn't move on otherwise.

'Back to your less interesting theory,' Sarah said. 'I suppose it's possible Barry was planning to leave with both the money and Christy.'

'If so, he changed his mind quick on Tuesday morning,' I said. 'At least about the Christy part.'

'I read somewhere that people can be unhappy in a relationship but not do anything about it, until they have an alternative.'

'A fresh lily pad for the frog to jump to.'

'Let's call him a toad. Frog's too good for him.'

'Now you sound like me,' I said, straightening to step away from the dishwasher. My butt was getting hot. 'But frog or toad, Margraves had second thoughts when he arrived here on Tuesday.'

'Given that, what was his alternative?' Sarah asked. 'Go back to Helena and pretend it never happened?'

'It's possible. So far as we know, Barry had no idea that Helena was even on to him.'

'And from what you said about his reaction to Christy, Helena wasn't going to catch them in the act no matter how long she stayed.'

'Which is another question. Did Helena actually leave on Tuesday and come back on Wednesday, like she said?'

'Does that really matter?' Sarah asked. 'Her husband died Tuesday morning and we know she was here then.'

'But the theft of Christy's—'

The door burst open. 'Look at what I found,' Christy exclaimed, holding up her arm.

'Speak of the devil,' I said, circling around from behind the serving area to where she stood.

Christy's face fell. 'I'm the devil?'

'Not you, your bracelet,' I said, waving for her to sit down. 'We were just talking about it.'

'Where did you find it?' Sarah asked, joining us at the table.

'In my coat pocket,' Christy said, taking off the wool coat in question and hanging it over the back of the chair. The thing was so long, half of it was on the floor as she tried to pull the chair out to sit. 'Can you believe it?

'Honestly, no.' Sarah was frowning. 'After all that whining, you never actually lost the thing?'

'Or had it stolen?' I asked.

'It's really a mystery.' Christy leaned forward, her hands tented. 'It must have just slipped off.'

'You do have skinny-ass wrists,' Sarah said, taking one and twisting it around to see the bracelet.

'Ouch.' Christy pulled back her arm.

'The bracelet is pretty loose,' I said.

'Right?' Christy was admiring the thing. 'Maybe it slipped when I was taking my gloves off and got caught up when I stuffed them in my pocket.'

I frowned. 'It was in your glove?'

'No, my pocket. But it could have slipped out of the glove or even just off my wrist and into the pocket.'

'Lucky for you,' Sarah said. 'It could just as easily have fallen onto the ground.'

'Oh, but then I'd have noticed, don't you think?'

I was thinking, but not about that precisely. 'What about the robbery?'

'I know,' Christy said, head going up and down. 'It's a curious thing, isn't it?'

Curiouser and curiouser. 'If there was no robbery, then where is the package Barry sent you?'

Christy held out both hands, palms up. 'I don't know. I guess I must have misplaced it.'

'You don't know?' Sarah repeated. 'You said it had a diamond in it, for God's sake. And how is it you never checked your pockets for the bracelet?'

Christy bristled, pushing her bottom lip out. 'A lot has happened, you know. The envelope arrived right after Barry died, after all. I was in no state to remember anything.'

'Apparently,' Sarah said. 'But even so, you invented a robbery and reported it to the police. That's a crime, isn't it, Maggy?'

'Probably,' I said, a little absentmindedly.

'Well, you'd better find that envelope,' Sarah continued, seeming to take Christy's absent-mindedness personally. 'Maggy says Barry was taking money out of their accounts and probably used it and their credit cards for your little gifts. Half that bracelet and whatever is in the envelope belongs to Helena.'

Sure. Sarah decides to torment Christy, and I'm the one who gets hurt. 'That was confidential,' I snapped at her.

But Christy was clutching the bracelet to her chest. 'She can't have it. He gave it to me. It's mine, right, Maggy?'

I held up my hands in surrender. 'I honestly have no idea who owns the bracelet. But I do think you were robbed.'

'You mean the envelope,' Christy said, a vertical frown wrinkle creasing her forehead between her eyes.

'And the bracelet.'

'Which is on her arm,' Sarah said, grumpily. 'And I don't know why you get so touchy about Pavlik.'

'I'm touchy when you repeat something that I told you in confidence,' I said. 'You promised not twenty minutes ago that you wouldn't repeat it.'

'Repeat what?' Christy was looking back and forth between the two of us.

'See?' Sarah asked. 'She doesn't remember anyway.'

Fine. 'Back to the bracelet, Christy. If it has been in your pocket since you reported it missing Wednesday night, why didn't you find it yesterday? Today is Friday.'

'Like I said.' Sarah was nodding.

Christy shrugged. 'I just didn't notice, I guess. Or maybe I wore a different jacket.'

'You were wearing that coat yesterday at the Morrison,' I pointed out.

'Was I?'

'Yes. I noticed it specifically when Helena attacked you.'

'The widow attacked her?' Sarah asked eagerly. 'Why didn't I get details?'

'It was more a lunge than an attack,' Christy said. 'We both fell on the couch.'

'And they ended up hugging and crying,' I said. 'Don't you see what I'm getting at?'

'That Christy and Helena are late-blooming lesbians as a result of being done wrong by the same man?' Sarah guessed.

'We are not,' Christy said. 'At least I'm not. Now.'

Sarah opened her mouth to pursue that.

'Enough.' I held up my hand. 'What I am trying to say is that Helena Margraves launched herself at Christy, landing on top of her. Christy was wearing this coat. The same coat in which *today* she found her bracelet.'

I could not paint a clearer picture, but Christy still couldn't see it. 'Huh?'

Sarah, however, threw me a look. 'Why don't you just say that Helena Margraves planted it in Christy's coat pocket?'

I sighed. 'Because it's not as much fun.'

'Wait,' Christy said, eyes wide. 'Helena put the bracelet in my coat?'

'You're right, Maggy,' Sarah said, sarcastically. 'That *was* fun.'

I ignored her. 'I think it's entirely possible Helena had the bracelet palmed and dropped it in your pocket. For one thing, I had noticed she didn't want Caron to help her look through her purse for the missing passport. That was before you arrived, Christy.'

'I wouldn't either,' Christy said, thrusting her chin into the air. 'My bag is sacrosanct.'

She should be more worried about liability. I had been inside that bag.

'But don't . . .' I'd been about to say 'don't you see' again but gave it up. 'Anyway, maybe Helena didn't want Caron to find something in her purse.'

'Her passport?' Christy guessed.

I shook my head. Christy might be smart under all that craziness, but she wasn't necessarily logical.

'The bracelet,' was Sarah's dry guess.

I nodded. 'Exactly. Then when Christy walked in, I turned back to see Helena with her hands in her pockets. I remember thinking I hoped she didn't have a gun.'

'But she did have my bracelet,' Christy said, finally catching on. 'And put it in my pocket as we fought.'

'Or hugged,' Sarah said, and turned to me. 'But why would she give it back?'

I shrugged. 'Probably afraid she was going to be caught with it. Christy's first words when she entered were, as I recall, "Did you steal my bracelet?"'

'How prescient of me,' Christy said, delighted with herself. 'So that solves the bracelet. But what about the envelope? Do you think she has that, too?'

I shrugged. 'Probably. And if it really was an unset diamond, it would be easy to hide.'

'That's genius,' Christy said. 'You would be a great criminal, Maggy.'

'Thanks.' Deducing done for now, I got to my feet as the bells on the door chimed.

'Maggy?' Kelly Anthony stuck her head in.

'Hi, Kelly.' There were things I wanted to ask her but debated doing it in front of Christy and blabbermouth Sarah.

As it turned out, I didn't get a chance.

'I'm looking for Christy Wrigley . . .' She caught sight of Christy behind me, even as Pavlik came up behind her.

'Would you accompany me to the station, Ms Wrigley?' Anthony asked. 'We have some questions.'

'If this is about the false robbery report,' Sarah said, 'it was just an honest mistake. Or a stupid mistake, depending on how you look at it.'

'Yes.' Christy pushed back her sleeve as she stood. 'The bracelet was in my coat pocket this whole time.' A shadow crossed her face. 'Or maybe not. Maggy thinks Helena did steal it, but then got scared and snuck it back into my pocket while we were on the couch. We're not sure about the envelope and maybe the diamond.'

Pavlik leveled a look at me. 'What am I supposed to take out of all that?'

'The robbery report from Wednesday night may be a mistake. Or not.'

Pavlik shook his head.

'Thing is,' Christy said, shrugging into her coat, 'Maggy says that Helena may own half of it all anyway, because the money came out of her and Barry's joint accounts.'

'I think it was Sarah who said that,' I corrected.

'I'm not sure that's true,' Christy continued. 'But if so, maybe I could pay her back in installments. I really do love this bracelet.' She sniffled. 'And it is the only thing that I have of Barry's now that he's gone.'

'Is it?' Deputy Anthony said, putting a hand on her arm to usher her to the door. 'Let's go talk about whether that's true.'

I tugged at Pavlik's sleeve as he started to follow them out. 'You can't possibly believe Christy killed Barry Margraves.'

'Of course not. You're her alibi.' A glimmer of a smile that faded. 'Unless you have something to tell me.'

'No,' I said. 'Then what are you questioning Christy about? Despite what she says, I know she'll give back the bracelet. And the envelope, if Helena doesn't already have it.'

Pavlik glanced toward Sarah, who was hovering nearby. She held up a hand in acknowledgment and disappeared in back.

'That was unusually accommodating of Sarah,' Pavlik said. 'She probably assumes she'll just worm it out of you when I've gone, anyway.'

'Probably,' I murmured noncommittedly. Then: 'Does Christy need a lawyer?'

It was a question designed to get Pavlik to open up, and he knew it. So he didn't. 'Yes.'

Damn. 'Criminal or civil?'

This time he did break a smile. 'Is the next question going to be "animal, vegetable or mineral"?'

'But what about Helena? Isn't she already in custody?'

'Not in custody. She's a person of interest.'

'You should see if she has that envelope.'

'The one that was supposedly stolen and has a diamond in it?'

'Supposedly. At least Christy assumed it was a diamond.'

'No, Christy is right. It is a diamond. And she should know because she wired the money for it.'

I put my hand to my forehead. 'Oh, my God. She said something on the phone to Barry about a wire, but she swore to me that she wasn't sending him money from her account.'

'She wasn't.' Pavlik had started for the door and now turned. 'In fact, she was doing just the opposite.'

'Christy?' I asked numbly, as through the window, Kelly Anthony loaded Christy into a squad car.

TWELVE

'Christy?' Sarah repeated. 'Fraud?'

Pavlik had been right about Sarah to a point, but my partner was not so much worming information out of me as I was letting it gush out full blast. I'd turned the 'open' sign to 'closed' and switched off the overhead lights, so Sarah and I were sitting in the quiet, semi-darkness.

'The money being pulled out of the Margraves' accounts,' I said in a low tone. 'They've traced the transactions back to Christy.'

'But didn't Christy tell you that it was Barry who asked her to do it?'

'So she said.'

'You don't believe her?'

'Yes, I do believe her. But that's what Pavlik is going to say.'

'Then *he* doesn't believe her.'

'Think about it. According to Christy, Barry gave her his permission and everything she needed to conduct these trans-actions. But with Barry dead—'

'What kind of transactions are we talking about?' Sarah interrupted.

'Beyond the diamond? Pavlik didn't say, but the word Christy used at the time was "trades". She said they had to be done when the market was open and the time difference between New York and wherever Barry was traveling in Europe made it difficult.'

'So he asked her to make them.'

'So she said.'

'There it is again.'

Both of us had our elbows on the table, heads on our hands.

'But as we know now,' I said, dropping one hand to thump the table. 'If Barry wanted a trade done while the US stock market was open, all he had to do was call his wife.'

'Unless he didn't want his wife to know,' Sarah said. 'How do we define "trade"?'

'Buying or selling, presumably? Though selling seems most likely in this case.'

Sarah's eyebrows went up. 'Why do you think that?'

'Because I also heard Christy telling Barry she'd made a "transfer". The trade would have been to liquidate the stock – or whatever it was – in order to transfer the proceeds out of the account.'

'That would account for Pavlik's "siphon". Do you want something to eat? Drink?'

'No.' My stomach was churning.

'But this was all at Barry's direction,' Sarah protested, getting up and picking up a cranberry juice we used – along with an orange, grapefruit and apple – for display purposes.

'You're not going to drink that, are you? It's been there for a year.'

'It's juice.' She twisted off the top and took a swig. 'And warm.'

Served her right. 'Now Barry is dead, and we have only Christy's word that she had his permission to make these trades. She certainly didn't have Helena's.'

'Yeah, what about that?' Sarah said, coming back to sit down with the juice. 'Didn't Christy notice there was another name on the account?'

'Assuming there was. When I was married, I had my own investment and retirement accounts from First Financial. Ted and I were each other's beneficiaries, of course, but—'

Sarah held up her hands. 'OK, so I'll stipulate that Helena might not have been on every account Barry had. But you just said you heard Christy talking to him about the transfer. Wouldn't that be proof she did it with his permission?'

'She'd taken the phone off speaker, so I was only hearing Christy's side of the conversation at that point. I'm not sure how much weight it would carry. Hopefully, there are emails or texts from him providing the numbers and giving her instructions.'

'Did you call Bernie?'

Bernie Egan was a corporate lawyer, but he had been good

enough to refer me to criminal attorneys in the past. I was starting to feel like I was taking advantage.

So I shrugged. 'I'm not sure I want to get Bernie involved this time.'

Sarah sat back. 'You think Christy did this.'

'I think Christy is a big girl and can find her own attorney. She's done it before.'

'For Ronny, and he ended up in the slammer.'

'Because he tried to kill me,' I reminded her, checking my phone. 'Nothing from Christy yet.'

There was a knock at the door. Sarah and I exchanged looks.

'We're closed,' I called.

The doorknob rattled and a voice said, 'It's locked.'

'Because we're closed,' Sarah muttered under her breath as she disappeared around the corner. 'Not that anybody gives a shit.'

I, actually, did.

'Sorry,' I said, going to the door. 'We had an emerg—'

'*You've* had an emergency?' Helena pushed in, trailing her omnipresent roller bag. 'Try finding out your husband is a cheater and a thief, all in one day.' She pulled a chair out from a table and replaced it with her bag before sitting on another. 'Oh, and dead, of course.'

'I'm sorry,' I said.

'*You're* sorry,' she started, and then waved the rest of the sentence off. 'I really am sorry. This angry, mouthy person isn't me.' She ran a hand through her dark hair. 'I just don't know what to say or do.'

Nor did I really. 'The police released you?'

This probably was not the thing to say. Helena's anger flared and then fizzled. 'I was brought in for questioning, not arrested. But, yes. They're done with me for now. They seem to have moved on to the other woman.'

'Christy?' I sat down, too. Some of this I was aware of already, but I wanted to hear it from Helena.

'Literally, like I said, the "other woman". For fraud.' Helena put both palms flat on the table and pulled in a long breath, before letting it back out. 'Such a nice antiseptic word for stealing everything I had. Everything we had.'

'Bank accounts, you mean?'

'Bank, investments. Even our charge cards.'

'They've been stolen?'

'The numbers, apparently. They're all charged up to the max.' She tapped one finger. 'And I thought a couple of plane tickets and some jewelry was the end of the world.'

'Are you saying Christy did all that?' I asked, appalled.

'Christy or Christy and Barry. But since he's dead . . .'

'Christy's left holding the bag.'

Her head jerked up. 'Forgive me if I don't feel sorry for her.'

'Of course,' I said. 'That was stupid of me. It's just that Christy . . . well, everything I know about her says she's not a thief.'

'Yet she stole my life and my husband.'

There was that. 'Christy said Barry gave her the account numbers. Told her to do a trade for him because he was out of the country.'

'She's lying.'

I cocked my head. 'I heard her on the phone with him.'

She pushed back from the table a little. 'When was this?'

'Tuesday morning before he arrived here. You can check his phone records.'

'Uh-uh. He wasn't using his regular cell phone for his little affair. I thought I'd told you that.'

And I'd forgotten. 'That's right. You said nothing was on his bill, so he must have a pay-as-you-go. Did the police find it?'

'On what was left of his body? I don't know.' Her lips were tight. Either trying not to cry or throw up.

'I'll ask,' I told her.

'Yes, do that. Help get your little friend off the hook.'

'I don't want . . . OK, I do want to help Christy, if she was just following orders of some kind.'

'From Barry, you mean?' Helena shrugged now, almost in surrender. 'It's possible, I suppose. I obviously didn't know the man, even after fifteen years of marriage. Maybe his plan all along was to hide our money in offshore accounts and then disappear with another woman. Any other woman.'

'I don't know about that. Things seemed to go awry when he got here,' I told her. 'Maybe Barry changed his mind. Do you have his computer? If he and Christy corresponded by email, he might have sent her the account information that way.'

'In Denver,' Helena said. 'My mother went to the house and got both the computer and a different form of identification for me and is overnighting them to the sheriff.'

'Your passport is still missing?'

'Yes. Which is in line with everything else. I feel like every part of my life has been stolen. Wiped off the board.'

'And then Christy accuses you of taking her tennis bracelet, too.' I was backing into the subject, best I could.

'Her bracelet which was purchased with *my* charge card? Yes. She has a nerve.' She held up a hand. 'But before you ask, no I did not.'

'She found it in her pocket.' I purposely did not say which pocket since I suspected Helena might have put it there.

'Figures.' She laughed humorlessly, not giving anything away. 'And I'll likely find my passport in the lining of my coat or something. Wish the same were true of everything else I've lost.'

I hesitated. 'Are you staying at the Morrison meanwhile?'

Her face tinged pink. 'I was at a motel across from the sheriff's department last night.'

I knew the place. 'You can't stay there. It's a rat trap.'

'Well, I'm not sure I'm welcome at Hotel Morrison, given the scene I made in the lobby yesterday.'

'Nobody cares about that.'

'I do.'

I stood up. 'Come on. I have an idea.'

'We're not going to your house, are we?' Helena asked nervously, as I started the Escape and went to back out of the parking space behind the shop.

Sarah had stayed hidden – and likely eavesdropping – in the office, so I hadn't bothered to tell her I was leaving.

'Heavens, no,' I said. 'Not that you wouldn't be welcome to stay, but—'

'For God's sake, I'm a total stranger. I shouldn't be welcome,' she said. 'For all you know, I killed my husband.'

I glanced sideways at her before pulling out onto Junction Road. 'Did you?'

'No.' She didn't look at me. 'But would I tell you if I did?'

'No.' We were both quiet as I made a left to go east on Brookhill Road.

'So . . . where are we going?'

'Downtown Milwaukee. The Slattery Arms.'

'That's where the sheriff said Barry stayed.'

'Exactly,' I said. 'We'll get you a room there and do some nosing around. Did you get his belongings from the hotel?'

Barry Margraves had not left a bag at the Morrison because it had been Helena staying there, not Barry. And Helena had packed up and left on Tuesday after her husband was killed. I could only assume that meant Barry's suitcase was still at the Slattery Arms, where he would logically have left it when he came to Brookhills to see Christy and never came back.

'His suitcase? No,' she said. 'I didn't have the heart to deal with it right now.'

'Then what was the hotel going to do with it?'

'Box it up and ship it originally,' she said. 'I figured that way I could decide whether or not to open it.'

'You said "originally"?'

She glanced sideways at me. 'Now that they're thinking Barry's death wasn't an accident, I don't know if plans have changed.'

Another example of the original assumption messing things up investigation-wise. But at least the suitcase hadn't been snowed-on like the crime scene was. Barry's belongings should be just as he had left them. Unless the hotel had already cleaned the room, boxed the personal effects and sent them out. 'Your husband definitely didn't have his computer with him here, though?'

'No. That is at home.' She glanced over at me. 'Are you thinking about the burner phone?'

'In his room? No, he would have taken that with him to go see Christy,' I said. 'But I'm curious to know what else he brought, aren't you?'

'Massage oil? Sex toys? Candles? Can't say I am.'

I couldn't imagine any of those things in connection with Christy, who was more the gloves, bleach and scrub brush type. But the little redhead had surprised me before.

'I have a connection at the Slattery Arms. If the sheriff hasn't confiscated your husband's things or they already haven't been shipped, would you mind if I took a look? You don't have to.'

She groaned. 'Fine. I will. Otherwise it'll kill me thinking you know something I don't.'

We were quiet for the rest of the drive east.

I finally broke the silence as we pulled into the Slattery Arms' circle entranceway. 'You identified your husband's body, right? And you're sure it's him?'

She was staring at me like I had lost my mind. 'Of course I am. I may say that I obviously didn't know him after all this, but after fifteen years, I certainly know what he looked like. Why do you ask?'

'Just something somebody said.' That somebody being Sarah. But Helena's comment earlier had resurrected it in my mind.

'Which was?'

I switched off the ignition. 'You said that maybe Barry had planned all along to transfer your money to offshore accounts and disappear.'

'With another woman. Yes, I said that.'

'It wouldn't have to be another woman.' I swung open the car door and, leaving the key in the ignition for the valet, climbed out. 'He could have just wanted to disappear.'

'But why?' Helena said, getting out of hers. 'We were happy. Or so I thought. He was not having a crisis at work. We weren't having financial problems.'

Which left 'the other woman', of course. 'I just thought that if you weren't absolutely sure it was him . . .'

'Because of the plow?' She gave a little shiver and came around to join me on the sidewalk as the valet got into the driver's seat. 'It was Barry. His face was' – she swallowed hard – 'intact.'

'I'm sorry,' I said, putting my hand on her shoulder.

'You watch too many movies,' she said, looking up at the façade of the Arms. 'Nice place, though.'

'I do. And it is,' I said, nodding thanks to the doorman.

'Who's your connection here?' she asked, following me through the grand entry doors.

'My ex-husband cheated with Rachel Slattery. And then married her.'

'And you and she are friends?' She stopped. 'You're obviously more forgiving than I am.'

That was up for debate.

THIRTEEN

'Believe me, I'm not that forgiving,' I said, stepping into the lobby of the Slattery Arms. 'Besides, Rachel Slattery is in jail.'

I held up a hand as Helena Margraves opened her mouth to ask the obvious question. 'Long story. But I'm still friends with her brother.'

I stepped up to the desk. 'Hi. I'm looking for Stephen Slattery?'

'Maggy?' A tousled blond head appeared from around the corner.

'Stephen,' I said, giving the six-foot body attached to that head a hug.

'It is so good to see you,' he said, holding me at arm's length. 'Beautiful as always.'

I was wishing I had changed out of my coffee-scented T-shirt and jeans. I loved Pavlik, but Stephen was drop-dead handsome in a little too high-toned kind of way. And he had a bit of a thing for me.

I took a moment to bask in it before turning to Helena. 'Helena Margraves, this is Stephen Slattery. Stephen owns and manages the Slattery Arms.'

Stephen took Helena's hand, giving her the full-on Slattery smile. 'Maggy exaggerates. My family owns the Arms. But she's right that I manage it.' He turned back to me. 'Mom and Dad have taken Mia to Disney World.'

Mia was Ted and Rachel's daughter. 'She's not quite two yet, is she?'

'Apparently they're easier to control at that age,' Stephen said. 'Mom and Dad have a condo in St Pete, so I suspect Disney is just an excuse to have her to themselves for a while.'

'I'm sure Ted can use the break,' I said.

Stephen grimaced. 'You'd think so, given he's a single dad right now . . .'

'Right now,' being the next twenty to life.

'But there's this rivalry.' He shook his head. 'I don't have to tell you how my mother, especially, can be.'

'Controlling and manipulative?' I suggested.

Stephen bowed his head with a laugh. 'Rachel did come by it honestly. Now I would love to believe you're here just for me, but knowing you, Maggy—'

'Also controlling and manipulative?'

Stephen cocked his head. 'Maybe that's why I'm crazy about you. You remind me of my mother.'

A shiver that I didn't bother to try to control ran down my spine.

Stephen chuckled again. 'OK, so out with it. What can I do for you?'

'Really for me,' Helena piped up, waving her hand. 'Remember me?'

'Sorry,' I said to her. Then to Stephen: 'Helena is Barry Margraves' wife.'

Widow.

His face changed. 'Oh, geez, I am so sorry for your loss, Mrs Margraves. And here we are chattering away.'

'Oh, please. No apologies necessary.' Even newly widowed Helena responded to the Slattery suave. 'And call me Helena.'

'Helena needs a room,' I told him.

'I think I can arrange that,' he said, waving us toward the counter where one of his desk clerks was waiting. 'For how many nights?'

'I don't know, quite honestly,' she told him, looking helpless.

'Not to worry,' he assured her. 'We'll start with one night at our family-and-friends rate and go from there.'

Until she got her passport. Assuming the sheriff let her leave. Who knew? The way things were going, she and Christy could be roomies.

'We understand Barry Margraves had a booking here,' I said, as the desk clerk handed Helena her key.

'Yes.' Glancing at the line forming behind us, Stephen gestured for us to follow him to his office. He closed the door behind us, rolled up the sleeves of his white dress shirt and sat down at his computer. 'Reservation for Barry Margraves arriving Monday and leaving on Wednesday,' he said, glancing up at us. 'But of course tragedy struck on Tuesday.'

I frowned and turned to Helena. 'I didn't think about it until now, but you and Barry both flew in from Denver on Monday. How did you avoid each other?'

She flushed. 'I saw Barry's flight confirmation for Monday afternoon, so I took the first morning flight out. Told him I was going to see my mother.' The last words faded away like she couldn't bear to repeat them.

'Your mother lives in Wisconsin?' Stephen asked pleasantly.

'Of course not. It was a lie, like everything Barry told me about his trip here.' She said it defensively.

'Oh,' was all Stephen said, seeming out of his depth. Though I had to believe a career hotelier had seen more than his share of cheating spouses and room hopping. Don't ask, don't tell.

'Barry's room,' I said to Stephen. 'Is it still as he left it?'

From Tuesday to today, which was Friday? Doubtful.

'Let's see, that was room three hundred and forty-one.' He tapped on the computer and sat back. 'There was an interim cleaning on Tuesday morning, since housekeeping knew it was a two-night booking. When housekeeping went in Wednesday morning to turn the room for the next reservation, they found it had not been vacated. Our day manager waited as long as he was able, but finally gathered Mr Margraves' belongings and repacked his suitcase so the room could be cleaned. I'm sorry.'

Helena held up a hand. 'I'd appreciate having my husband's things now, if I could.'

Stephen shook his head ruefully. 'I'm afraid when we realized that Mr Margraves had been the victim of an accident, I contacted the sheriff's department. They asked that we hold his bag for their pickup. I'm sure after they're done—'

I leaned forward. 'When?'

'When what?'

'When are they picking up the suitcase?'

'This afternoon, the deputy said. Then—'

'So show it to us.' I was on my feet.

'I don't know if—'

'Did anybody tell you not to?' I asked reasonably. 'Your manager already handled everything, so fingerprints aren't an issue. And if it helps' – I reached into my coat pocket – 'I'll wear gloves.'

'Those are mittens,' Stephen pointed out.

'Wait,' Helena dug through her purse and pulled out a black cloth pair, much more appropriate than my red and white striped mitties.

'Neither of them is exactly police issue,' Stephen said, pushing his chair back with a sigh. He opened a drawer as he stood up. 'These will do.'

He dangled two pairs of nitrile gloves. Just the ticket.

Stephen, bless him, brought the suitcase in and set it on his conference table for Helena and me to go through. 'I'll stand watch for the coppers outside,' he said with a grin, closing the door behind him.

'He's only half-kidding,' I told Helena as I took off my jacket and laid it on a chair. 'Stephen looks high-class, but he's got the soul of a cat burglar.'

'He *looks* like a politician,' Helena said. 'Do we trust him?'

'We do. Besides, all we're doing is going through your belongings.'

'Barry's belongings,' she corrected.

'Same. At least now.'

Her phone buzzed and she checked a message. 'Aw, geez, Mom.'

She held it up. 'I asked my mother to send my driver's license and Barry's computer and she didn't get around to it until just now. Good thing I didn't ask her for a kidney.'

I laughed. 'I hope you told her to send it overnight or it'll be on five-day ground. At least that's what my mom would have done.'

'Oh, it was *toooo* expensive,' she said, mimicking her mom's – or maybe it was my mom's – voice. She pulled a sheath of folded papers from the front zipper pocket and separated out a blue folder. 'Of course, *his* passport is here.'

'Which doesn't help you much.' Or him, these days.

'Boarding pass, hotel and flight reservations, directions, receipts.' Helena was picking through the folded papers. 'Barry insists on printing things out, when it's all on his phone anyway. I tell him it's a waste of pa—' Her voice broke, as she turned the pile over like she could not bear to see them.

Christy's name and address were scribbled on the back.

I pretended that I didn't notice. 'Can you unzip the suit-case? I'm having trouble with these gloves.'

'It's what I found.' Her voice was a little hoarse. 'Why I came here.'

'Barry wrote down Christy's name and address,' I said quietly.

'Yes. On the back of the very charge card bill that had the jewelry purchase.' She laughed, but it was more like a sob. 'It's not like I had to be a great detective.'

I didn't know what to say. 'No. I guess not.'

Helena closed her eyes and took a deep breath, gathering herself. As she did, I snagged the papers and, folding them again, slid them under my coat on the chair. No reason to have them flashing 'CHEATER, CHEATER, CHEATER' in front of her.

We had things to do.

For Helena's part, once she opened her eyes, she steeled herself to unzip the suitcase, pretending to be interested in the contents. 'Jeans, tennies, the T-shirt he sleeps in . . .'

She sat back sniffling.

'It's OK,' I said, patting her arm.

'OK? Nothing in my life is OK now. And nothing here tells us anything we don't already know.'

I was lifting out folded boxer shorts and socks, tied into pairs. 'Maybe what's not here will tell us more.'

'I don't see his iPhone, if that's what you mean.' She rubbed her forehead. 'He always kept it on him or in the front zipper pocket of this bag. Let me double-check.' She slipped her hand into the pocket that had held the papers and passport. 'Nope.'

'It's possible Barry had both phones on him. I know he had the one, at least, because' – I was going to say I saw it in his hand when he was hit, but instead said – 'Detective Anthony got your phone number from it.'

But Helena seemed fixated. 'If Barry left his phone on the dresser or nightstand charging, the manager might have just put it inside the bag.' She was working her way across the suitcase bottom and then up to the side pockets and around.

'Stephen said it was the day manager who did the packing,' I said, surrendering to her need to know. 'Which means he should be on duty now. I can ask.'

I stuck my head out the door and relayed my question.

'Stephen is certain the phone would have been placed in the bag with everything else,' I told Helena on my return, shutting the door again.

'Of course he is.' She'd moved away from the bag and was frowning. 'The alternative is that his manager is careless at best or, at worst, a crook.'

Returning to the suitcase, I went about replacing the shorts and socks. 'I asked him to double-check with the manager just in case. And we'll also talk to Deputy Anthony. See if he had it on him.'

That seemed to placate Helena a bit. 'Tell her it's an old one – three or four generations back. I was always telling him to enable tracking, just in case he lost it, and here we are.'

The man was cheating. Allowing his wife to track his iPhone was the last thing he'd do. Not that I said that either.

'Barry did stay in touch, though,' Helena continued, a little misty. 'Even on an overnight trip. But maybe the calls home were to cover for what he was really do— What?'

'It's just odd.' I had stepped back from the suitcase, eyeing it. 'There are no dressy clothes. No gifts. No indication he was having a . . .' I hesitated. Tryst sounded too cutesy, affair too long term. I settled for: '. . . assignation.'

'Besides the paper with his mistress' name and address,' Helena said, leaning on the chair back.

'Yes.' I slid my jacket further over the offending paper.

'Right.' Rousing herself, Helena opened her husband's kit bag. 'Toothpaste, toothbrush, razor. But on the bright side, as you say, no lube, no condoms, no Viag—'

Stephen's artfully raised voice from outside the office interrupted. 'Deputy Anthony is here? Tell her I'll be right with her.'

He stuck his head in. 'Done? The deputy is here.'

'Just a sec,' I said, piling the clothes and kit bag back neatly.

'Here you go,' Helena said, handing me the passport. I flipped through it before sliding it into the zipper pocket. Barry had not been quite the world traveler Christy had made out.

I glanced up as Stephen came in the room. 'Any luck with Barry's phone?'

'Sorry. He says no phone, charging or otherwise.'

'Thanks for checking, I said, zipping the suitcase and standing it back up.

'I'll take that out to her,' Stephen said, lifting the handle. 'Do you want to stay here or duck out the back?'

'See what I told you, Helena? Heart of a cat burglar,' I said.

Helena actually laughed. 'If we go out the back, I can come back through the lobby with my suitcase like a proper hotel guest.' She held out her hand. 'Thank you, Mr Slattery.'

'Stephen. And anything you need, let me know.'

They both preceded me out the door – Stephen turning left, Helena right. As I picked up my coat to follow, I saw the papers with Christy's scribbled information on the chair.

Stephen had already taken the suitcase to Deputy Anthony. I couldn't very well chase after her, could I? I eyed the waste-basket for a micro-second, then stuffed the wad in my purse and hurried after Helena.

Stephen must have had the valet bring the Escape around because Helena was already at the car. Or, more precisely, she was behind it, ducking down.

'Who are you hiding from?' I whispered as I joined her.

'The deputy.' She gestured to Kelly Anthony, who was maneuvering Barry's bag out of the hotel.

'Why? She doesn't know we just rifled through the contents of that bag.'

'True.' She straightened but didn't quite step out of the shadow of the vehicle. 'Police just make me nervous.'

I felt my eyebrows shoot up. 'Any reason for that?'

'No.' She glanced sideways at me. 'Authority figures, in general, intimidate me. I find it hard to see them as regular people. Take the sheriff. Good-looking, but I'd sleep next to him with one eye open.'

'I do.'

Now Helena's eyes flew open and she did a stutter step, causing Deputy Anthony to glance over her shoulder as she trundled Barry Margrave's bag toward her squad car.

'You . . . um.' Helena kept her voice low, eyes on the deputy's back. 'You and the sheriff . . .'

'Are we a couple? Yes. Actually, we're getting married.' Time and date to be determined.

'That's so nice,' she said, trying to cover her embarrassment. 'Did you meet at the coffeehouse?'

'We did. But not the current location. The first one collapsed.'

'Financially?'

'Physically,' I clarified, shaking my head. 'Pavlik suspected I'd murdered my partner.'

'When the building collapsed.'

'Oh, no, earlier.'

She was trying to work it out. 'Your partner Sarah?'

'Heavens, no,' I said. 'Sarah's still alive.'

'Of course,' she concurred. 'This would be your *dead* partner.'

'Exactly.' I couldn't help myself. 'For what it's worth, Caron Egan was my partner, too. You know, the woman who owns the Morrison?'

'And is alive.' She was getting the hang of it.

'But a suspect in Patricia's murder, as well.'

'Patricia.'

'The dead one.'

'Right.' A glimmer of a grin. 'Small world, Brookhills. Apparently filled with victims, suspects, criminals and coppers.'

'It feels like that sometimes.' I laughed and opened the back of the Escape to get her bag.

'Anything else you need?' I asked as I set it on the ground.

'No.' She stuck out her hand. 'But thank you.'

'You're welcome.'

As I climbed into the driver's seat and turned the ignition, I wondered if Helena fully appreciated that she was in the suspect category herself.

A knock at the window startled me.

Stephen Slattery made a circular motion with his hand, indicating that he wanted me to roll down the window.

'You know that gesture went out with crank windows,' I told him once I had lowered it.

'I do,' he said. 'But miming pushing a button or just pointing down doesn't have the panache. Have time for a drink?'

I glanced at the dashboard clock. Four thirty p.m. Too early to go home, but if I went back to Uncommon Grounds, I would have to help Sarah close. Assuming she had actually opened.

I turned off the ignition.

FOURTEEN

'It's five o'clock somewhere,' I said, as I slid onto a brass-studded leather stool in the Slattery Arms lobby bar.

'Five thirty-five in New York,' Stephen said, hitching himself up on the stool next to mine. 'What will you have?'

'Sauvignon Blanc,' I said. 'The drier the better.'

Stephen cocked his head. 'Has it been that long? I thought you were a red wine woman.'

'I am. And I like oaky Chardonnays when I drink white. This is to keep me from ordering more than one.'

'Because I'm such a stud you can't trust yourself.' When he smiled, a dimple appeared on his right cheek. And he knew it.

I patted the cheek. 'Because it's poor form for the sheriff's fiancée to get a DUI.'

'Ouch,' Stephen said, pulling back in mock offense. 'Way to remind me you're already taken.'

'You're only flirting with me because I am.'

'Untrue,' he said, indicating something to the bartender. 'I flirted with you before Pavlik. And after Ted.'

'Actually,' I said, thinking back. 'It was early Pavlik. But prior to our moving in together and certainly before our engagement.'

'Meaning I'm not a scoundrel.'

You gotta love a man who uses the word scoundrel. 'Oh, but you are.' I took a sip of the white wine the bartender had poured. 'This is a Chardonnay. And oaky and delicious.'

'Good palate,' Stephen said, admiringly.

I pointed at the bottle the bartender had set down. 'Cakebread Chardonnay from Napa Valley. Ted and I used to love it.'

He put his fist to his heart. 'Both the ex and the fiancée have been invoked now.'

I grinned. 'I will still only have one glass, but thank you. This is delicious.'

'You're welcome.' He took a sip of his. 'And I agree.'

'And thanks, too, for getting Helena a room and giving us the time to search through the suitcase.'

'First of all, the "Friend and Family" rate is not much of a discount, so no need to thank me.' He smiled at my pained expression. 'Secondly, they were her husband's things. All I did was give her time to look them over before they were confiscated, at least for a bit.' His expression changed. 'She didn't slip out anything incriminating, did she? Hemlock or an asp, perhaps?'

'Nothing so romantic,' I said. 'In fact, nothing romantic at all, which is kind of odd.'

Stephen took a beat. 'If poison and snakes are romantic to you, I think I'm glad we never got together.'

'Me, too,' I said, squeezing his hand. 'So what do you think? Married man lies to his wife and flies to town to meet the woman he's been cyber-courting for months on the side. Wouldn't he arrive with a gift? Or just flowers if nothing else?'

'This is Barry Margraves? Who's the woman?'

'Christy Wrigley.'

'I don't think I know her.'

'Very possible. She lives across from our shop and helps out occasionally.'

'And is it Christy or Helena who's suspected in his murder?' he asked.

'Why do you think it's murder?'

'Because you're asking questions.'

Good point.

Stephen continued, 'But the weapon. How does one plot a murder using a snowplow?'

Another good point. 'I think it would have to be a crime of opportunity. The snowplow was there and . . .' Sounded implausible, even to me.

'I get it,' Stephen said helpfully. 'Like finding a gun on the street and shooting somebody with it.'

'Somebody you have a grudge against and just happens to be there,' I said. 'It does stretch the imagination. But if somebody did it, we know it was not Christy. She and I were in the store and saw Barry Margraves killed.'

'That's a nice change.' Stephen patted my hand. 'You can't be suspected for once.'

Nor could Stephen's murderous sister. Jail being the best alibi. But I did not say that. 'Right.'

'Terribly traumatic for Christy to see her lover mowed down in front of her,' Stephen said. 'For you, too. But you're an old hand at this. And he was not your lover, after all.' His eyes narrowed. 'Or was he?'

'He was not,' I told him. 'And, strangely, people dying in front of me never gets old.' I sat up straight. 'That sounded awful. I meant I never get used to it. Always traumatic. Bad.'

Stephen suppressed a grin. 'Of course. But back to your victim not arriving with courting gifts. He was married, so maybe he planned to pick something up here in the gift shop.'

I wrinkled my nose. 'Hotel gift shop gifts? Kind of tacky.'

'We have a very nice gift shop,' Stephen said. 'And a jewelry store.'

'I'm sure you do,' I said. 'In fact, if you could check with them to see if Barry Margraves made any purchases, I'd appreciate it.'

'Walked right into that one, didn't I?' he said ruefully. 'I will do that.'

'Thank you,' I said, smiling. 'He'd already sent Christy a diamond tennis bracelet, which Helena tipped to. That's the reason she flew out here. To track down the other woman.'

'Then the cat was out of the bag.'

'Exactly.' I had a thought. 'I have to send a quick text to Pavlik.'

Mock sigh. 'Fine.'

I tapped for a few seconds and then set down the phone, so as not to miss a reply.

'Telling him you're going to be late?'

'Asking whether Barry Margraves had an iPhone on him. Since it wasn't in the room or in the suitcase, he had to have both phones with him.'

'Both?'

'He apparently had a separate phone for conducting the affair.'

'Smart,' Stephen said, draining his glass. He picked up the bottle. 'Can I top you off?'

'Thanks, but no,' I said, finishing my Chard and sliding off the bar stool. 'It was delicious and this has been fun, but I must go.'

'Must you?' Deep gaze in the eyes.

I laughed. 'Yes, I must. Thank you again.'

'You're—'

I was out the door before I heard the welcome part.

'I'd forgotten how charming Stephen is,' I said to Sarah. 'Good taste in wine, too.'

'Apparently so,' she said sourly. 'I'm surprised you came back to help me close.'

'Me, too,' I admitted. 'I had no intention of doing so, but my car just headed to Uncommon Grounds of its own volition.'

'At least the car has a conscience,' she said. 'And speaking of which, what about Pavlik?'

'He said Margraves had the iPhone on him, which makes sense since Kelly Anthony said she found Helena's number on it. He wouldn't use the burner, which is still missing, to call his wife.'

Sarah, who had stooped to plug in the vacuum cleaner, straightened. 'What are you talking about?'

'Margraves.' I switched on the vacuum.

She switched it off. 'I meant what about Pavlik? Is he all right with you having drinks with strange, good-looking men in the middle of the day?'

'It was almost five and Stephen's not strange. Pavlik knows there's nothing to worry about.' Though he had called Stephen my old boyfriend. So maybe he would mind. 'I'll tell him.'

'Come clean, huh? Just in case somebody saw you?'

I shrugged. 'It was the lobby bar.'

'Idiot.' She pressed the switch.

I unpressed it. 'I am not cheating or lying. I don't need to hide having a drink with an old friend.'

'So you say.' On again the vacuum went.

Giving up, I went to get a damp rag to wipe the tables while she vacuumed.

'So what's the deal?' she asked as she finally switched the vacuum off.

'With what?' I had finished my wiping and was gathering the dirty rags to take home. Finally.

'The phone. You said somebody found one?' She hit the retract button for the vacuum cord.

The thing whipped around and nearly took my eye out as it snaked back into its hole. 'If you guide the cord in, it won't do that.'

'But I like it when it does that,' she said, with a grin. 'Now, the phone?'

'Barry Margraves' iPhone. He had that on him, but he had another one and we can't find it.'

'Why another one?'

'I told you – a burner or pay-as-you go. He and Helena had a joint plan, meaning calls from both their regular phones were on the same bill.'

'And he wasn't stupid enough to chance that.'

'No, Helena checked.' I was thinking. 'Barry had a phone in his hand when he was hit, remember? Maybe that wasn't the iPhone the sheriff's office has. Maybe it was the burner and it went flying on impact.'

Sarah was frowning. 'I wasn't there, remember? You were here with Christy and called me after.'

I had started for the door and now turned. 'That's right. Where exactly were you when I called?'

'Somewhere not driving a snowplow, so just get that out of your head.'

'Gone.' I balled my fingers next to my forehead and then released them quickly. 'Poof.'

'Honestly,' she said, shaking her head. 'I don't come close to being a viable suspect. I didn't know the man. You at least had talked to him on the phone.'

'I had, hadn't I?' I said, thinking about that. 'When Christy handed me the phone.'

'And an hour later, the guy was dead.'

'Then he had to have called from his burner, right?'

'Maybe, maybe not,' Sarah shrugged. 'If he used his iPhone, it would show up as a recent call on the phone, itself, unless he deleted it. And on his bill, even if he did.'

'True. I'd like to get a look at the phone – or, better yet, the bill.'

'Maybe Pavlik will let you if you sweet-talk him like you did Slattery.'

Maybe so.

Or not.

'You know I can't do that, Maggy,' Pavlik said when I got home. He sniffed as he hugged me hello. 'Chardonnay?'

Damn, the man was good. 'I had a glass with Stephen at the Slattery Arms.'

'When you were pumping him for information as I said you would.'

'Cuz you are so smart.' I nuzzled him.

'And you are so full of it,' he said, hugging me. 'Now what did Slattery have to tell you?'

'Nothing much,' I said, following him into the living room. 'Margraves never came back to his room on Tuesday, as we well know. The day manager packed up his things. In fact, Kelly Anthony just picked them up. We just missed her.'

'She mentioned that she saw your Escape at the hotel. Who is we?'

'Me and Helena. She's staying there tonight.' I frowned. 'How did Kelly know it was my Escape?'

'Educated guess. And the "Proud mom of a gay man" sticker might have helped.'

I do love my Eric. I grinned. 'OK, so Kelly arrived while we were there.'

'Did you talk Slattery into letting you go through the stuff?'

Busted. 'Yes. But we used gloves.'

Pavlik looked skyward. 'Of course you did.'

'Nitrile ones,' I continued. 'Not my ratty mittens or anything.'

Now he laughed. 'Find anything?'

'No, which is why I asked you about phones. You have the iPhone, but Barry had to have another, a burner, since Helena didn't find any calls to Christy on their joint bills.'

'And it wasn't in his things.'

'No, but I saw a phone in his hand as he stepped into the road. It might have gone flying when he was hit and still be buried in the snow somewhere.'

'And you're not out looking for it?'

'Too dark.' And cold, according to Sarah, who had refused to help me. 'Not that we'd find anything your deputies didn't find that day.'

'You're jollying me along,' Pavlik said. 'You know full well there was no reason to search for a second phone the day of the incident.'

'True. But now that there is the possibility that Christy and Barry were in cahoots, syphoning money out of the joint accounts and hiding it, that phone could be important.'

'Cahoots, huh?' Pavlik settled onto the couch and waved me down to sit next to him.

I snuggled in. 'Unless, of course, you found communication between the two of them on the iPhone.'

Pavlik kissed the top of my head. 'Directions to Christy's house in the maps program, but no calls or texts to her number.'

I sat up, nearly bopping him. 'Yet I know he called her maybe an hour before, because I talked to him. There has to be another phone.'

'Unless he called from the hotel before he left.'

That had not occurred to me. 'And caught a ride from there after he hung up.' Getting to Brookhills from the Slattery Arms in a snowstorm in less than an hour would have been tight, but doable. 'But that call aside, Christy said they spoke regularly. If there's no indication of that on the iPhone . . .'

'He had to have another,' Pavlik agreed.

'If Margraves dropped it when he was hit, it could have been buried by Harold's plow or any of the others that came through.'

'And here we are three days later,' Pavlik said, shaking his head. 'That mobile could be anywhere, including under that giant pile of frozen snow the truck plowed into.'

'Does this mean it won't be found until spring?'

'No, it means Anthony will need to get Public Works out with shovels tomorrow morning.'

'Or flamethrowers?' I suggested.

'Not sure that's a good idea, but we'll let Sanitation or whoever they send decide.'

I pulled back to see Pavlik's face. 'You're taking this pretty seriously.'

Pavlik snagged an arm around me. 'Only because you're right. Christy's phone has an incoming call from "Barry" just an hour and four minutes before 911 got the call from your phone.'

'When I reported Margraves being hit by the plow.' Of course, they would have checked Christy's phone. I only wished I had when I had the opportunity.

'Exactly. The call to Christy wasn't from the iPhone we have in our possession, yet you're corroborating that it was Margraves calling.'

'Yes, I spoke to him. I assume there were previous calls from that same number on Christy's phone?'

'More than I cared to count,' Pavlik said. 'Going back nearly four months.'

That meant that everything Christy had told us about the relationship was true, not a figment of her imagination. 'And what about texts? Do they confirm she was instructed to make those trades? Wire money?'

'Afraid not,' Pavlik said. 'We're still sifting through, but so far there's nothing explicit. In one voicemail, he says he's calling to see if she "took care of it", but no details.'

'Christy said he gave her routing and account numbers, but I suppose he did that over the phone. I mean as they were talking, not texting.'

'It's safer,' Pavlik acknowledged. 'And, obviously, it leaves no record. Which means we still have only Christy's word that she was making the transactions at Margraves' behest.'

Ugh. 'Is she in custody?'

'Not yet,' Pavlik said.

'Good.' I slid away and dug my phone out of my pocket, punching in a few words and then hitting send.

'What are you doing?'

'Texting Christy to help me open tomorrow.'

'Because you need her or because you think you can pry something out of her that we haven't?'

'Both?' I tried, settling back.

'Well, just so you know,' Pavlik said, nuzzling my neck, 'Christy might not be in custody, but her cell phone is.'

FIFTEEN

Happily, I had been able to reach Christy and she joined me in the coffeehouse at six a.m. Saturday morning. Unfortunately, I had not thought to let Sarah know she wasn't needed.

'You have got to be kidding me.' Morning person, Sarah was not. 'I dragged my ass out of bed and—'

'Shh,' I said, glancing over my shoulder to where Christy was hanging up her coat. 'If you want to go home, do it. I just needed to talk to Christy before she' – I lowered my voice another decibel – 'gets arrested.'

'Arrested?' Sarah repeated, not bothering to lower hers.

'Who's being arrested?' Christy asked, coming to join us. 'Hi Sarah.'

'Hi.' A dark look at me.

'Maybe Helena,' I fibbed. 'Who knows?'

'Poor thing,' Christy said, wiping her finger across a table for dirt. 'Sticky.'

'Is not,' Sarah grumbled. 'I washed that table myself.'

Christy ignored her, going to the back.

'Let her clean if she wants to,' I hissed to Sarah.

'I thought you might be talking about me,' Christy said, reappearing with a navy towel and spray bottle.

'I was just telling Sarah you do a better job cleaning than we do. Thank you so much for coming in.'

'Happy to.' She sprayed what smelled like pure bleach on the table. 'How did you know to call me on my landline? Did Sheriff Pavlik tell you they took my mobile?'

'I didn't know that,' I lied, lifting my eyebrows. 'Did I call you on your house phone? I must have pressed the wrong one.'

Sarah glanced at me suspiciously and back again to Christy. 'You still have a landline?'

'Of course.' She sniffed, probably because of the fumes.

'In case there's an emergency and we lose electricity or the cell towers go down, I can still use it. You don't have one, Sarah?'

'My not being a dinosaur, no,' Sarah said as she turned away to hang up her own coat.

'Well, I think it's very smart of you, Christy,' I said. 'I should activate mine again.'

'Now that you're with the sheriff, you probably don't need one,' she said, wiping the table. 'He probably has all sorts of communications devices – satellite phones, drones and all, in case of natural disaster or nuclear war.'

I would take my apocalypse later, thank you very much. 'Probably.'

'Drones?' Sarah said. 'What you do with those? Send notes like carrier pigeons?'

'Shows what you know,' Christy said, sticking her nose in the air, even as she continued to scrub. 'Drones can be used as portable cell towers.'

'Really,' I said, genuinely interested. 'How—'

'I'll send you some articles,' Christy offered, waving off the subject. 'But let's get back to me getting arrested.'

'Why would you be arrested?'

'Please, Maggy,' Christy said, giving one final rub to the imaginary spot. 'Don't play stupid.'

'But she's so good at it,' Sarah kibitzed with a snarky smile.

'You both know that the sheriff thinks I might have taken money out of Barry's account without his permission.' Christy straightened up with the navy towel which was bleaching white in spots before our very eyes.

I decided to ignore it. 'That's true. But he is sending people out to search for Barry's mobile phone this morning. Assuming they find it, it should prove he gave you the account numbers and all.'

'I don't see how. He relayed it all to me as we talked on the phone, so I could write it down.'

'Where?' I asked.

'In my notebook, of course.' She picked up the spray bottle. 'Along with usernames and passwords for his accounts.'

'He gave you those, too?' Sarah demanded.

'Of course,' she said. 'How else was I going to get into the accounts online?'

How else indeed.

She kept talking as she sprayed another table. 'Silly Barry, he pretty much used the same password and username for everything.'

'Silly Barry,' I repeated.

'You probably do the same thing,' Sarah told me.

'I do not,' I countered. 'I use different ones and can never remember them.'

'That means you write them down,' Christy said. 'Which isn't good. We'll have to talk about cyber security, Maggy.'

Right now the little potential hacker was the last person I wanted advice from.

'Barry hadn't even set up his security questions,' Christy continued. 'I had to do all that before I could get to anything else.' She set down the spray bottle. 'I hate to say it, Barry being dead and all, but he wasn't very organized.'

'Maybe Helena set up the accounts,' I suggested.

'Maybe so. Barry was detail-oriented in so many other ways.' She sniffled. 'That's why we were so perfect together.'

'Except for that detail of his being married,' Sarah reminded her.

'Yes, that.' Christy pulled out a chair, wiping it off with the cloth before sitting. 'I just don't know what to think about him.'

'That he was a slimeball?' Sarah offered.

I wasn't sure if I was glad Sarah was there or not.

Good thing Christy wasn't easily offended. 'I guess he was. But maybe I just fall for that kind of bad boy. Like Ronny.' She held up a hand. 'No offence.'

'None taken,' Ronny's step-cousin said. 'He's a slimeball too.'

'And a killer,' I reminded them both.

'That's true,' Christy said, brightening. 'Barry wasn't that, at least.'

Sensing an opening. I pulled out the chair across from her and sat. 'But what was he, do you suppose?'

'What do you mean?'

'You know that the Margraves accounts were emptied.'
Helena had confided this little nugget, so I wasn't revealing
anything I had learned from Pavlik alone.

'Emptied?' Christy's eyes were wide. 'No, I didn't know
that.'

'And you didn't *do* that either?' Sarah asked, picking up
the now navy and white rag and sniffing it. She coughed.

'Did I empty their accounts?' Christy said. 'Of course not.
I just sold a few securities and then transferred the money out
of the brokerage account, so Barry could pay some bills.' Her
face reddened. 'I thought for a diamond.'

'The one that's still missing,' I said. 'In the manila
envelope.'

'Yes,' Christy said. 'And now I'll never know for sure what
was in it.'

'Then there may not even be a diamond?' Sarah asked,
tossing down the rag in disgust. 'Why are we even talking
about it?'

Pavlik told me that money had been wired for the purchase
of a diamond, presumably the one in the missing envelope, but
I wasn't free to tell Christy and Sarah that. 'Back to the
Margraves accounts. If you didn't empty them, Christy, then
Barry must have done it.'

'But why?' Realization dawned on Christy's face. 'Because
he planned to run away with me?'

'Sure,' Sarah said. 'And the two of you would live happily
ever after on some tropical island, spending his and the
betrayed wife's money.'

'Oh,' Christy said, her hands balled up under her chin. 'That
sounds wonderful.'

'It sounds like fraud,' I said. 'Which is what you're going
to be formally charged with if you're not careful.'

'Don't forget murder,' Sarah said.

'But Maggy and I were together when Barry was killed,'
Christy said.

'Then you must have hired somebody.' Sarah hung onto a
new theory like Mocha did with a bone Frank coveted. 'Or
you and Maggy are in it together.'

'Cahoots,' I said.

They both looked at me.

'Sorry,' I said. 'Just something that keeps popping into my head. But, in answer to your question, Sarah: no, Christy did not kill Barry and neither did I.'

'Fine.' Her arms were crossed. 'Though I didn't phrase it as a question.'

'Statement, even worse,' Christy said, miffed. 'Why would I murder Barry? I loved him. Or thought I did.'

Loved, past tense. Today was Saturday and Barry had been mowed down in front of us on Tuesday. Four days and Christy already seemed to be viewing him in the rearview mirror. I guessed that was resilience. Or psychopathy.

Now Christy drew in a breath, her eyes bugging out. 'Or maybe he's not dead.'

'I tried that,' Sarah said. 'Maggy says Barry's dead as a doornail, flat as a pancake.'

'I'm afraid so,' I said, trying to soften it. 'Good theory, Christy, but Helena identified him.'

'Maybe she's in . . . what was your word?'

'Cahoots,' I said. 'But there's also—'

Footsteps pounded up the front steps and the door opened. 'Can I use your bathroom?'

'The Plow Man Cometh,' I said, as Harold Byerly made his way to the bathroom, parka hood up and boots tracking dirty snow.

'Now, Maggy,' Sarah said. 'Harold is just using the bathroom.'

I gave her side-eye. 'Aren't we being charitable, all of a sudden. The man needs a good gastroenterologist.'

'Or more fiber in his diet,' Christy said in a chippy tone.

'Or less,' I said, as the door opened again and Deputy Anthony entered. 'Morning, Kelly. Can I get you a coffee?'

'Five, please,' she said, stripping off her gloves. 'I've got four guys from Public Works digging through snow looking for that phone.'

'What phone?' Christy asked, as Sarah went back to get the coffee.

Kelly Anthony just lifted her eyebrows and gave me a dark

look, presumably placing the blame for today's task squarely on my shoulders.

I turned to Christy. 'I told you. We think Barry had a second phone he used to communicate with you. But we – or the authorities – haven't found it.'

'Ohhh,' Christy said. 'That's why you were so interested in my landline, Maggy. And why Detective Anthony took my cell phone.'

For her part, Deputy Anthony did not comment.

Not that Christy paused for one, anyway.

'Say,' she said, getting up from the table and approaching the deputy. 'Do you think—'

'Umm, Christy,' I said, pointing. 'You have something—'

But the redhead didn't pause for me, either. 'We were just talking and Maggy thinks it's possible that Barry faked his death.'

I held up both hands. 'I didn't say that. Just the opposite, in fact.'

Christy balled her fists on her hips. 'Well, you said it was a good theory.'

'I was placating you,' I said. 'I also told you that Helena had identified him—'

'And might be in cahoots.'

'I never—'

But Kelly Anthony was just shaking her head. 'I don't know what you all are up to, but the man was identified with dental records and fingerprints.'

Fingerprints, that was interesting. 'Margraves' prints were on file? Did he have a criminal record?'

I was the target of another one of those looks. 'Fingerprints are used for everything these days from opening your cell phone to passport ID for frequent travelers. You don't have to have a "criminal record", as you put it.'

I sensed I was not Deputy Anthony's favorite person right now.

'Barry did travel a lot,' Christy was saying. 'I'm sure he had some sort of special clearance.'

A door opened and closed. Harold Byerly emerged from the hallway to join us just as Sarah handed Kelly Anthony a cardboard tray holding four coffees. 'I've got the fifth one on the counter,' she said, hitching her thumb over her shoulder.

'Give it to Harold,' Anthony said, pushing her way out the door with the coffees.

'Somebody's a little surly this morning,' Sarah said, watching her go. 'She didn't even pay.'

'I think it's on me,' I said. 'I'm the one who suggested the missing phone might be in a snow pile.' I turned to Harold. 'How are things, Harold? No repercussions from . . .' I gestured toward the street.

'Mowing down the love of my life?' Christy suggested.

The woman was all over the place. One moment she's left Barry in the past, the next moment he's not dead. And now, suddenly, he's the love of her life again.

Harold just picked up the fifth to-go cup. 'Why do you think I'm digging out snow piles instead of driving my truck? Can't say I didn't deserve it though. Leaving my truck unattended and all.'

Punishment or not, I was surprised Harold had been tapped to participate in the search for the cell phone, given he was involved in the incident. However negligent he might have been, though, Harold had no reason to want Margraves dead. Or to hide evidence if he should come across the phone.

'You were in a real hurry that morning,' I said to him.

'It's not easy to find an available bathroom at that time of the morning in a snowstorm,' Harold told us. 'I said hallelujah when I saw you were open. Literally, yelled "hallelujah" and jumped right out of the truck.'

'Bless you,' Christy said. 'We were glad to be there for you, weren't we, Maggy?'

Harold had her at 'hallelujah'. The woman was a chameleon. 'Of course.'

'Damn bathroom stank for hours,' Sarah said. 'Say hallelujah to that one.'

'Hallelujah!' Christy piped up, raising both hands over her head.

But Harold was sheepish. 'Sorry. I love pad thai, but—'

'It doesn't love you. I know,' I said, seeing my opportunity for getting the narrative from the horse's mouth. 'Now you saw that we were open, parked your truck in front of Clare's, hopped down and ran right in here, right?'

'Not thinking to lock it,' Byerly said ruefully. 'That was my cardinal sin, according to my supervisor.'

'And the keys?' I asked.

He clucked his teeth. 'In the ignition.'

'Yeah, that's not good,' I agreed. 'In the ignition with the truck running?'

'You know,' he said, cocking his head, 'I can't say for sure anymore. I could have sworn I shut it off, but I guess I was wrong.'

I wasn't so sure of that.

Harold held up the to-go cup. 'Can I pay you for this?'

'Your coffee is on me, just like the rest of them,' I said.

Christy preceded Harold to the door and pushed it open for him.

'Christy,' I said, as Harold nodded gratefully and left. 'I think you sat—'

But the redhead was hanging out the door. 'Rebecca! Over here.'

I went to the window to see Rebecca step off Christy's porch and cross the street.

'I was just putting a note in your mailbox saying I was sorry I missed you,' Rebecca said, entering the coffeehouse. 'Hello, all.'

'It's my fault,' Christy said. 'Maggy needed my help and I completely forgot you and I had planned to go out for breakfast.'

'If you want to go now, Christy, that's fine,' I said, feeling guilty for having disturbed their plans. Besides, I had gotten all I wanted out of the woman for now.

'But you said you needed me.' Christy apparently had a need to be needed.

'And I did. But that was before I knew that Sarah was coming in.' It wasn't necessarily a lie. I never could be sure Sarah would be in – at least on time. 'Now that she's here, you—'

'But I just saw Sarah going out the back,' Rebecca said. 'From the train platform to the parking lot.'

Frowning, I stuck my head in the office. Sure enough. The sneak's coat was gone.

I came back into the main dining room. 'I guess Sarah did have to leave.'

'Well then, I'll just stay, Maggy,' Christy said, picking up her bleach-soaked cloth and turning her bleach-blotched butt at me to wipe another table. 'You can depend on me.'

Goody.

Rebecca stayed on for coffee before she left to get on with her day. Commuters came and went and Christy cleaned and cleaned. And talked and talked.

'If it's all right, Maggy?'

'Yes?' I had shut her out in self-defense and now she was waving her towel – I'd taken away the bleach – to get my attention.

'The mailman just came so I'm going to run over to my place and get it, OK?' She glanced up at the clock. 'It's only four, so it should be quiet enough.'

I thought I could make it through while she crossed the street and back. 'Of course, go ahead and take your time. I'll be fine.'

I sat down at a table and laid my head on my crossed arms, like naptime in kindergarten, enjoying the silence. But seemingly not two minutes later, footsteps pounded up the steps and the door slammed open.

'Maggy!' Christy called. 'You're not going to believe this.'

'What?' I asked, a bit irritably, raising my head. I had been looking forward to my ten minutes of peace.

She tossed something onto the table in front of me, and I followed my nose down to it.

A manila envelope addressed to Christy Wrigley. And with Barry Margraves' return address.

SIXTEEN

I picked up the manila envelope. 'This is *the* envelope? The one you said went missing from your underwear drawer?'

Along with the bracelet, which also was no longer missing.

'*Lingerie* drawer.' Christy sat down across from me and picked up the envelope. 'But, yes. The very one. Look at the cancellation date. January nineteenth. That was Tuesday, which is when it was delivered to me. The day of Barry's death.'

And now here it was Saturday. Christy's address had been circled, and I traced it with my fingertip. 'Somebody found it and put it back in your mailbox?' I remembered Rebecca on her porch.

'No, that's the odd thing,' Christy said. 'I saw the mail carrier slip it into the box just now. That's why I was so eager to go across and get it. You must have thought me odd, running out like that.'

No odder than usual. And, besides, I was busy being grateful. 'Are you going to open it?'

'I don't know,' Christy said. 'Do you think I should? What would the sheriff want me to do?'

Pavlik would want us to go out and hand it to Kelly Anthony. But if I said that out loud, I wouldn't have deniability. 'Can you feel anything in it?'

She ran her fingers back and forth across the envelope like it was covered in braille. She stopped. 'Maybe a lump here?'

I felt the lower left corner, where I detected a pea-size bump. 'Maybe so.'

We both stared at the envelope between us, hands in our laps now.

'Open it,' I said.

She hesitated and then grabbed the envelope and tore it open in one motion.

A big ol' diamond fell out.

* * *

'Don't touch it,' I warned Christy, getting up.

'Oops.' She was balancing it on her left ring finger. Startled, she let go and the thing bounced on the envelope and then rolled off onto the floor.

'Oh, my God,' I said, getting onto my hands and knees and crawling to where I had seen it come to a stop. Once there I stuck my hand out, keeping my eyes on the diamond. 'Glove.'

'What?' Christy was standing now.

'Glove,' I said. 'You know, the things you wear nearly continually? I don't want to leave prints.'

'But I've already touched it.'

Like I said, I didn't want to leave *my* prints. 'Just give me a napkin, if you don't have a glove.'

'No, I have a glove,' she said, going to her purse. 'Nitrile, latex or rubber?'

I felt my eyes start to roll and righted them. 'Nitrile. Please.'

She handed me one.

I stretched it over my hand and picked up the diamond, placing it back on the envelope. 'Watch, but don't touch. I'll see if Anthony is still here.'

'I wouldn't have touched it, if you'd told me not to sooner,' Christy was saying as I went to the door. 'In fact, you're the one who said open it.'

Couldn't argue with that. I stepped out on the porch and was relieved to see Anthony was nowhere in sight, though the public works guys were still digging the snow mound where the plow had been stuck.

I went back and got my phone, speed-dialling Pavlik.

'You found what?' he asked when he picked up.

'The envelope that Christy reported stolen. The one she thought had a diamond in it? Well, it does.'

'You opened it.'

'Christy opened it.' I was a snitch. Especially unforgiveable since I told her to do it.

'Is Anthony still out front?'

'No, she's gone.' I didn't know if they'd found something or the deputy had just stepped away. Either way, I preferred dealing with Pavlik, given Kelly's earlier mood. 'Want me to bring it to you?'

Sure, why not close early again.

'No, I'm nearby. I'll just stop in.'

'Oh, OK,' I said, a little surprised. 'Great.'

I rung off.

'What did he say?' Christy had the diamond, which looked to be three or four karats to my uneducated eye, in the palm of her now gloved hand.

'That he'd stop by to get it. Will you put that down?'

'I have a glove on.'

Yes, she did. 'OK, but let me get a picture.'

'Ooh, good idea.' Christy held the diamond up next to her face and smiled for the camera.

'I meant just the dia— OK, fine.' I obligingly took the shot and then had her hold the diamond on her palm again, and just snapped that. Then I pieced together the envelope and took a third shot of that.

As I set the phone down, Pavlik came up the steps.

'You *were* close,' I said, closing the door behind him. I would have given him a kiss, but this was an official visit. It would be unseemly.

'Just driving back from the Slattery Arms to the office,' Pavlik said.

'You saw Helena?'

'No, your boyfriend,' Pavlik said, taking blue gloves out of his pocket and slipping them on. As he did, I saw him take in the fact that both Christy and I wore a single matching glove.

'You have a boyfriend, Maggy?' Christy was saying disapprovingly. 'I may have poor taste in men, but I do restrict it to one at a time.'

'The sheriff is being facetious,' I told her.

Pavlik picked up the diamond, which was sitting innocently on the envelope now. 'Have you handled it?'

'Maggy wanted me to take a picture with it.'

A withering look from Pavlik.

'That's not quite how . . .' Oh, what the hell. 'Christy handled the diamond with her bare hands. We both handled the envelope.'

A tight smile. 'Well, luckily we have elimination prints from both of you on file.'

'Oh, yes,' Christy said, perkily. 'That is lucky. And we put on gloves after, just in case.'

Pavlik didn't close his eyes and count to ten. Three, maybe. Then slipping the diamond into the envelope, he put the whole thing into an evidence bag. 'You say this was delivered by the mail courier?'

'Yes,' Christy said. 'Just this afternoon. I saw him and I rushed right over to get it, didn't I, Maggy?'

'She did,' I told Pavlik.

'But this is the envelope that was delivered to you on Tuesday?' Pavlik asked. 'You're sure?'

'Yes.' Her head was pumping up and down. 'I put it in my lingerie' – a glance at me – 'drawer.'

'And reported it missing on Wednesday evening,' Pavlik said. 'You didn't look in that drawer between Tuesday when you put the envelope in and Wednesday when you discovered it was gone?'

'Well, of course,' Christy said, seeming affronted. 'I do change my under . . . lingerie, you know. Sometimes two or three times a day, if—'

Pavlik held up his hand. 'I understand. But you didn't see the envelope when you opened the drawer?'

'Well, no.' Christy wrinkled her brow. 'I had put it in the back, you see. Under the bras and panties that are pretty, but I don't wear every day. I was saving them for when Barry—'

Hand went up again. 'And the bracelet. You also kept that in that drawer.'

Christy pushed up her sleeve to reveal the subject of discussion. 'Yes, but not under the lingerie with the envelope. I put it in a sock, on top. Because I was wearing it every day.'

'Sock,' Pavlik repeated.

'A clean one,' Christy said a little defensively.

Pavlik looked at me.

'Socks are good places.' I shrugged. 'They cushion things.'

'Exactly,' Christy said, nose in the air.

Pavlik held up both hands now. 'I'm not questioning the wisdom of your storage methods. But you did say you wore the bracelet on Tuesday.'

'Yes, and when I took it off, I put it in the sock on top of the good panties and bras.'

'Which, in turn, were on top of the envelope by then,' Pavlik said.

Impatience. 'I told you that.'

'You didn't wear the bracelet on Wednesday?' I asked, taking over to give Pavlik a break. 'I didn't see you that day.'

'No, I was in mourning. Rebecca came here and got us both coffee, remember?'

'I do. You said it was only when you were packing to spend the night at Rebecca's that you realized the bracelet and envelope were gone.'

'Yes. First the bracelet, since I was going to take it.'

'In its sock?' Pavlik asked, checking his watch.

I resisted a smile.

'Yes. Watches pack beautifully in socks, too, by the way,' she said, nodding at his. 'They don't scratch, you know.'

'Excellent idea,' I said, wanting to move on. 'But back to the bracelet, Christy. When you went to pack it, the—'

Pavlik interrupted. 'Was it an easily identifiable sock?'

'Blue and black striped,' Christy said. 'I lost its match years ago.'

'But you kept the single sock for—'

'Jewelry, of course,' Christy said nodding. 'Or whatever.'

'Whatever.' Pavlik seemed mystified.

'So, sock and bracelet are gone.' I pressed ahead. 'Then you think to look for the envelope?'

'Yes. Rebecca and I went through the drawer systematically. The envelope was gone.' She pointed. 'Well, I guess it had to be, because here it is back.'

'Yes, it is,' Pavlik said, tucking it away in his inside coat pocket. 'And you found the bracelet in your coat pocket on Friday. But no sock?'

'You're right.' Christy's eyes got wide. 'The bracelet and envelope are back, but my sock is still missing.'

I touched her shoulder. 'Isn't is possible you did take the bracelet out of the drawer on Wednesday and just mislaid the sock? You were under a lot of stress.'

'I suppose,' she said, doubtfully.

'These things happen,' Pavlik said. 'Maggy put the ice cream in the refrigerator just last night.'

'I did?' Ice cream is serious business.

'I saved it in time,' Pavlik assured me. 'My point is that we've all done things without thinking.'

Christy was nodding. 'Once I put my coffee in the micro-wave to reheat and then realized the cup was still on the kitchen counter.'

'Then what had you put in the microwave?' I asked.

'My cell phone.' Christy had picked up my own phone and was admiring the photo of her posing with the diamond.

I fought the impulse to snatch it out of her hand and walked Pavlik to the door. 'Sorry about our handling the evidence.'

'I should probably be glad somebody didn't bleach it.' He sniffed, wrinkling his nose. 'Smells like a laundromat in here.'

'Christy has been cleaning.' Stepping out onto the porch, I wrapped my arms around myself to keep warm. 'What did Helena have to say?'

'You don't believe I went to see Slattery?'

'Jealous lover?' I pressed my lips together to keep from smiling. 'I believe that you may have seen Stephen, but that Helena was your reason for going.'

'Anthony was busy with the excavations, so I went to pick up Barry Margraves' laptop.'

Helena's mom must have overnighted the package after all – good for her. 'Did she also send an ID for Helena so she can get on a plane? Assuming you'll let her leave, that is.'

'She did and Helena already was on the phone booking a flight as I left. We have no reason to keep her here. She didn't steal her own money.'

'Or run over her husband who was cheating on her?'

'Your husband cheated on you and you didn't run him over with a snowplow.'

I sighed. 'It was autumn. And we had a son.'

'Good to know you have principles.' He kissed the top of my head.

'Some.' I was wondering where all this left Christy. Other than holding the bag. 'I don't suppose you've had a chance to look at the computer.'

'Not yet.' Pavlik started down the steps. 'I may be late tonight.'

I leaned down to give him a kiss. 'Do what you have to do.'

And report back to me, I thought, closing the door.

Frank and I were watching a movie in bed when Pavlik got in.

'Shove over, Frank,' the sheriff said. 'You're taking the whole bed.'

Frank jumped down with a harrumph as Pavlik sat on the edge of the bed to take off his shoes. The sheepdog went to join Mocha on the dog bed. The chihuahua did not give an inch, so Frank ended up partly on and mostly off the bed.

I muted the sound of the movie. 'You've had a long day.'

'Long and non-productive.' He stood up and took off his pants, draping them over a chair.

'The computer?'

'No emails from or to Christy, no communication with Christy of any type. But then he would not leave evidence of an affair on his computer where his wife could find it, would he?'

'Not if he's smart.' Ted had not been smart. I just hadn't looked. 'No dating site portal?'

'Hell, no. That would be really stupid. We're recovering the deleted emails and browsing history, but that's going to take a while.'

'What about financials? Bank sites and investments?'

'Those are there and he accessed them recently. Not exactly a cyber genius. His usernames and passwords—'

'Were all the same, Christy said.' The words were out of my mouth before I realized how damning they would sound.

Pavlik had been unbuttoning his shirt and stopped.

I felt my face get warm. 'Christy said she added security questions and answers for better security.'

'She did, which gave our guys some trouble until I realized the questions and answers were authored by her, not the Margraves.'

'So "mother's middle name".'

'Actually, it wasn't even that tough. City of residence was Brookhills. Instrument was piano. Father's name was Wrigley. And like that.'

Oh, Christy. 'Though if you didn't know they applied to Christy, you'd have a hell of a time answering for the Margraves.'

'As we did,' Pavlik said. 'Helena Margraves couldn't get in either. Or provide us with answers that worked.'

'Think about it, though,' I said, sitting up to adjust my pillow. 'If you did suspect Christy had done the questions, the answers would be a roadmap to her. Search "piano", "Brookhills", "Wrigley" and there she would be: Christy Wrigley, piano teacher, Brookhills, WI. Would she have been that transparent if Barry hadn't given her permission to access the accounts in the first place?'

'Christy microwaved her phone,' Pavlik pointed out. 'She may not always be functioning on all cylinders.'

'A mistake anybody could make,' I told him.

'No, you would refrigerate yours, not microwave it. Which might keep space aliens from hacking it but wouldn't fry it.'

Good to know. 'I actually Googled "phone in microwave". There are a surprising number of people who have done it accidentally. And a few on purpose.'

'To *what* purpose?'

'You know, someone read somewhere that it would shield their private information. Unfortunately, they neglected to continue to the next paragraph that said don't turn the microwave on. Another thought the microwave would charge the phone. Another, dry it out after they dropped it in the toilet.'

'Sanitize it, too, maybe,' Pavlik said.

'Speaking of phones,' I said. 'Did Kelly have any luck finding the burner?'

'No. And she and the public works people are none too happy with you.'

'I got that idea when she stopped in for coffee. I assume you told them it was my idea?'

He pulled his favorite sleeping T-shirt over his head. 'They just seemed to know.'

Funny how that works.

He picked up the remote. 'Do you mind if I turn this off? I have to be up early tomorrow to drive to Chicago.'

I was surprised. 'But tomorrow is Sunday.'

'And my father's birthday, remember?'

Pavlik's mom had died less than a year ago and we tried to stay in touch with his dad as much as we could. I grimaced now. 'I completely forgot. I'm working.'

'Dad knows,' Pavlik said, rubbing his cold feet on my leg. 'We're going to spend a boys' day.'

'He'll like that,' I said, giving a little shiver and moving my leg out of range. 'You'll be back tomorrow night or are you staying over?'

'Back.'

I could tell he was already drifting.

'What about the transfers from the Margraves' accounts?' I asked before I lost him to sleep completely. 'Have you found where the money was sent?'

He roused. 'Financial crimes is looking into the wire transfers, but it was Margraves' credit card that was used to buy the diamond you so kindly handed over today along with the tennis bracelet and plane ticket.'

'The one for him and Helena to fly to London,' I remembered.

'Uh-huh.'

'When was that supposed to be?'

No reply.

'Pavlik.'

A low snore resonated from his open mouth. The sheriff was asleep.

I, on the other hand, was not the least bit sleepy. Leaning off the bed, I snagged my phone and ear buds from the nightstand and, shielding the screen with my pillow so the light wouldn't bother Pavlik, punched up *The Age of Adaline*, the movie Frank and I had been watching.

Tuning down the volume so it was merely background in my ear, I tried to think.

The plane ticket was curious. Christy certainly wouldn't have purchased a ticket for Helena and Barry to fly off to

London. And I was pretty sure that Kelly Anthony had told us the ticket was in their names. That meant Barry purchased it, right?

I sat up.

Barry insisted on printing out things. 'Boarding passes, hotel and flight reservations, directions, receipts,' Helena had said.

And I just happened to have those very things he had printed out in my purse.

Slipping out of bed quietly, I padded into the living room where I had left my bag. Not even the dogs stirred.

Pulling out the folded papers, I flattened them on the coffee table. Boarding pass for Barry Margraves from Denver to Milwaukee, three fifteen Monday afternoon. That checked out.

Reservation for Slattery Arms in his name, one room for two, for two nights. That made me pause. Was the 'two' in the 'guest(s) per room' field just the default in the reservation site or a specific request Barry had made? But why specify a double room, which would raise red flags should Helena see it? Christy lived here and if all had gone as well as it seemed Barry had hoped, they could have stayed at her house.

I moved on to the last sheet of paper. It was a print-out of recent credit card transactions, with items highlighted in fluorescent yellow. Tiffany's would have been the diamond bracelet. Tracing down the transaction dates with my finger, I found the purchase of a single plane ticket DEN to MKE to SAN, Denver to Milwaukee to San Diego. Then another purchase posted two days earlier, a booking for MARGRAVES/BAR/ HEL to LHR, London Heathrow.

Not much more detail. Airline abbreviation, date of departure, MKE-ORD-LHR. I frowned. MKE, not DEN. And the date was tomorrow, Sunday.

I sat back on the couch, tucking my cold feet under me as I considered. Maybe Barry had planned to stay in Brookhills until then. But the hotel reservation had only been through Tuesday night, not through Saturday night for a Sunday departure.

So maybe the hotel room *was* just for him and he figured he would stay with Christy the rest of the time? But then he had met her and . . . what?

And why would he be flying with *Helena* from Milwaukee to London, assuming she was the 'HEL'?

Folding the papers again, I creased the fold with my fingernail, trying to remember what Barry had said before he was killed on Tuesday. Something about that he hadn't expected 'this, whatever this is.' And when I said I was going to call the police, he threatened to do the same, saying he'd do the honors as he stepped backwards off the curb and into the street with the phone in his hand.

I squeezed my eyes tightly closed, trying to see that phone in my mind's eye. Was it an iPhone or something else? An iPhone, I thought, not so different than mine or Sarah's, maybe a little older.

Opening my eyes, I focused on the scribbled address on the back of the folded papers. Christy Wrigley, 12 Junction Road, Brookhills, WI . . .

I frowned, trying to remember where I had seen the address in that particular form before.

'Of course,' I said. 'The envelope.'

Which was now in police custody. But I had a photo.

Stealthily, I tiptoed back to my nightstand and picked up my cell, returning to the couch. Frank roused and followed me back, collapsing with his giant head on my feet for a pillow.

Scrolling through the photos, I slowed at Christy's headshot with the diamond and continued on to the torn envelope. One half had the return address, the other Christy's street address, which was identical to the one on the back of the bill, with one exception.

'Different handwriting.'

SEVENTEEN

Pavlik was already gone when I awoke the next morning. I had not awakened him with my discovery, thinking I'd tell him in the morn . . .

OK, that's not true. I was banking on Pavlik being gone. That way I had an excuse to keep my theory to myself and maybe confirm and even build on it before turning over what I knew to the police.

And what was that theory? It wasn't fully formed, but if Barry had written Christy's address on the back of the bill Helena had discovered, then he had not addressed the envelope with the diamond.

Were there explanations? Of course. Somebody – the diamond merchant? – could have sent the envelope for Barry, putting the Margraves' return address on it for convenience sake. But that's the very reason I wanted to think through it all again in the light of day.

I wasn't due in to work until eleven, so I made myself a cup of coffee and sat down at the kitchen table with the papers from Barry's suitcase. The credit card charges, in particular.

I scanned the three highlighted items:

The charge at Tiffany's for just over $12,000 for the bracelet.

Another with the merchant notation 'Gemology' for nearly three times that amount.

Both Christy-related and both highlighted.

Two plane tickets MKE-ORD-LHR.

'Highlighted, too, but maybe not Christy-related,' I said to Mocha, who had just hopped up on the chair across from me. We knew that Helena found this print-out and Christy's address written on the back of it. Did she highlight the unusual charges intending to ask Barry about them?

I checked the time, just past nine. Maybe I could catch Helena at the hotel before she left and ask her.

I picked up my phone.

'Thank you for waiting,' I told the accommodating widow when she opened the door of her room on the sixth floor of the Slattery.

'Your call made me curious,' she said, stepping aside to let me in. 'My flight is at one p.m., so I need to be downstairs getting a ride-share by eleven.'

The time was now ten thirty. 'Give me twenty minutes now and I'll take you to the airport myself.'

'Deal.' She swept her hand toward a couch. 'Have a seat.'

'Nice room,' I said, looking around at the well-appointed suite, with its vaulted ceiling.

'And nice bill,' she said, picking up a sheet of paper from the coffee table. 'Your friend didn't give me a discount, from what I can see.'

'He said he'd give you family and friends pricing,' I said. 'But knowing his mother, that wouldn't be much of a discount. And Stephen must answer to his mother, believe me.'

'Wise of you to choose the sheriff,' she said with a sly smile. 'Mother-in-laws are forever.'

'As my ex has found out,' I said.

'That's right,' Helena said. 'Your ex married Stephen's sister.'

'Rachel,' I said. 'Karma is a bitch and so is Mother Slattery. Sometimes I feel sorry for Ted.'

'I bet you do.' She set down the hotel bill. 'But you said you had something to show me?'

I pulled the papers from Barry's suitcase out of my purse. 'You said that you had seen Christy's address on the back of this paper.'

'Yes. That's how I knew who she was and where to find her.'

I flattened the papers. 'And Christy's name and address here is in Barry's handwriting?'

'I told you that.' She checked her watch.

'Did you also see what was on the reverse side?' I turned over the paper.

'The charge card transactions?' She sat down next to me

and pulled the bill closer. 'Barry must have printed this from the website. I almost had a heart attack when I saw it.'

'Then it was you who highlighted these entries?' I pointed at the three.

'Highlight them? No. I wanted to burn the thing when I saw it. Or better yet, stuff it down Barry's throat.'

'This one.' I pointed at the Heathrow ticket. 'Did you plan to fly to Heathrow from Milwaukee with him for some reason?'

'Have you lost your mind?' she said, not unreasonably. 'I didn't even know Barry was in Milwaukee in the first place. And with his mistress, no less. I certainly didn't fly here to go on holiday with him. *Or* kill him, I might add.'

Always good to know. 'Then if you didn't highlight these transactions, your husband must have.'

She was staring at me, uncomprehendingly. 'I assume so. Why?'

I pulled my phone from my purse and punched up the picture of the envelope to show her. 'This envelope arrived at Christy's address with a diamond in it. I assume it's what the thirty-four thousand, seven hundred and eighty-nine dollars to Gemology was for.'

At my words, Helena closed her eyes and seemed to count to the full ten before opening them. 'I will stipulate that my beloved husband was a cheating son of a bitch. I don't need to have you put more proof in front of me.'

'I have proof of something,' I said. 'But it's not what you think.'

I enlarged the photo. 'Look at the envelope, Helena. It's addressed to Christy at the same address you saw on the back of the credit card transactions. But I don't think it's the same handwriting.'

She cocked her head before reaching out for my phone to study the photo again. 'That's not Barry's handwriting.'

'But it is your return address?'

'It is.' She handed the phone back to me. 'What does it mean? He had somebody else send it to her?'

'Maybe,' I said, setting the phone down. 'But combine that with the highlighted bill, I can't help but wonder—'

Helena was losing patience. 'I really need to finish packing,' she said, getting to her feet. 'If you're just cogitating on something, you can do that without me.'

'Wait.' I held up my hand and – unlike my dogs and her husband – Helena obeyed. And then even sat for good measure. Her husband would be alive today if he had taken orders that well.

But there had been something else going on with Barry. I was almost certain of it.

I continued. 'Forget that Barry was your husband and that you believe he was cheating. If you just saw this paper, what would you think?'

She took it again. 'That somebody had marked the questionable purchases, I guess. Things that he wanted to check on or keep track of. But—'

'But,' I said significantly, 'maybe that's exactly what Barry did. He saw the charges and realized there were purchases he hadn't made.'

'If he didn't make them, then why not just ask me about them?' Helena demanded.

It was a good question, but not hard to answer. 'Two obvious jewelry purchases? Maybe he was afraid you'd jump to conclusions and hoped he could clear things up before you ever saw them.'

'But I wouldn't have jumped . . .' She stopped herself and then took a long breath before starting again. 'About two years after we got married, Barry had what he called a "slip".' She waved her hands. 'Detail aren't important, but I told him if it ever happened again, I'd leave him.'

'Then he had a lot at stake,' I said quietly.

'Yes. Yes, he did.'

We sat in silence for a second. Helena roused herself. 'Are you suggesting that Barry came here for the same reason I did – to find out who this Christy is?'

'I guess I am. Or at least I'm suggesting it's a possibility.'

'But think about what you're saying. It would mean that your friend Christy isn't a slut sleeping with a married man, but that she is an outright thief.'

Fraud, Pavlik had said when they brought Christy in for questioning.

Helena had tilted her head to look me in the eye. 'Are you prepared for that?'

'Honestly, no,' I said. 'I can see how Christy could be duped, but to just steal outright?' I shook my head. 'I don't think it's in her DNA.'

Helena was frowning. 'I found Christy because Barry had written down her address. If what you're saying is true, how did he get it in the first place?'

'Probably called Tiffany's or the gemology place and they gave it to him.' Another thought came to me. 'The security questions she set up would have pointed to her, too, but I don't think financial institutions will give them to you if you say you've lost them. They just make you do new ones.'

'The what?' Helena seemed genuinely confused.

'Christy added security questions to Barry's accounts.'

'For security from whom? She's the thief.'

'That's one of the reasons this whole thing doesn't make sense to me. Christy told me she beefed up security because the passwords were the same on everything.'

Helena cast her eyes skyward – or vaulted ceiling-ward, in this case. 'Our first dog's name and birthday. He died ten years ago and so Barry figured nobody could guess it. Nothing I said could move him to change them up. I can't imagine how *she* managed it.' Helena sounded more hurt than resentful.

'Christy? She didn't change usernames or passwords, but she did make up her own security questions when the website cued her to do it for authentication purposes. And she answered them with her own information.'

'Like her mother's maiden name, rather than Barry's?' Helena asked, shifting uncomfortably on the couch.

'She didn't know his, I guess, so she answered with what she did know.'

'How very convenient for her.' Helena pulled the brocade pillow out from behind her and punched it twice before throwing it across the room.

I was happy it wasn't me, since I was within arms' reach as well. 'To be fair, she said she couldn't access the accounts without adding them.'

'Well, boo-hoo. Then how about staying the hell out of the accounts?' Helena said. 'And my life while she was at it.'

I sighed, shaking my head. 'I know. But Christy swore that Barry gave her permission to go into the accounts. I assume she intended to give him the answers.'

'Good of her.' Sarcastic now, and she had every right. 'What does the sheriff think about all this? Have they arrested her?'

'Pavlik doesn't know about the handwriting not matching yet.' I admitted, feeling my face redden. 'Or my suspicion that Barry might have been as in the dark about what was going on as you were.'

'I thought you slept with the sheriff,' she said. 'One eye open, remember?'

'I do remember,' I said. 'He left to visit his dad in Chicago early today before I had a chance to tell him.'

'Really.'

'Besides, I wasn't certain,' I admitted. 'I needed to make sure that you hadn't made the notations on the bill and confirm that it wasn't Barry's handwriting on the envelope.'

'Where is the envelope now?' she asked. 'And the diamond?'

'The sheriff's department has it,' I told her.

'And the bracelet?'

'Last I knew, Christy still has it.' I was trying to read Helena's expression. 'Why do you ask?'

'Well, it's evidence, too, right? First she said it was stolen and then she miraculously finds it in her pocket.'

I had suspected the bracelet had been placed there by Helena. But now everything had turned on its ear. 'You don't know anything about that, right?'

'Why would I? I just hope that Tiffany's takes returns.'

I didn't want to be there if the two women squared off again over the jewelry. Although the way it was shaping up for Christy, she might not have need of it for a few years. 'We'd better go if you're going to catch your plane.'

Helena stood. 'My flight's not until four. I lied to get rid of you.'

'Nice.'

'I am nice,' she said. 'Which is why I didn't hang up when you called or slam the door in your face when you got here.'

I would call that more passive aggressive than nice, but OK.

'Let's go,' Helena said, beckoning me to get up.

'Go where?' I asked, acquiescing. 'You just told me your flight wasn't until four. Do you want to sit in the airport for four hours?'

'No. Which is why I'm going wherever you're going next.' Helena extended the handle of her roller bag. 'This is my life you're playing detective with. My husband, who is dead for no apparent reason. I want in.'

Then 'in', I thought, she shall get.

'You're late,' Sarah called from the back as I opened the door of Uncommon Grounds.

'My fault,' Helena said, following me in from the porch.

'You don't have to say that,' I told her. 'That's Sarah's greeting whenever I come in, no matter how early or late I am.'

'Maybe.' Sarah appeared. 'What are you doing here?'

'Me? I'd like a latte,' Helena said, pulling off her coat. 'Is our little thief here?'

'Christy?' Sarah asked, seeming bemused and more than a little entertained. 'She's not working today.'

'Good,' I said. 'We can talk freely.'

'Works for me.' Sarah lifted a latte mug for Helena to see. 'For here, I assume?'

'The drink can wait,' Helena said, waving for us to join her at a table by the window. 'Come sit.'

Sarah did as she was told, another monumental achievement, and we filled her in.

Sarah was sitting back in her chair shaking her head as we finished. 'Are you telling me that Barry Margraves came here not to meet the new love of his life, but to find the woman who was stealing from him?'

'That's pretty much it,' I told her. 'Or at least what we suspect.'

'What about the account information?' Sarah asked. 'Numbers, passwords? If Barry didn't give them to Christy, where did they come from?'

That stopped me. I glanced at Helena. 'I don't know the answer to that. Have you had any indication you've been hacked or had your identities stolen?'

'You mean other than having every last cent sucked out of our accounts?' Helena asked. 'And every credit card charged to the max with the exception of the one I keep for business?'

It was the very definition of being hacked, of course.

'And thank God I had that,' Helena was saying, 'given the "special" rate your friend charged me at the Slattery.'

Yeah, yeah, yeah – try to do somebody a favor. While simultaneously sniffing out information, of course. But back to the hack: 'How in the world would Christy pull off something like this by herself?'

'Who says she's in it by herself?' Sarah said. 'Don't you think her dumping Ronny came out of nowhere?'

'Ronny? How could he . . . oh, God.' The last thing I wanted was that psycho back in our lives since I still had one. No thanks to him.

'It makes sense,' Sarah said, leaning forward. 'Ronny is a master manipulator and as gullible as Christy is—'

'Who's Ronny?' Helena asked.

'Christy's not that gullible. At least I don't think so.' I shook my head. 'When I heard her talking about wire transfers, I was afraid Barry might be stealing from *her*. Certainly not the other way around.'

'Who's Ronny?' Helena repeated.

'Christy's boyfriend before she met Barry.' Or didn't meet Barry. 'And Sarah's cousin.'

'Step-cousin, thank you very much,' Sarah said, getting up. 'Anybody else want a coffee?'

'Sure,' Helena said. 'Assuming then you will get back here and explain to me how your cousin is involved.'

'Step-cousin,' Sarah said again, disappearing into the service area.

'I'm not even sure step-cousin is correct,' I told Helena. 'Ronny's father Kornell married Sarah's Auntie Vi late in life.'

'Meaning there's no nature or nurture about this,' Sarah said from the window as she pulled espresso shots. 'Ronny is plain up batshit crazy and that comes from Kornell and his family. Nothing to do with us Kingstons.'

Helena glanced at me.

I shrugged. 'It's true. Kornell was pretty out there, too.'

'And that was before the train hit him,' Sarah contributed.

'You don't mean *this* train,' Helena said, pointing to the 'Way to Trains' sign above the corridor to the platform.

'Unfortunately, yes,' I said. 'He was hard of hearing and—'

'Nearly blind,' Sarah said. 'He should never have been driving, but you couldn't tell the crazy old coot anything.'

Helena had her legs crossed and now her foot convulsively kicked me. 'Sorry.'

I moved my chair a bit away.

'You do seem to have a problem here, though,' Helena said, foot still bouncing up and down. 'People being hit by unlikely . . . things.'

Trains, snowplows – not so unusual at a train station in the winter in Wisconsin, but I could see how it might appear.

'Flat whites?' Sarah asked, appearing at the table with two drinks.

'Umm, yes,' Helena said, wrapping her hands around the cup Sarah slid to her.

I took the other and Sarah retrieved hers and sat down with it. 'If you put it in perspective, there's only been those two accidents in the year since we've been open here. The odds of another happening anytime soon have to be astronomical.'

That was true, though it didn't change the fact that Helena's husband had already been victim of one of them.

'But back to Christy,' Sarah continued. 'I agree that Christy isn't a criminal mastermind, but what if Ronny hatched the plot.'

'And that plot was what?' I asked.

'Identity theft,' Sarah said, coming up from her sip of flat white with a milk foam mustache. 'Christy pretends to dump him and – poor lonely thing – goes fishing for men.'

'Fishing.' I rubbed at my own upper lip.

She took the hint and licked hers off. 'Yes, fishing with an "F" or a "P H", however you want to spell it.'

Cute.

'Then bingo,' Sarah continued, 'she lands a rich one.'

'We're not rich,' objected Helena, who had lifted her drink and now set it down again.

'No?' Sarah said. 'Sure couldn't tell that from the Google Earth of your house. Looked plenty big to me.'

'You do have an inground pool,' I reminded her. 'And a Mercedes parked in the drive—'

'You Google Earthed my house?' Helena interrupted as if the cyber-intrusion might be the last straw.

'Christy Google Earthed your house,' I said, cringing a bit. 'She showed it to us. Sorry.'

'That's OK,' Helena said, uncrossing her leg and putting both feet flat on the ground, like she wanted to flee. 'I guess.'

But Sarah was on a roll, Helena's feelings be damned. 'Now once Christy's found her target, she sets about stealing his personal information.'

'How?' I asked. 'Christy's not a cyber-criminal. She's a piano teacher.'

'I told you,' Sarah insisted. 'She's a piano teacher with a boyfriend surrounded by criminals twenty-four/seven. I'm sure Ronny could get a few tips from his cellmates to pass on to his accomplice outside.'

His accomplice being Christy. 'Pavlik has Christy's mobile. He could see if there's been any recent contact between Christy and Ronny.'

'She might have another phone,' Helena said, getting in the spirit.

'The prison records would show who Ronny talked with, too,' I said. 'And speaking of burner phones, there is no trace of the burner phone we assumed Barry had. Maybe because—'

'Because he never had one,' Helena said, her eyes getting moist. 'Barry was a victim, not a cheat.'

'We're saying Christy's whole dating thing, the new love of her life, was a ruse?' I asked. 'Why bother? Why not just steal the money?'

'To explain the gifts and trips maybe,' Sarah suggested. 'I have to hand it to Christy. That was one hell of an act.'

I wasn't quite buying it. At least not all of it. 'But I talked to the man on the phone.'

'You talked to Barry?' Helena asked.

'Or somebody who said it was him,' I said, turning to her. 'Do you have a recording of Barry's voice?'

'Probably somewhere on my phone,' Helena said. 'I'll—'

'You know what this means?' Sarah interrupted. 'Our gal Christy had a motive for killing Margraves.'

'Wait. Identity theft and stealing is bad enough,' I protested. 'But murder? Besides, Christy was with me when Barry was hit by the plow.'

'You saw it?' Helena's voice was quiet as she traced a zig-zag pattern on the table with her index finger. The leg had crossed again.

I put my hand over hers to still it. 'Yes. I am so sorry.'

'Was it . . .' She cleared her throat. 'Did he suffer?'

Assuming Barry Margraves had died at first impact, as I'd told Sarah, I was certain he literally didn't know what hit him, but that would sound too pat. 'No, he didn't suffer. It was just all too quick. Over in a second.'

'Good.' She was staring down at the table.

'Let me get you a latte,' Sarah said, taking Helena's undrunk, if not untouched, flat white.

One might think my partner was being sensitive to Helena's feelings, but I knew she was escaping them.

'It was eas—' Helena struggled to get the words out. 'It was easier to be angry with Barry. To think that he'd been cheating on me when he died. Now . . . I feel like I've betrayed him by believing the worst of him.'

'You had every reason to be suspicious,' I said. 'No use beating yourself up for being human.'

'Human is one thing,' Helena said, meeting my eyes. 'But I flew here like a crazy woman instead of sitting down with my husband of more than a decade and asking him to explain. I'm the one who betrayed him by not giving him the benefit of the doubt.'

'So you ask, and he denies. It gets ugly.' Sarah had stuck her head out of the service window. 'As it is, Barry died never knowing what you suspected, right?'

Helena blinked. 'Well, yes. I guess.'

'Then no worries.' Sarah disappeared.

Helena turned to me with a frown. 'Did she say, "no worries"?'

'I think she means it could have been worse.' I said. Explaining Sarah was always a challenge. But this time, I thought she was right. 'As it is, Barry didn't believe you betrayed him, and he apparently didn't betray you.'

'Apparently,' she repeated. 'But he's still dead, and I don't know why.'

'We *will* find out,' I told her.

'Yes, *we* will.' She seemed to rally. 'I'm going to cancel my flight.'

Sarah came around the corner with the latte. 'Now where did we leave off?'

'Trying to figure out how Christy could have killed Barry,' Helena said. 'While standing with Maggy.'

'Cahoots,' I said, glancing across the street.

'Cahoots?' Helena's forehead wrinkled.

'It's apparently the word of the week,' Sarah explained.

'I'm just saying that Christy, if she did this, would have needed a partner,' I said.

'She did have a partner: Ronny,' Sarah said. 'I told you.'

'I mean a physical partner who isn't behind bars. One who could drive a snowplow,' I said.

'What about that driver? Harold?' Helena asked. 'Are we absolutely certain that he wasn't driving the truck?'

'"We" are,' I said, suppressing a smile. Now I knew how Pavlik felt when I invited myself into his investigations. 'Harold Byerly was in our bathroom from twenty minutes prior to Barry being killed until maybe thirty minutes after.'

'The room smelled like dead skunk a full three hours later,' Sarah assured her. 'This was no quick drop-one-and-out, believe me.'

'I . . . I do, I guess,' Helena said, wrinkling her nose.

Movement on Christy's porch across the way caught my eye. The door had opened and now she stepped out. As she lifted the lid of the mailbox, she seemed to sense me watching and turned to look, shielding her eyes against the glare of the sun off the snow.

I raised my hand to wave, but she apparently didn't see me, just retrieved her mail and went back inside.

It triggered a memory. 'We should talk to Christy. I'd like a look at her notebook.'

'What notebook?' Helena had gotten to her feet and now paused. 'Sorry, I keep asking the questions, but I have absolutely no answers.'

'That's OK,' I said, standing myself. 'I think we're going to get those answers very soon.'

EIGHTEEN

I had to ring the bell twice before Christy came to the door, her phone in hand.

'. . . how long?' she was saying into it. 'Of course. You should.'

'Sorry,' she said, after another three minutes of one-sided banalities before she finally hung up. 'Rebecca was on the phone, and I didn't want to be rude.'

'To her or us?' Sarah asked sourly. 'We're still standing on the porch. You could at least have let us in while—'

'That's fine,' I said to Christy with a smile. 'Could we come in now?'

'Of course.' She stepped aside to let us pass by. 'I'm afraid the house is a mess.'

'This is a mess?' Helena whispered to me as we passed through the living room.

'By Christy's standards.' The only furniture in the room was Christy's grand piano and its bench. If I squinted, I might be able to see a speck of dust on the piano's lacquered finish. But I doubted it.

'Are you moving?' Sarah asked.

'No, why do you ask?' Christy led us into her kitchen and waved for us to sit. Since there were only two chairs at the table, we all stayed standing.

'Because there's nothing here,' Sarah said, scowling. 'Did you list the place again?'

Sarah deemed any listing she didn't have as traitorous. Even though she was no longer practicing real estate.

'No,' Christy said, shaking her head. 'But I put a lot in storage when it was on the market. I think it makes the house seem ever so much larger.'

'You didn't get it out of storage when you decided to stay?' I asked. 'That was a year ago.'

'I know,' Christy said, her eyes wide. 'Can you believe

I never really needed all those things? I feel so much freer now.'

I was saved from answering when she turned to Helena. 'Has Barry's body been released? I'd love to attend the funeral if you don't mind.'

'I mind,' Helena said.

'Oh, OK.' Christy pointed again to the table. 'Please, Maggy and Helena, sit.'

'And me?' Sarah asked sourly.

'Help me get two more chairs?' Christy asked, opening the still-splintered back door and leading the way out.

Helena and I looked at each other, before taking our seats as ordered. At Helena's place was a single placemat with a setting of plate, knife, spoon and fork. A cloth napkin that had been tortured into the shape of a rose adorned the plate.

'This is so, so sad,' Helena said, shaking her head.

'I used to think so,' I said. 'But Christy is Christy. And that means if she's eating by herself, she's not going to do it sitting on the living room couch watching television for company like the rest of us do.'

'She doesn't have a couch. Or a television,' Helena pointed out.

'True. I'm just saying that I kind of respect that even eating alone, she sits down at the table and does it up properly.'

'Does what up properly?' Christy asked, coming in with a folding lawn chair. Sarah was behind her with an oversized bucket with the hardware store name on it.

'The rose napkin is beautiful,' I said with a genuine smile. 'I hope we didn't interrupt your lunch.'

'Not at all,' she said, unfolding the green and white checked lawn chair. 'Please, Sarah sit.'

Sarah set down the bucket. 'No, I'm fine—'

'Please.' When Christy used that tone, you didn't mess with her.

Sarah sat on the lawn chair, her butt hitting the floor as the woven plastic webbing stretched. 'Thanks.'

Christy flipped over the bucket and sat on it. Then she stood up. 'Oh! Would anybody like something to drink? I can wash the glass.' She pointed at a tumbler draining in the rack by the sink.

'No, thanks,' I said, as Sarah opened her mouth to say worse. 'We were just concerned about you. With the police and all.'

'It is worrisome,' Christy confirmed, re-centering herself on the bucket. 'The police think I stole Barry's account information. But he gave it to me. Honestly.'

This last was directed to Helena.

'How did he give it to you?' she asked. 'On the phone? Email? Text?'

I was impressed that Helena was asking pertinent questions instead of knocking Christy right off her bucket. The two women were about the same height, but I thought the brunette could take the redhead easily if she wanted to.

'Over the phone,' Christy said. 'But what's odd is that the sheriff's department can't find any record of the calls from Barry's side.'

'What number did you have for him?' I asked.

Christy recited it, and I glanced at Helena.

She shook her head. 'That's not Barry's number. At least not the iPhone.'

'And the sheriff's department hasn't found another,' I said.

'No, they haven't, that's just the problem,' Christy said. 'They think I'm making it up.'

'And you're not?' Sarah asked.

'Of course not,' she said indignantly.

Sarah raised her hands. 'Just making sure. What about Ronny?'

'I told you,' Christy said. 'I don't love him anymore. I know he's your cousin, Sarah, but that's just the way it is.'

'I *meant* is Ronny involved?' Sarah asked. 'Did he maybe feed you the account numbers and tell you how to use them?'

Christy's head snapped up. 'Whatever are you talking about? This had nothing to do with Ronny. I haven't talked to him for months.'

'We can check, you know,' Sarah said. 'The prison keeps records.'

'Of course, I know,' Christy said, angrily leaning forward on her bucket. 'I'm the one who went to see Ronny every visiting day. I didn't see any of the family doing that.'

'He's . . . not . . . my . . . family,' Sarah said, bitingly.

'That may be,' Christy said, folding her hands on her lap, 'but you're all the family he has. Has ever had.'

Sarah opened her mouth and then closed it again.

'Yeah, Sarah,' I said, and got a dirty look. It was reward enough.

My partner finally cleared her throat. 'Fine. I'll visit him. Once. If you tell us the truth.'

'Thank you,' Christy said. 'And I am telling you the truth. Barry gave me the account numbers and access information. I sold what he told me to and transferred the money. Two transactions, that was it.'

'Two transactions?' Helena's forehead wrinkled as she leaned forward. 'I thought you were going to tell us the truth.'

'I am,' Christy said, turning to her.

'You emptied all our accounts.' Helena was unfolding the rose.

'I did not,' Christy said, scowling.

'Did so.' The rose was no more.

'Did not,' Christy said snatching the napkin from her. 'Barry gave me the account numbers and I wrote them down in a notebook. Then I did the two transactions. That was it.'

'Can we see the notebook?' I asked.

Christy frowned. 'The deputy took it. My phone, too, but that they just gave back.'

Well, that was good news at least. 'You said you put some security questions in place?'

'Oh, yes.' Christy, suddenly apologetic, turned to Helena. 'I couldn't get into the accounts without doing that. I'll give you the questions and answers and you can change them. No reason my information should be on Barry's accounts now.' She sniffled.

'That's kind of you,' Helena said slowly, seeming to take a new tack. 'Now tell me. How did you and Barry meet? On a dating site, I understand?'

'Well, yes.' Christy seemed startled, but also a little relieved. 'Things hadn't been going well with Ronny. Jail and all, you know.' She rolled her eyes. 'I was telling Rebecca and she said I deserved better. And asked if I had thought about online dating. I set up a profile and, presto, Barry answered.'

'Rebecca?' Helena glanced at me.

'Yes, Rebecca Penn, down the street,' Christy continued. 'You've probably seen her. She's about your height and with dark hair, too. In fact, when I saw you cross the street just now, I thought it was her. But then I realized, "Wait – I'm on the phone with Rebecca. Duh."'

Duh, indeed. 'Speaking of your phone,' I said. 'Do you have a voicemail from Barry saved?'

'Well, yes,' Christy said, glancing at Helena uncomfortably. 'I kept one particularly because it was just so very Barry.' She sighed.

'Could I hear it, do you think?' Helena instinctively seemed to know where I was heading with this.

Christy tilted her head. 'Poor dear, you want to hear his voice again, too. It's just that . . . well, it may hurt your feelings. Being that he left it for me and all.'

'Is it dirty?' Sarah could always be counted on to ask the uncomfortable question. And be absolutely comfortable doing it. 'Phone sex is inevitable, I suppose, your being so far apart.'

'I told you we weren't.' Christy frowned. 'Having phone sex, I mean. I'm just trying to be sensitive to Helena's feelings.'

'You were phone-banging her husband,' Sarah said. 'A little late to be thinking about her feelings.'

'I was not phone banging him, which is a filthy way of putting it anyway.' Christy was folding the napkin on her lap. A swan maybe, this time. 'And I told you I didn't know he was married.'

'Of course you didn't,' Helena said soothingly. 'And don't worry about the content of the message. I just want to hear Barry's voice one last time.'

'I so understand,' Christy said, setting aside the napkin bird to get up.

As she disappeared down the hallway toward her bedroom, I turned to Sarah. 'Are you really going to visit Ronny?'

'Of course not,' she said, pushing herself up and out of the lawn chair.

'You broke the chair,' Helena said, pointing at the hole in the weave where Sarah's butt had been.

'I think it's more that it broke me,' she said, rubbing where she'd landed. She craned her neck to see around the corner. 'Think she has a bed in her—'

'Here it is,' Christy's voice said, from down the hall. Sarah backed off and went to lean against the kitchen counter.

'Don't you want to sit?' our hostess asked her. 'You can have my bucket if that chair . . . oh, dear. Did it break?' She looked like she was going to cry. 'It was my parents'.'

'I'm sure it was,' Sarah said. 'But sadly aluminum tubing and plastic webbing doesn't last forever.'

'No.' Christy was trying to reweave the disintegrating webbing.

'You can get new webbing,' I told her. 'It'll be practically brand new.'

'I suppose,' she said, running her hand along the frame. 'But it won't be the same.'

OK, time to get off the lawn chair. 'Did you find the phone with Barry's call?'

'Oh, yes.' She tore herself away from the damaged heirloom and pulled the phone from her pocket to punch up voicemail. When she found the one she wanted, she hit the 'play' arrow.

'Hello, my dear,' the voice said, and I recognized it as the man I'd spoken to when Christy thrust the phone at me on Tuesday morning. 'Sorry that I missed you, but my project here just ended. I'll phone you from Heathrow before I fly out.'

I looked at Helena, but Sarah jumped in. '*That's* the message you kept? My insurance agent could have left that. Or my plumber.'

'Your plumber calls you "dear"?' I asked.

'No, but my insurance agent does. He's very British.'

'And that's why I love this message,' Christy said with a pout. 'Barry says "prō-ject" and he'll "phone" me. And he talks about Heathrow. He was so . . . so continental, don't you think, Helena?' She asked it like the two were Sister Wives.

'Absolutely not,' Helena said, and then turned to me. 'That's not Barry's voice. Not even close.'

She was right. I should have realized when I spoke to the
real Barry on the street. Between the storm and the drama of
the moment, it just hadn't sunk in.

Apparently for Christy, either. She seemed astonished.
'But—'

'But nothing,' Helena continued. 'Barry doesn't say "my
dear", for one thing. He says "sweetie", if anything.' Her voice
broke. 'He's not . . . well, he's not one to be mushy, he'd call
it. And he certainly doesn't pronounce "project" like that. Or
fly in or out of Heathrow, for that matter.'

She turned to me. 'You saw. You paged through his passport.'

I did, but I didn't realize she'd seen me. 'There weren't
many stamps, and none for Heathrow, that I saw.'

So no London trips, until the one scheduled for . . . was it
today?

'. . . Except for our honeymoon in the Bahamas,' Helena
was saying. She cocked her head. 'Maggy?'

I had snagged my purse from the floor and was digging
through it, praying.

Yup, the sheath of papers was still there. I pulled out the
credit card transactions and traced down the list to the third
highlighted entry. Flight booked for today, as I thought. 'Barry
and Helena Margraves. Milwaukee to Chicago O'Hare and
then on to London.' I looked up. 'The fake Barry booked this,
that's why the real Barry highlighted it. He hadn't made the
purchase.'

'The fake Barry?' Christy repeated.

'I'm afraid so,' I said to her. 'And he knew they'd be leaving
from Milwaukee, not Denver.'

Helena was watching me. 'But who is "they"? Not me,
certainly.'

'Yet, your passport was stolen,' I said.

'Are you suggesting somebody else planned to use it?'
Helena asked. 'But why steal my passport and not Barry's? It
was still with his things at the Slattery.'

'Maybe that's why . . . they couldn't get hold of it,' I said.

'It's easy to make up a false passport,' Christy said.

Our heads all swiveled her way.

'Or so Ronny told me,' she said, turning red. 'Once.'

'The jailbait's former girlfriend is right,' Sarah said. 'If somebody could plan all of this, they sure could come up with a false passport if they needed to. But who are they?'

Who indeed?

I was thinking back to the unexplained. The diamond in the plain manila envelope. The robbery of the bracelet and the diamond envelope the night after Barry's death. The disappearance of both and then the reappearance of same – the one in Christy's pocket and the other in the mail.

An envelope reposted. Why? Because somebody was afraid it would be found on them and blow everything.

And the bracelet. 'Did you put the bracelet in Christy's pocket?' I asked suddenly.

'What? Who, me?' Helena stuttered.

'Yes, and this is important. So please don't lie.'

She took a deep breath. 'Yes.'

'You told me you didn't steal it,' Christy said, looking terribly disappointed with the other woman.

'And I told you that it was my money that bought it in the first place,' Helena said. 'But no, I didn't steal it. I . . . this sounds crazy, but I found it in my coat pocket, too.'

'And put it in Christy's.'

'Exactly.'

'When did you find it?' I asked.

'That same day as I was looking through everything for my passport. There it was.'

I cocked my head. 'But you realized the passport was missing at the airport. You must have gone through your pockets there, right?'

'Yes, of course. I reached into my pocket as my ride-share driver was unloading my suitcase. My passport was missing but the bracelet was there.'

'Did you have your coat on?'

'No, it was too heavy, and the car was warm. I . . .' She stopped. 'I gave it to the driver to put with my suitcase.'

'Then maybe it fell out in the trunk of the car,' Christy said. 'The passport, I mean.'

'And the bracelet hopped in?' I asked. 'What did this ride-share driver look like?'

'Very nice looking,' Helena said. 'Blond hair and a' – her eyes flew open wide and met mine – 'Canadian accent.'

'I knew it.'

'Knew what?' Sarah demanded. 'You two are being cryptic, and I hate cryptic.'

Everybody hates cryptic. But it was kind of fun. 'Canadians pronounce certain words differently. Words like—'

'Prō-ject,' Sarah said, comprehending. 'Long "o" vowel sounds where we use short.'

'But what does that mean?' Christy asked. 'Who is Canadian?'

'You know him, Christy,' I said. 'We all do, and you even told me he's driving ride-share these days?'

'Who?' Sarah had had enough.

'Michael Penn.'

'It all makes sense,' I said, as we hurried down the block to what had been Penn and Ink. 'I saw Rebecca hand Michael the two to-go cups so she could pull out an envelope and mail it Wednesday morning. I just didn't put it together.'

'The envelope with the diamond?' Christy asked, trying to keep up in more ways than one. 'But why did she have it?'

'Because she stole it when she stayed with you Tuesday night,' I said. 'That and the bracelet.'

'Are you saying that Rebecca and Michael did this all together?' Sarah asked. 'In—'

'Cahoots, yes.'

'But if that's true,' Helena asked, 'why would she give it back?'

'Because it was the least of what they'd stolen, but the most incriminating. Think of it, things were falling apart, but the money already had been siphoned off and transferred to offshore accounts. All they had to do was get out of here quickly and access the money while everybody was still looking at Christy. Nobody would be the wiser until it was too late.' I led the way up Rebecca's sidewalk and rang the bell.

'You think this Michael planted the bracelet in my coat when he took it out of the trunk and handed it to me?' Helena asked.

'And stole your passport. He'd already re-mailed the envelope to arrive a day or two later. Or depending on the mail carrier, be returned to sender. Either way, it wouldn't lead to them.' No answer forthcoming from within, I lifted the lid of the mailbox and peeked in. Empty. 'I even saw Rebecca on your porch checking for the mail the day it was re-delivered.'

'She was going to re-steal it?' Sarah tried the door. 'Open.'

'You can't go in,' Christy said.

'The hell I can't.'

I followed her in and up the stairs to the living quarters. 'Maybe to re-steal it. Or just see if it had been delivered.'

Sarah had gone down the hall and now stuck her head out of Rebecca's bedroom. 'No sign of anybody, but the drawers are open like the place was searched.'

Or somebody packed in a hurry. I joined her in the bedroom, Christy and Helena on my heels. 'No suitcase in the closet,' I said, opening the door. 'Though she may not—'

Christy gasped. She was pointing at something on the floor of the closet.

I reached in and fished it out. A single blue and black striped sock.

'Oh, Rebecca,' Christy wailed, hand to her mouth.

I turned to Helena. 'Do you have the airline app on your phone? Could you pull up Barry's reservation to Heathrow?'

'No, I don't think—'

'I've got it,' Christy said, having gathered herself. She pulled out her phone. 'Let's see, reservation for MKE-ORD-LHR. Leaves today at five p.m.' She did a double-take.

'What?' I asked.

She held up the screen. 'Two checked in.'

NINETEEN

'Rebecca is pretending to be me,' Helena said. 'You said she and I look similar, Christy.'

'You do,' Christy said, pocketing the phone to lean down to pick up her sock. 'If I could be fooled, I don't see how TSA will tell the difference between the real-life Helena and the photo on your passport.'

'Which she has, of course.' As I said it, I heard a car start up and went to the bedroom window in time to see a black SUV squeal around the corner to head east on Brookhill Road. 'That's them. We still have time to catch them.'

'C'mon,' Sarah yelled. 'The Firebird is out front.'

We ran for Sarah's yellow 1975 Firebird, which she'd left parked on the street. It was closer than my Escape in the lot behind the coffeehouse, but significantly less roomy. And the other disadvantage of the Firebird was it was driven by Sarah.

'Hurry,' Christy urged, as Sarah searched her pocket for the key to unlock the driver's side door.

'Pretty car,' Helena said, 'but no keyless entry.'

'Sure there is,' Sarah said, swinging open the door. 'If I don't lock it, I don't need a key.'

'And she always locks it,' I said, waiting at the passenger door for her to climb in and reach over to pull up the lock. When she did, I swung open the door and stepped back to let Helena climb into the back before I got in.

'My God,' Helena said folding the front seat. 'There isn't a back seat.'

'There is,' Sarah said, getting into the driver seat. 'I just took out the cushions. It'll ride a little rough.'

An understatement. Having experience with the Firebird, I pointed for Christy to take the back with Helena and took the shotgun position next to Sarah myself.

'Michael looks nothing like Barry, though,' Christy said, crawling in next to Helena. 'Seatbelts?'

'They're there,' Sarah said, firing up the Firebird. 'Under the blanket.'

Which she was using to cover the metal springs.

'That means they would have had to fake Barry's passport regardless,' I said, fastening my own seatbelt. 'Though they might have been able to change the picture on the original if they'd gotten hold of it.'

'The ride-share guy was about the same build, but a blond, like I said.' Helena grabbed the back of my seat to steady herself as we peeled away from the curb. 'He could have dyed his hair, I suppose. But assuming it was this Michael, how could he be certain he got my fare?'

'Probably just waited for someone wanting a ride from the Slattery to the airport,' I said. 'And jumped on it.'

'It's not that hard,' Christy said. 'I've never driven ride-share, but I've done grocery delivery.'

Sarah's head twisted around, even as she was making a squealing left turn onto Brookhill Road. 'And the relevance of that would be?'

'It uses an app, too,' Christy said, shifting her bum a bit. 'The order – or fare, in the case of ride-share – pops up and you decide whether to take it based on size of purchase, maybe, or the store to be shopped. For grocery delivery, I like to cherry-pick people I know because they tend to increase the tip when they see it's me.'

'That's kind of awkward, isn't it?' Helena asked. 'Shaming your friends into giving you a bigger tip?'

Christy shrugged. 'No different than if I was serving them in a restaurant. Girl's gotta make a living.'

'But what if the person looking for a ride wasn't Helena?' Sarah asked from the front seat. 'There are probably lots of requests for rides to the airport from a hotel.'

'He might get the first name before he agrees to give the ride,' Christy said, her brow wrinkled. 'But if not, once Michael did accept the fare, he'd get the name. If it wasn't Helena, he could just cancel. Or say he couldn't find them.'

'Wouldn't he get in trouble for that?' Helena asked. 'I mean with the ride-share company.'

'You *are* nice,' Christy said, pivoting to look her straight in the face. 'I'm sorry about the whole husband-stealing thing.'

'Thanks for that,' Helena said. 'But—'

'Ooh! Ooh!' Christy was raising her hand, like she was in class.

'Yes, Christy?' I said.

'Was it Michael's car that dropped off Barry that day, too?' She turned away from Helena and whispered, 'Before he was . . . you know.'

'She knows he was killed,' Sarah said, gunning the car from the right lane of Brookhill Road onto the entrance ramp of the freeway. 'You don't have to whisper.'

'I'm just trying to be as nice as she is,' Christy said, pouting a little.

'I'm not that nice,' Helena said. 'Maggy, did you see the car Barry got out of?'

'Not really,' I told her. 'Christy?'

'A black SUV, but I was more focused on the man who got out of it.' Her face reddened. 'And the snow was really coming down hard.'

'It could have been Michael driving the car,' I said. 'He'd have to monitor the ride requests from the Slattery like we think he did the Morrison.'

'It's a much bigger hotel,' Sarah said, flooring the Firebird to get around a pickup. 'And how would he and Rebecca know Barry was there? Or even in Brookhills?'

'She' – Helena nodded to Christy – 'gave them access to our accounts and charge card bills. First thing a hotel does when you make a guaranteed reservation is put a pending charge to your account.'

Christy opened her mouth to protest and then closed it. And opened it again. 'I may also have written down the user-name and password you and Barry use for pretty much everything.'

'In your notebook,' I said. 'Rebecca saw it?'

'I might have shown it to her.' Christy seemed about to cry. 'But I don't understand. Rebecca was lying to me this whole time?'

'Like a rug,' Sarah said.

'What?'

'Yes, Rebecca was lying,' I told Christy, not bothering to explain. 'She used you to steal Barry and Helena's money.'

'But Barry gave me the account numbers,' she protested. 'Or . . . are you're saying it was Michael who did?'

'Michael was the one you – we – were talking to,' I reminded her gently. 'Helena said the voicemail wasn't Barry, so it had to have been Michael.'

'But wouldn't I have recognized Michael's voice?' Christy asked.

'How well do you really know him?' I asked. 'Besides, he could have used a cheap voice changer.'

'There are even apps for that,' Sarah said. 'Free online.'

I wasn't surprised.

'Oh, my God,' Christy said, putting her hand over her mouth. 'All the private things we said to each other, the plans we made.'

None of us knew what to say to that.

When I turned, I saw Helena had her arm around the redhead. 'Get angry, sweetie. It's easier than being sad.'

Christy sniffled, thinking about that. 'But if Michael was the one who gave me your accounts and all, where did he get them?'

'I guess we were the victims of identity theft after all,' Helena said. 'It just wasn't you.' She sat up straight. 'In fact, we got a notification . . . oh, it must be a year ago, that a local hardware store was hacked, and our information might have been compromised. Nothing happened and we just forgot about it.'

'Until now.' I pointed. 'Take this exit, Sarah.'

Sarah veered hard right onto the ramp over the complaints of the butts in the back. 'So how did this work? Christy makes contact with Barry on the dating site and Helena and Michael go hunting for his hacked information on the dark web?'

'The other way around,' I said. 'Christy and Barry never made contact, or at least I don't think they did.'

'Then Barry—' Helena started.

'Never went onto the dating service, never intended to cheat on you. Rebecca and Michael had your account information and created a dating profile in Barry's name. Then Rebecca made sure that Christy put up a profile. Fake Barry responded.'

'All this time . . .' There were tears in Christy's voice. 'Rebecca and this Barry were playing me?'

'Fake Barry,' Helena reminded her. 'If my husband had been cheating with you, I'm sure he would have been a real gentleman.'

Christy sniffed. 'Thank you.'

'You know what I don't understand?' Sarah asked, making another scooting right off the freeway and onto the airport spur. 'Why did they need Christy at all? They had the information, why not just steal the money?'

'Christy seemed the perfect scapegoat,' I said. 'The transactions would be traced back to her. Unfortunately for them, Christy is a little compulsive—'

'A little?' from Sarah.

'And couldn't help but add security questions and tidy up the accounts.'

'That's true,' Helena said. 'Barry said he couldn't get into the credit card site. Maybe that's when he decided to take a closer look at the charges.'

'You would have noticed big items like the bracelet and diamond eventually when the paper bills arrived at the house,' I said, 'but Rebecca and Michael planned to be well away by then. Instead, Barry called the charge card company for current charges that hadn't been billed yet.'

'And printed them out,' Helena said. 'Which is when I saw them.'

'Allowing both of you to track Christy down,' I said.

'Then both of you came to Brookhills for the same reason?' Christy asked.

'Independently, but on the same day,' Helena said. 'I thought he was cheating, and he thought I'd think he was cheating.'

'You were perfect for each other.' Christy sighed.

'We thought so.' Helena gave Christy's shoulder a squeeze. Christy leaned her head against her new buddy.

'There's still the snowplow, you know,' Sarah said. 'Who flattened Barry?'

'It almost has to be Rebecca,' I said, 'if we're right that

Michael had just dropped Barry off. Though I guess Michael could have parked the car and climbed into the plow as we were talking. It would have been tight timing, though.'

'Then you think this was premeditated?' Helena asked. 'They planned to kill Barry? What about me?'

'It couldn't have been planned,' I said, thinking about it. 'Or Michael could have easily done away with Barry on the way over.'

'True,' Sarah said, turning onto the final approach to the airport departures. 'Why wait to commit murder by snowplow?'

'That's why I think they were just tracking him at that point, trying to figure out how much . . . There they are!' I pointed to the skywalk from the parking garage to the terminal. 'Stop!'

'What, here?' Sarah slammed on the brakes, sending all of us lurching forward.

'Good enough,' I said, throwing the door open.

I ran for the terminal door without waiting to see if anyone else was in pursuit with me.

Inside, I did a quick scan of the airline ticket windows. Nothing. But Rebecca and Michael had been on the skywalk, meaning they'd enter the terminal on the same level as security and the departure gates, which was one floor up.

Glancing at the people with strollers and wheelchairs backed up at the elevators, I sprinted for the escalators. Annoyingly, there were travelers on them, too. Dodging around the stationary people and bags, I ran up the moving steps hoping I wouldn't pass Rebecca and Michael going the opposite direction down to ticketing and baggage check. Though at least that would give me more time to stop them.

As it was, I didn't know what I was going to do when I did catch up with them, except I was determined to stop them from going through TSA.

At the top of the escalator, I caught sight of my targets crossing from the skywalk toward the security line with no luggage other than carry-on wheelie bags. The stanchions for the switchback security lines were empty and the TSA officer checking passports only had three other people in front of him.

'Stop!' I yelled.

Rebecca and Michael turned. Rebecca was wearing a winter hat, newly cut bangs to match Helena's hair peeking out. She shoved Michael to keep going into the stanchioned line.

He glanced back at me and she shoved again, urging him to cut the line by going under the red velvet ropes. By the time I reached the security point, two people had entered the queue behind them, and Rebecca and Michael were at the TSA desk.

'Don't let them through,' I called, pushing past the two passengers and ducking under the rope. 'Their passports are fake.'

The agent looked up from the passport he held. 'Step back, please. Behind the blue line.'

'Maggy,' Michael said, his face white. He was still holding his – or the fake Barry Margraves' – passport.

I ignored him, pointing at the passport and boarding pass the agent held. 'This woman is not Helena Margraves.'

'She's crazy,' Rebecca said, pressing closer to the agent. 'We're going to miss our flight.'

The officer separated the boarding pass from the passport and put the latter face down on his scanner. It beeped. He picked up the boarding pass. 'And just how do you know this isn't Helena Margraves?'

'Because this is,' a voice behind me proclaimed as the real Helena's fist connected with the fake one's jaw.

TWENTY

'I know that I was in Chicago,' Pavlik said that night, as he took his bag from the trunk of the car. 'But you could have called Anthony.'

'I know,' I said, lifting his coat out and closing the trunk. 'And I did call her. It was just a little late.'

'You mean you called from the detention room in the airport,' he said as we walked toward the house.

'They do take this kind of thing seriously.' Punching (Helena). Hair-pulling (Christy). Parking in a loading zone (Sarah). The only thing they had on me was cutting the security line.

Happily, false passports trumped all of the above, and they'd held Michael and Rebecca, as well. The Heathrow flight took off without them.

Now Pavlik put his arm around my neck and pulled me close. 'Slugging somebody at security can get you into big trouble.'

'Helena had every right,' I said, lifting my face to plant a kiss on his cheek. 'Rebecca even cut her hair into bangs so she looked like Helena. And to add insult to injury, they were bad bangs. No feathering at all.'

'I'm sure that means something,' Pavlik said.

'It does,' I said, stopping short of the porch. 'It's just that if you don't feather or razor cut a fringe, the hair lays too flat, too Buster Brown-like.'

Pavlik raised his hand. 'I stipulate the bangs were bad.'

'Wise man.' I could hear the two dogs inside scrabbling against the door. 'Sit with me?' I gestured to the porch steps and offered him his coat.

He nodded and set down his bag to pull on the coat.

'Well done,' he said, sitting on the top step next to me.

'What, sitting here?' I snuggled under his arm for warmth. 'Under the cold dark sky?'

'Solving this. Brookhills resident Rebecca Penn running visitor Barry Margraves down with a snowplow? It boggles the imagination.'

'Crime of opportunity,' I said. 'Rebecca and Michael knew Barry had booked a flight to Milwaukee, because they could see all his transactions, thanks to Christy. They had to assume he'd tipped to their scheme and got nervous.'

'Helena too? Did they know she was coming?'

'I wondered about that,' I said. 'But Helena's flight wasn't on the list of current credit card transactions when I saw it.'

'And Barry's was.'

'Correct. Turns out that Helena used her business credit card – one that hadn't been hacked – not wanting Barry to know what she was doing.'

'Smart.'

'It was. Barry, on the other hand, continued to use the same card that the gifts and London ticket had been purchased on. I think he must have been in a panic, though, and was counting on the San Diego trip to cover for his coming here.'

'Hence the circuitous flight from Denver to San Diego via Milwaukee.'

'Correct.' I leaned my head on his shoulder. 'Barry had cheated on Helena and she forgave him.'

'Recently?' Pavlik seemed surprised.

'No, early in their marriage. He promised her it would never happen again, and he kept that promise.'

'Though the charge card purchases seemed to prove otherwise.'

'Which is why he wanted to get to the bottom of them without Helena ever knowing.' I sighed. 'So far as he knew when he died, she never did.'

'I guess that's some comfort,' Pavlik said. 'Or not. The man did nothing wrong.'

'Other than trying to protect his wife a little too much,' I said. 'Don't ever do that with me, OK?'

'OK. If I find charges for gifts to another woman on my charge card, you're the first person I'll come to.'

I laughed. 'It does sound like a stupid thing to do, doesn't it? But if only Barry had, he might still be alive.'

'But divorced.'

'Maybe,' I said. 'I had Barry down as a bad guy from the start. Cheating on Helena, emptying their accounts, lying to Christy.'

'He was, when you think about it. Except it wasn't really Barry.'

I shook my head. 'Which is what led us off on countless wild goose chases.'

'Like searching for the burner phone,' Pavlik said. 'Which didn't exist. Public Works is going to send you a bill for weekend double-overtime.'

'Kelly seems to have forgiven me,' I said.

'Kelly wasn't one of the Works people out digging for hours,' Pavlik said.

'Street looks nice, though,' I said brightly, and then sobered. 'I hope Harold is off the hook.'

'He is to a point. He still left his plow unattended, with the key in it.'

'Helena must have been watching for Michael to drop off Barry,' I said. 'They knew what he looked like, after all, essentially everything about him. As you say, the snowplow was parked with the key in it, just across from their house.'

'According to Anthony, Rebecca admitted she'd crossed the street from her house to get a better view because the plow was blocking her. The door of the truck was sitting ajar and after Margraves got out of the car and Michael drove past, she climbed up into the cab of the truck.'

'That sounds, if not pre-meditated . . .'

'Your crime of opportunity. Rebecca was desperate, as it turns out.'

I turned. 'Desperate how?'

'She was broke. We had no reason to look into her financials until today, but she went through all her savings and then some in the last year.'

'Living in New York,' I said, remembering. 'She said it was expensive. That's why she came back.'

'She rented a place that was way over her means.'

'She was going to make it big,' I said, tucking my hands into my coat pockets. 'Michael and Wisconsin were the only things holding her back from being a real artist. Or so she thought.'

'Even real artists don't necessarily make a lot of money,' Pavlik said. 'Probably just the opposite and they certainly don't make enough to support the lifestyle she was living there. She ran up a lot of debt.'

'And had to come back here. But she and Michael already had dissolved their business. He was hurting, too, driving ride-share just to survive.'

'Yet they found a way,' Pavlik said.

'I think Rebecca found a way.'

'You never liked her, did you?' Pavlik teased me.

'Nope, though I tried to when I saw how good she was being to Christy. But that was a lie, too.' I shook my head. 'I knew that Rebecca was bitter after her sister was killed and things went bad for her and Michael. I just didn't know she was a psycho maniac.'

'She didn't like her sister much from what I recall.'

'I'm not sure Rebecca likes anybody but herself,' I said. 'Or wants them to be happy.'

'I'll say. She told you I was cheating. With her sister.'

I sat up straight. 'That's true, isn't it? Back then I assumed she was just mistaken, but maybe she was trying to manipulate me the way she manipulated Michael and Christy.'

'You don't manipulate easily.'

'When it comes to my man, I guess I don't.' I linked my arm with his, sliding my hand into his coat pocket. 'I just hope Christy doesn't go running back to Ronny.'

'"Go running back" is a stretch, given the guy is in jail.'

'True, but that's what made him safe,' I said. 'She went out of her comfort zone when Rebecca convinced her to try the dating site. It all turned out to be a lie, even Rebecca's friendship. They broke Christy's heart and nearly got her thrown in jail.'

'How is she taking it?' Pavlik asked.

'Surprisingly well,' I said. 'Did I tell you that she jumped Rebecca when she tried to get back up after Helena punched her? I thought she was going to pull Rebecca's ugly bangs right out of her head.' I smiled. 'I was kind of proud.'

'Your little girl has grown up,' Pavlik agreed.

'Actually, she has. I have a lot of respect for the way she doesn't let anything get her down. But I admit I'm glad Amy will be back Tuesday.'

'I understand Helena Margraves is flying back to Denver tomorrow.'

'Talk about resiliency. Helena lost her husband twice. Once when she thought he was cheating and then again to the snow-plow. And she's so damned nice, she's even become friends with Christy.'

'Who didn't steal her husband, after all,' Pavlik pointed out. 'But you said before that it was Rebecca who manipulated Michael. Do you honestly think he was duped?'

I cocked my head. 'I think Michael is in love with Rebecca and has been ever since I've known them. He was crushed when she left. We barely saw him.'

'So she comes back and he's willing to do anything for her. Michael does admit he helped her steal Margraves' identity, but says it was Rebecca manipulating the accounts through Christy.'

'And Rebecca who killed Barry,' I said. 'And also Rebecca who stole the bracelet and diamond from Christy's house the night she stayed with her.'

'But Michael planted the bracelet on Helena and re-mailed the diamond from what you said.'

'Yes, and Michael stole Helena's passport.' I sighed. 'Wonder what the unset diamond was for. It seems an odd thing.'

'Maybe he was going to propose to Rebecca.'

'A romantic,' I said, standing up and brushing myself off.

'You want a diamond?' Pavlik asked. 'I can't get you one that big, I'm afraid.'

'Actually.' I put out my hand to help him up. 'I'd much prefer a large peperoni pizza and a couple puppies drooling on my toes. You?'

'You've got yourself a deal.'